POINTE OF DARKNESS

POINTE OF DARKNESS

LA DARK SERIES

PARIS ANDREN

Pointe of Darkness: LA Dark Series
Copyright © 2016 by Paris Andren

J JAF Publishing, LLC
jjafpublishing.com

Cover design: SelfPubBookCovers.com/FrinaArt
Book design by Maureen Cutajar, gopublished.com

ISBN: 978-1-944599-00-3

In loving memory of my Andrea

Acknowledgements

IN ALL HONESTY and with great humility, there are too many people that I would like to thank and acknowledge. My family, my friends, and strangers alike have all stepped forward and without hesitation to embrace and support me through this journey. I would have never succeeded without all of you. However, there are a few people that I must name, and will list them here letting them know how much their support has meant.

Kevin, Louise, Cory, Leah, Trina, John, Ann, Erica, Lex, Jacquie, Ali, Nadia, Kelly_Ann, Janna, Diane, Laura, Little Mary, Vicki, Sha, Lithena, Denise, Luthaniel, Tess, and Greg. I would also like to thank my editor for her wonderful input and her lovely, 'virtual' red pen of grammatical correctness.

POINTE OF DARKNESS

❧ 1 ❧

AVA

Floating...disconnected...fading in and out...blessed darkness.
Pain. The rancid smell of vomit.
Pain. The darkness pulled me under again.
Pain. Demanding and relentless, a harsh master awaiting a response.
Flashes of hazy events, but no real memory.
Only...Pain.

I TRIED TO SWALLOW past a lump of unbearable dryness, but it felt as if razor blades had shredded my throat and vocal cords. The taste of vomit and copper pennies coated my tongue as I swept it along lips that were chapped and probed corners that were raw. The noxious scent of days old milk and wet, dirty asphalt after a brief rain perfumed my labored breathing, until I was all but choking on it. Straining but yet determined, I pulled my cheek out of the filth.

Light filtered from the mouth of the alley, but it was too weak to penetrate the darkness of my distant corner. Gusting eddies of pirouetting trash floated pieces of debris into my hot, gritty eyes making it difficult to pry them open without more pain.

There was an urgency to the staccato pace of my heart that could not be denied and was screaming, "Ava, get up and get away. Now!" I didn't understand what was happening, but I couldn't deny the demanding nature of my heartbeat.

Palms flat against the wet ground, I extended my arms until they were trembling with strain. A whimpered cry escaped my raw throat, resonating through my head like a sirens wail. Ignoring the pain, I continued to push until I was sitting up and resting on bent knees, with my ankles tucked under me. With my head bowed and chin resting upon my chest, I prayed that, between my spinning head and labored breathing, I didn't fall over.

The last thing I wanted to do was move, but the urgency to leave was undeniable. Bracing a hand against the brick wall next to me, I stumbled to a stand. As my legs were buckling, I pressed my hip harder into the wall, causing bits of mortar to dig in, bruising it further. What was one more bruise, when I felt littered with them; my body was used and broken.

My breath caught in the back of my throat as waves of pain and nausea swept through me again. God, what had happened to me? I couldn't remember anything and wasn't sure I wanted to.

I moved away from my little hidey-hole towards the entrance of the alley, with my feet dragging and breath hitching. The pain and nausea continued unabated, threatening to bring me back to my knees. Each shuffling step was pure torture, as places within my body ached and burned relentlessly. Damn it! I hadn't even been introduced to those places yet.

Stopping to catch my breath, I sagged against the brick wall for a short break. I needed strength before breaching the alley entrance, as my head was spinning and I was still dizzy. I wiped my forehead impatiently with the back of my hand, before the sweat could drip into my stinging eyes, and then let them drift shut for a moment. Listening to my surroundings, all was quiet except for the slight freeway noise off in the distance and the low music coming from the left.

I peeked around the corner to the right, nearly losing my balance in the process. Streetlights illuminated the empty storefronts and deserted streets, but after seeing nothing and no one, I turned back to the left. Where was a cop when I so obviously needed one? Most days it seemed I tripped over one at every corner. If I jaywalked, would one show up? I shook my head at my rambling thoughts.

Stepping from the protection of the alley, I ventured left towards the mysterious music. Hugging the storefronts, I used the walls and windows as a crutch to keep me upright and moving forward. My vision was still skewed, but I could see that there was light shining on the sidewalk up ahead. Quickening my pace, I stumbled to reach this beacon of light, a safe harbor in my muddled head.

A sigh escaped when I reached the illuminated door and placed my back against the cool glass, letting it chill my fevered skin. My body couldn't decide if it was hot or cold, bouncing back and forth between them. I didn't understand why, but nothing was making sense and it hurt my head to think about it. Resting here a moment seemed like a good idea, as I was so tired and my eyes were determined to close. It was only for a moment and then my world was tilting again.

Eyes snapping open and arms pinwheeling, I fell backwards, as the door was opened behind me. Since neither my body, nor my brain, were functioning well, coordinating their efforts was far beyond my current mental capacity. I was braced for impact and rigid with anticipated pain, though I managed to land safe and gentle— cradled within leather clad arms, but with a startled, "Oomph!"

I knew I should have been frightened and scrambling to get away. I didn't know this man, but at this point nothing short of death could have hurt much worse. Though being dead wouldn't hurt, I supposed. Great, now I've gone completely mad. I couldn't keep up with the randomness of my thoughts.

My next random—the incredible clean and masculine scent of the arms cradling me. I took in a deep breath, letting his scent envelope me, until the scent was all but begging me to snuggle in deeper. Why resist, he felt safe and I decided to trust that instinct, though perhaps that misguided trust had led me to here in the first place. I couldn't deal with that right now; later I'd try to figure it all out. Right now the darkness was pulling at me and the need to give in was too tempting, but not before I saw who was holding me so gently.

Lifting my eyes, I tried to focus on my savior. His face was blurred by the bright lights overhead, which had surrounded him in a halo of sorts. I tried to pull his features together and managed only a vague impression of a fallen angel. Squinting and straining to see something more distinct from his face, I was hit by the clarity of his bright blue eyes. Unable to look away, I was held captive within forever and ushered gently towards the darkness. A final sigh escaped my chapped lips, as I was consumed, and my world of pain was chased away.

❧ 2 ❧

AVA

Earlier In The Month

"DANIEL? HEY IT'S Ava. I'm on my way," I squealed into my cell.

"Now your friend Willow is expecting me...right? What if I arrive earlier than expected? She's okay with having me as a roommate? I mean she doesn't know me. What if we don't get along? What if she doesn't like me? God, what am I doing? Daniel, it's too soon."

"Ava stop! It's time, honey," he said with a tone of regret and sadness, but he was right, it was time.

"Everything is all set. You guys will get along famously, I guarantee it. You have the address I texted you, off Melrose...in Hollywood?"

"I do. It's loaded into McCoy's GPS. Daniel, thank you for setting all this up for me. Okay, I'll be heading out in a few. Oh and Daniel, when you see Mason would you please tell him that I can't wait for all of us to get together. That is, if he can pry himself away from the ladies."

"I know right? That's what being the star quarterback will

get you. Sure gives a whole new meaning to the concept of tail-gating," Daniel stated deadpan.

I choked on the water I had just taken a sip of, laughing and snorting uncontrollably.

"You're a mess Daniel, but you crack me up. It's been way too long since I've laughed this hard. I'll call you once I've arrived in LA and get settled. Bye love, talk to you soon."

I ran my thumb across my screen, ending the call. Leaning against my powder blue VW Bug that I'd named McCoy, I stared at the only home I'd ever known. It had been sold and the equity used to pay off the remainder of Maman's medical bills. I was well and truly alone in the world now, an orphan in essence. Though I was twenty-two and an adult, I was still without any family, except for my best friends Mason Alexander and Daniel Creighton. We'd been the best of friends since I moved to Palm Springs from New York, when I was three years old.

Maman, as I'd always called her, adopted me when I was three, after my mother and grandparents had died in a car accident. I don't remember much about them, but Maman had kept them alive for me, through stories and videos. She had met my mother, Grace, while dancing for the New York City Ballet and they had become inseparable. Fast friends she had always called them. When my entire family had died, Maman chose to stop dancing and moved us from New York to Palm Springs. Talk about cities that were polar opposites. She'd given up every-thing, her career, her life, everything...just for me. It didn't matter that technically she wasn't my mother, in all the ways that mattered, she most certainly was. I didn't know anything about my father, other than he had taken off before I was born. Whatever!

After moving to Palm Springs, Maman had founded Made-moiselle's Ballet en Pointe Studio, as a way to support us. She was French and perhaps a tad proud, but I couldn't help but love her, eccentricities and all. I started dancing in her classes when I was just three. She had thought it would help to keep me occupied and channel my grief. Of course at three I didn't understand any of that, I just wanted to wear ballet shoes and a tutu. As the years had progressed, ballet had become my one true passion, almost to the exclusion of everything else. My dream had always been to dance as a principal ballerina with a large company, much like the Los Angeles Ballet. I had planned to pursue the career Maman had given up for me, a tribute to her beautiful legacy. Not only had she been my mother, but she had been my best friend and we had done everything together. I didn't have many girlfriends in high school because I'd had her and she'd been the perfect best friend.

Five years ago she'd been diagnosed with cervical and uterine cancer. Multiple rounds of chemotherapy and radiation had left her too weak and too tired to teach, breaking her heart. I had taken her place, teaching ballet at the studio to support us. As the end had neared, I'd stopped teaching to care for her fulltime. Luckily, I'd been able to sell the studio to a former student who had moved back to the area. Selling it had enabled me to care for Maman and pay off what was left of her medical bills at the time.

She had fought hard these past five years, but in the end, nothing could be done. We had long since exhausted the radiation and chemotherapy options. I'd delayed pursuing a career in ballet these past four years, staying in Palm Springs to care for her. She had given up the career she had so loved to raise me so I figured I could pursue dancing later. My time with her would be limited and she was far more important to me. She was my rock and I didn't know what I was going to do without her or how I would survive.

It had been six months now since I laid Maman to rest. My two best friends, Mason and Daniel, had come home from LA for the funeral. I wouldn't have made it through that day without them. I was thankful she was no longer suffering and in pain, but that didn't make her passing any less painful for me. During the last six months, I had settled her business affairs and...grieved. I thought I was finally ready to join my best friends in LA. We had always planned to move to LA together, sharing a bungalow in Hollywood or Santa Monica. I had wanted to pursue dance, Daniel had wanted to be an attorney, and Mason had wanted to play football for which he had received a full ride as the starting quarterback at USC. They were both graduating with honors in June. I had broken our pact made as kids, turning our trio into a duo, but they had understood. They'd loved Maman just as much as I had, though they had always called her Chloe...Chloe DeLaney.

"Recalculating."

Arghhh...If that bitch says recalculating one more time in her snotty British accent, I'm gonna have to choke the bitch. Damn LA traffic and road closures. This wasn't my first trip to LA, but these closures were taking me away from my normal route.

"Arriving at your location on the right...in five hundred feet."

Miss Snotty got lucky this time. Oh yes she did!

I pulled up to the cutest apartment building ever. Oh this is just what I had imagined. Retro looking, but renovated, with white stucco, two stories, a red clay tiled roof and four steps up to a central landing area. Our apartment was on the right and there was a small courtyard on that side, towards the back. I could hear the strains of a beautifully haunting violin piece coming from that direction.

Drawn towards its sadness, with the melancholy resonating through my grieving soul, I had the desire to dance for the first time in six months. As I walked toward the violinist, my body was swaying to the music. Closing my eyes, I visualized what my movements would be and how I would represent the music. Dropping my bag, I started dancing. My movements were fluid, evocative, a translation of how the music spoke to me. How I felt it. Sometimes a song would evoke an immediate yearning within me and I couldn't deny the pull, the need to dance. It had always been this way. I was so lost in the music and my own head, that when the song ended, it was much like waking from a dream.

I focused my eyes on the violinist, when I noticed the music had stopped. Her violin and bow were held in her left hand and with her right hand she was reaching out to shake mine in greeting.

"I am Willow Sinclair. That was some beautiful dancing, girl. You are so going to nail that audition."

As I shook her hand, I smiled at that statement. Hope reins eternal and all that.

Willow returned the smile. "You must be Ava."

I couldn't help but notice how tiny she was. She barely reached my chin, though I was tallish, at five foot eight. Her little hand seemed almost child-like in my grip.

"Pegged it in one," I said, shaking her hand in return. "Ava DeLaney. I loved that piece you were playing. The melancholy of it spoke to me." I blushed at the characterization of her music.

"Thank you. I'm glad you liked it. It kinda matched my mood from earlier, but it's getting better by the minute," she said with a wink.

Willow turned a little to her right, placing her violin in its case, which gave me a chance to look her over. She was petite, but rather curvy, kinda fun-sized. She wore a curve-hugging blue tank top, paired with a hot pink ballet skirt. On her dainty feet she wore pink and green Chucks. I'd noticed she was sporting a small nose piercing on the right and I could see she had several colorful tattoos. But, what was so striking on Willow was all of that pale skin and wavy auburn hair. Even pulled up into a messy ponytail, like it was now, she was in a word...gorgeous.

I felt downright dowdy in comparison. I tended to dress more retro and today had worn black capris pants, with matching ballet flats. I had on a pale pink, short sleeved shirt that I had taken the tails and tied at my waist. My dark chestnut hair was pulled back into its customary bun and secured at my nape. Otherwise I was kinda plain. My nose was rather little and upturned, my mouth too big. I had a serious case of Angelina Jolie lips, but instead of feeling sexy, I felt like that quacking duck on TV.

Looking up, I noticed Willow had been checking me out as well, both of us learning what we could about our new roommate. We looked at each other and had started laughing; we had both been so obvious. Once we stopped giggling like two loons, we went to the front where my car was parked and unloaded all of my stuff.

What I'd learned about Willow that first day was that we were destined to be the best of friends. I loved that girl and her mad violin skills.

❧ 3 ❧

AVA

I WAS PLANNING TO participate in the open auditions at the Los Angeles Ballet. While still in Palm Springs, I had found a dance group to join that wasn't far from my new apartment. I'd left early so I could walk over and enjoy the temperate spring day. I'd wanted to warm-up before class started, taking my time to get acquainted with the studio. Having danced with the Ballet de L'Opera de Paris, Madame, who leads the group, was well respected within the community. I was giddy with excitement and reached the studio early just as planned, but when I walked through the doors, at least twenty dancers were in various stages of warming up. Well hell, so much for being early, now I felt late and conspicuous. I felt a blush creeping up the pale skin of my neck, like a neon sign for my discomfort. Taking a deep breath to center myself, I walked over to where Madame was chatting with a female dancer.

As I approached the pair, the dancer gave me a very thorough inspection that ended with her looking down her nose at me. How someone, more than half a head shorter than me, could manage that was a bit of a mystery. But I'll be damned if she didn't stare at me, as if I weren't good enough to be in the same stratosphere as her metaphorical tutu. She was beautiful, I'd give her that. Pale blonde hair, blue eyes, and normal sized lips, but her scowl quite ruined the overall effect. They halted their conversation, as I made my way over to them.

Giving a brief curtsy, I introduced myself. One gaze was inquisitive, the other hostile.

"Good morning, Madame. My name is Ava DeLaney. We spoke briefly about my joining your dance group."

Madame's right eyebrow winged up in inquisition. "Yes, mademoiselle, but I had thought to see you last week."

Good Lord, this wasn't going well. "Pardon Madame, I was still getting settled into my new apartment."

I definitely couldn't confess to watching old episodes of MadTv on Netflix with Willow, as I was pretty sure that would have been frowned upon. Or that we had hit a few dance clubs. Damn that girl was corrupting me already. She was exponentially more worldly than I was, but we meshed so well, as I tempered her crazy.

"Mademoiselle Ava, please get warmed up. We start in twenty minutes."

Wasn't that just freakin' peachy, I thought to myself.

I headed towards the corner of the studio, where I had seen an empty bench. Once I arrived, I kicked off my Toms and stripped out of my grey skirt and pink sweater. Underneath, I was dressed in a conservative black leotard, footless nude tights, and light blue ballet pantaloons. I pulled my pointe shoes and leg warmers out of my bag and sat down to put them on. A low murmur of conversation floated through the studio, along with a recorded piano piece that played softly in the background.

I went through my usual warm-up, starting with ankle rolls as I tried to ignore the fact that I had become the center of attention, though they were mostly discreet about it. I met a few inquisitive eyes, nodding my head in acknowledgment. Most seemed curious, as if to express: hey who's the new girl? A few, that blonde included, acted like acknowledging me was beneath them. Whatever, note to self, blondie will not be my new BFF.

Madame called the dancers to attention and we all hustled to grab a spot at one of the bars lined around the room. We went through a group warm-up, with Madame calling out various exercises as we went along. It felt incredible to work my dance muscles again. It had been so long, over six months, since I had wanted to dance again, but I knew the time was right.

Madame explained we would dance individually first and she gave us a sequence of moves she wanted us to perform. The class broke into little practice groups. Apparently, we were back in elementary school at recess, picking teams and I wasn't chosen. I was on my own.

When practice time was over, we each took a turn traveling across the floor, performing the sequence as Madame had asked. I watched the other dancers as I waited and I appreciated how Madame had called out encouraging instructions or corrections as needed to each person's form or step. My turn approached and though I was a little stressed, I knew I could perform what she asked and luckily I had a good memory for choreography.

A male dancer I'd been watching went next and boy was he ever good. He was tall at over six foot, and he had blonde hair and dark eyes or at least I thought they were dark. I would have loved to partner with him. He was graceful, in a masculine way, and carried himself with a confidence that boarded on cocky. His jumps were dynamic and I couldn't help but blush at all that maleness front and center. I was mesmerized by the play of his muscles under his tights...they left little to the imagination, hugging his glorious ass and thighs, while cupping his genitals so lovingly.

Lost in my head while imagining us performing a pas de deux, I almost missed my cue. But, as I traveled across the floor with the music pouring over and through me, I performed the sequence with grace and surety, ending with ten fouette's, in a single/double combo. I could definitely hold my head high after that and walked or rather pranced back to my spot in line. Maman would have been so proud. I noticed that after my turn across the floor, some of the dancers had warmed up to me, while others were decidedly cooler. I mentally shrugged my shoulders.

Next we were to pair up with one of the male dancers, performing a pas de deux, but since there were more females than males, we would have to double team the guys. Good Lord that sounded a bit wicked, I giggled to myself. I looked around feeling like it was recess yet again, when Mr. Hotness himself walked over to me.

"Marcus," was all he said, as an introduction, then continued, "and you're new."

Last time I checked my name was Ava, I smirked to myself.

"Ava," I stated as I shook the hand he'd held out in greeting.

"Well, Ava, you'll be needing a partner and since you don't know anyone yet, I'm volunteering," he said, as more of a command than an inquiry and with a smile that said, he was quite proud of himself. He obviously got whatever he wanted, whenever he wanted it...he seemed like a spoiled brat. I agreed however and we listened as Madame explained what she was wanting us to do. It seemed straight forward enough, nothing too difficult, but I hadn't partnered in a while, so I was nervous about screwing up and about trusting Marcus not to drop me. It was time to put my big girl tutu on...I knew I could do this.

Marcus and I were practicing when Madame called upon us to go first. Really, no pressure here, and I'm sure it had nothing to do with me coming in today instead of last week. I rolled my eyes, well in my mind I did. I understood though, put the new girl on the spot and see how she performs under pressure.

We walked over to what would be considered center stage and waited for the music to start. I could feel the heat creeping over my chest and up my neck, my pale skin blushing hotly. I hoped everyone would think I was just hot, considering it was overly warm in the studio. That thought had just crossed my mind, when I felt something skate along the base of my neck. A brief touch, that was barely there, and then Marcus was distracting me with his warm breath tickling my ear, saying, "What a lovely blush, Ava."

So much for being inconspicuous, I thought as I took a deep breath. I shook off my nerves and focused on the choreography of our performance. Marcus was a capable partner and I was immediately relieved and at ease. We managed the moves as Madame had wanted, each performing perfectly and in sync. I floated across the floor effortlessly, lost to the music and feeling beautiful in this moment. As we neared the end of the routine and the lift that I was nervous about, I chose to let go and give it over to Marcus, trusting in him completely. My worry was for not, as we performed it beautifully and without issue. Madame and the class, well most of the class, applauded when we finished and now I was most definitely beet red. I curtsied and Marcus bowed before we moved off to allow the other dancers a turn.

"That was wonderful, Ava," Marcus said, with his dark eyes staring down at me as he ran his finger along my blushing cheek. "I felt the exact moment you let go and submitted so beautifully," he said with a little nod, the meaning of which escaped me, then he left to partner with the other girls.

I was watching the other dancers perform their routines; all so wonderful and each with their own strengths, that I didn't notice blondie sidling up to me. For a pretty girl, she sure had an ugly personality which came through loud and clear with the venom she spewed at me.

"Don't think you're even close to our league. Marcus wouldn't stoop to partnering with a nobody. After open auditions, we'll both be principals with the LA Ballet and you won't even make the company. Just step off before you get hurt."

With that little ditty, blondie flounced away, though her departure lost some of its punch, when she tripped and stumbled while glaring back at me over her shoulder. I raised my hand to cover the smile creeping across my face. Seriously, were we in grade school? Who says that crap?

Class was ending when Madame approached me. I noticed the closer she got, the quieter the room became. I wasn't sure what to expect, but I would face whatever criticisms she had for me with dignity and honor.

"Very well done, mademoiselle Ava, you moved beautifully to the music. You dance with an innocent wonder I have not seen in some time. Where are you planning to audition?"

"Thank you, Madame. I had thought to audition for the Los Angeles Ballet."

"Excellent! Open auditions are about a month away, at the end of March. They are in need of a beautifully skilled principal dancer, one that can deliver innocence and beauty, but with such passion. You will be a perfect fit."

"Wow...thank you for your confidence." I was surely glowing red about now.

"But mademoiselle, you have much work to do. I expect you to be here six days a week until then. I will personally train you, but you must commit fully, no half measures, mademoiselle Ava. Agreed?"

"Yes, Madame. I won't let you down."

We nodded to each other and broke apart. The noise level increased immediately, with everyone chattering like magpies about what had just gone down. By their response, I'm assuming Madame did not offer private coaching. I wasn't sure what to make of that either, but I'd happily take whatever she was willing to offer. I went back to the bench in the corner to take off my pointe shoes and get ready to leave. I was at the front door when Madame called out to me.

"I will see you at eight a.m. mademoiselle Ava."

And there it was...I had a private ballet coach and the Madame at that. I would be floating all the way home. Marcus walked out at the same time and offered to walk me home. I was reluctant at first, but what could it hurt. We walked leisurely along the street towards my apartment, chatting amicably.

"You are a very beautiful dancer Ava, but I'm sure you are aware of that," he said as he gently touched my lower back, ushering me along.

Marcus was looking down at me with this little smirk gracing his lips. Now that we were outside and close together, I could see that Marcus did indeed have very dark brown eyes, almost black, quite an unusual combination with blonde hair. Gah, he really was just too beautiful for words. I wasn't sure what to make of him yet, but then we had only just met today. But the memory of that little caress along my neck caused shivers and had a blush stealing its way up my neck...damn it, not again.

"Are you cold? I have another sweater you could wear."

"No I'm fine, but thank you, Marcus."

I was looking down at the sidewalk when I replied, so that way he wouldn't see the discomfort swimming in my eyes. I was an open book or so I'd been told repeatedly. I didn't want him to see, nor did I want to acknowledge, that I was remembering that caress along my neck and our pas de deux together. I most definitely didn't want him knowing how the hot press of his hand against my lower back was affecting me. However, when I dared a glance up at him, peeking through my eyelashes, it was clear by the look in his eyes that I was fooling no one, least of all him.

We continued walking towards my apartment making small talk along the way and astutely ignored the undercurrent to our conversation. I learned that he and blondie, otherwise known as Natalia Vinokourov, were both auditioning for the LA Ballet. They had once been a couple he told me, which explained her hostility towards me. Did she think I was going to throw him down and have my wicked way with him? I mean seriously I just met the guy, holy hotness or not, I didn't even know him. People were plain weird.

The closer we got to my apartment, the more nervous I became. When we arrived at my building, things became quickly awkward because I had no intention of inviting him in. He must have realized I was struggling with what to do because he leaned forward kissing my cheek with a light press of his lips and stated that he would see me over the next couple of weeks. Madame had apparently asked Marcus to come partner with me in preparation for auditions next month, giving me about six weeks of training. I appreciated what she was doing for me. I felt at home with her, as she reminded me of Maman...stern, yet encouraging. She spoke French as well, which was a comfort to me, having grown up speaking it every day.

"Okay then, Marcus, thank you for seeing me home and I'll see you at Madame's tomorrow. I truly appreciate your help."

"Oh, it's entirely my pleasure Ava, see you soon."

I stood there for a moment, watching him walk away and I reflected on how my morning had played out. Madame had taken me under her wing, I'm not sure why, but whatever the reason was I so freaking loved it. I couldn't wait to fill in Willow, Daniel, and Mason on how everything had gone, especially with Madame and Marcus. He was clearly a talented dancer and his help would be invaluable.

❦ 4 ❧

AVA

"MASON!" I HOLLERED out as I waved my arms wildly. I ran towards Mason whose eyes were growing larger the closer I got, what with screaming and launching myself at him. It was heavenly to feel my best friend's arms wrapped around me. I had missed him and Daniel with an uncontrollable ache. We were family in every sense of the word, except for biology, which accounted for very little in my book.

"Ava, Ava...what am I to do with you crazy girl, you could have unmanned me with one misplaced knee." He was laughing as he chided me. We had always been like this. I'd started launching myself at him as soon as he was strong enough to hold me, which had been from a fairly young age, since I had always been rather light from ballet, though strong.

"Lord, how I've missed you..." My voice trailed off as the raw emotion from all the changes in my life overtook my ability to speak. Tears gathered in my eyes, but I blinked them back refusing their fall; I'd cried enough. Plus I was happy, not really sad in this moment.

"I'm starving, Mason, let's get something to eat. I've been wanting to try this great little bistro off Melrose that Daniel recommended." I loved the apartment that Willow and I shared; it was close to everything. I'd been here for a few weeks now and had settled in nicely. Daniel had been right in pairing Willow and I as roommates, we had become fast friends.

Mason and I walked from my apartment enjoying the spring weather in LA. "I'll warn you now though, I want to know everything that's been going on with you." I tried to affect an air of innocent query, but I wasn't fooling Mason by the look in his steady gaze. I just smiled in return.

The bistro was a few blocks away and we had seated ourselves in the courtyard out back, so that way we could continue enjoying the warm sunshine. We ordered, and then got down to the very serious business of catching up. I wanted to know all the little details that short telephone conversations and texting just couldn't cover.

"All right, Mason, spill it...what's been going on with your love life, school, future plans, football...leave nothing out. No detail is too small," I said while batting my eyelashes at him.

Mason burst out laughing and choked on the water he had just sipped. Oops!

"You don't want much, do you. Shall I tell you my blood type, the last time I had sex, and when my last poop was?"

"Well...I happen to know that your blood type is O negative, oddly enough just like mine, but yes all of those other details will do nicely, though Mason, do keep your bowel habits to yourself to allow for a little bit of mystery won't you?" I gave him my very best stern look. He just laughed at me.

"Okay, Ava, you win, though I won't be telling you everything. Graduation is in May, as you know, but at this point all of my focus has been on the NFL Combine next week. Remember, that's where all the recruiters come to check out those players wanting to enter the NFL Draft. So, I'm actually taking a test tomorrow, which was scheduled for next week, so that I can leave early and arrive at the combine ahead of schedule. You know how I hate being behind and running late. My future plans and football, at this point, go hand in hand. I'll re-evaluate after the combine and the draft, as to what I'll do next. Everything hinges on those two things. As a quarterback, it's hard to say, the last few years didn't see many first round picks and none last year. What else was it you had wanted to know? Let's see, this morning after a nice cup of joe and armed with the paper, I had..."

"Mason!" I said with exasperation. "I don't want to know. Now what about your love life...hmmm? Have you a girlfriend, a steady friend with benefits? What's up? Do tell and I want all the details!"

"No, Ava, there are just some things that should be kept from little sisters," he said and winked at me.

I reached across the table and patted his hand, saying, "It's fine, Mason, I don't really need to know. I just wanted to be sure you were happy." He turned his hand over to hold my smaller one in his, making me feel small and cherished.

"I'm happy, Ava. Life is good my beautiful friend. I'm thankful to see you smiling again. The move here has been good for you, though I understood your need to regroup and mourn. I miss Chole too. She would be incredibly proud of you for what you're doing with your life and what you are about to accomplish. I have no doubt you will be chosen by the LA Ballet. How are the practice sessions coming along with Madame and that Marcus guy?"

A slight chill worked its way down my spine and I shivered uncontrollably.

"Are you chilly, Ava? We can go inside."

"No, I'm not cold. It's the mention of Marcus. I can't really explain, but something about him bothers me. You know I haven't dated, not really and it's probably just that he's rather good looking. But...sometimes I'm a bit uncomfortable with the way he looks at me, like he can see inside me and would devour me whole if given the chance." A self-conscious laugh escaped. "I'm sure I'm over-reacting. You know I've never turned heads before, so it's just a new sensation for me, having someone be so overly attentive."

"Ava, trust your instincts. You're a beautiful woman and men will be falling all over themselves to have you. If this Marcus keeps bothering you, I want to know." He placed his finger under my chin when I had looked down at my hands. "I mean it, Ava, listen to what I am saying. Men are pigs, I should know, they will do whatever they can to get at you. Let Daniel or I know, okay? We will have a little chat with this Marcus or anyone else for that matter. You're our sister, Ava, and ours to protect."

"I promise, Mason. Tomorrow is our practice solo performances at The Shrine Auditorium." I raised my hand to stop him from speaking. "Before you pester me again, no, I haven't changed my mind. I want to do it alone. At least this first time. Please understand, as I'm nervous enough already."

"I know, Ava. We wouldn't want you to be uncomfortable. You'll be exceptional. Have faith that you're very talented, Ava, I should know. I watched Chole train you all those years...you're more than ready."

At the mention of my mother's name again, my heart pinched with how much I missed her, but I knew she would be proud. I really felt that now was my time and I was more than ready to make my mark on the LA ballet community.

"Thank you, Mason, I feel more than ready. I'm coming into ballet at an age older than most, but hopefully that will give me an edge of maturity that younger artists lack. Well, I'm not exactly old," I said with a chuckle of self-deprecation. "I'm just older than the average ballerina just starting her career, but I will use whatever I have to my advantage."

"Oh, Ava, you are many things, but average is not one of them," Mason said with a wink and a kiss on my cheek. "Come on, let's go back to your apartment. Daniel is going to meet us there. I thought the three of us and Willow could hang out for a while since I'll be leaving and will be out of town for well over a week."

"Don't you want to study for your test?"

"If I don't know the material by now, cramming surely won't help, and might actually confuse the issue. I'll do well, Ava, don't worry."

We walked at a leisurely pace back to my apartment, stopping at a few shops along the way allowing time for Willow and Daniel to arrive. We planned to watch some NetFlix and relax. I was trying not to be too anxious about tomorrow, but my stomach kept turning somersaults. I was ready, but spending this evening with my family would help soothe my nerves, especially if Willow had her way and we watched MadTv...that crazy girl was obsessed.

"Is Willow still bingeing on MadTv?"

I swung my head towards Mason, saying, "Are you listening to my thoughts again. How the hell did you know what I was thinking?"

"I've told you before, Ava, what you think is written across that beautiful face of yours or in your silver eyes. You're fairly transparent." He smiled down at me, like the brother he was.

"I know, Mason, more's the pity." I sighed, mumbling the last little bit to myself. I needed to work on the art of masking my thoughts and feelings, though easier said than done. I didn't think I would ever adapt to the cut-throat atmosphere of LA, it just wasn't instinctual for me, but I would make it here. I would make both of my mothers proud, there just wasn't any other options. Chloe gave up so much for me. I would realize and fulfill her dreams and mine as well.

❦ 5 ❧

AVA

WHEN MADAME TOLD us our practice solo performances would be at The Shrine Auditorium, I hadn't appreciated the magnitude of what that would feel like. The Shrine was a historical landmark that had opened in 1926, and it hosted such prestigious events as the Oscar's. It was located on the University of Southern California's campus and while I had seen it on numerous occasions from the outside, I had never breached its doors...and wow, it did not disappoint. I couldn't keep my eyes or head still, as I kept scanning every bit of the majestic building, soaking in the history and the atmosphere.

Madame started clapping her hands, a sure sign she wanted our attention. Pulling away from the beautiful auditorium to focus on her, my gaze ran across to Marcus and Natalia off to the side. The tension was so heavy between them that I could feel it from across the stage and saw it when Natalia raised her hand to slap Marcus. He easily caught her wrist, causing her to yelp out in pain. I started towards them when Madame called out...

"Okay, everyone, come here. Come together so I do not have to yell. Marcus, Natalia...please, come join the group."

They rejoined the rest of us at center stage. Marcus was looking his normal, charming self. Natalia however, was rubbing her wrist as she made her way over, but stopped when she saw me watching her.

"We must all thank Natalia's uncle, Mr. Vinokourov. His generosity has allowed us to perform our solo routines here, at the beautiful Shrine Auditorium. What an incredible opportunity for all of you. Please perform at your best today. Treat this moment as if it were the day of your auditions."

Turning as a group, we could see the outline of a figure seated a few rows back. As a group, we either bowed or curtsied to thank him. The other dancers had family members in the audience too, they were just a bit further back. Willow, Mason, and Daniel had been begging to come today until the last moment, but I'd been adamant about wanting to go it alone this time.

"Now, you all know the order with which to perform, but for those of you with short term memory loss," she sniffed a little hmmm, then continued, "I have posted the list on the wall in back. Refer to that, should you be unsure when your turn is. Let's get started. Good luck to you all."

I was about three quarters of the way down the list, so I would be waiting for a while. I kept myself loosened up by doing little routines, nothing too fatiguing, while visualizing my solo in my head. Marcus was up next, so I walked to the side of the stage to watch. He was a dynamic, explosive dancer and reminded me of the male dancers at the Bolshoi, in Russia. Strong and commanding while taking over the stage; owning it without apology. I loved watching him, but I had found over the last few weeks, during our work with Madame, that I didn't enjoy dancing with him. There was something about the way he treated me and handled me during our partnering that I didn't like...it made my stomach knot with uneasiness. Shaking off the feeling of disquiet, I watched Marcus finish his solo, which had been exceptional. Natalia was next on the list to perform and stood off to my left waiting.

"Good luck, Natalia." She'd looked my way without acknowledging me, then took the stage.

"Well, that went well," I muttered under my breath.

"Don't worry about Natalia, she's always nervous before taking the stage. She wasn't ignoring you."

I jumped when Marcus, who had evidently snuck up behind me, whispered into my ear. His warm breath, tickling across my ear, sent unpleasant shivers down my spine. I took a step forward and turned to face him.

"Since Natalia does ignore me or shoot daggers at me with her squinty blue eyes, I'm pretty sure she did mean to ignore me. I'm not blind, nor stupid Marcus, not everyone gets along. It's okay though, we don't have to be BFFs. What was going on with the two of you earlier?"

"You've got a sassy little mouth," he said, as he smiled and stepped towards me. "Don't you, Ava?" Though his smile never reached his dark eyes.

I stepped back, turning to watch Natalia, giving Marcus my back. Natalia was very good; had beautiful lines and lovely arches. She flowed across the stage and nailed her leaps effortlessly. When she finished, I clapped despite her animosity towards me. I walked away from Marcus to get ready, my turn was coming up.

When I took center stage, I stood for a moment to appreciate the atmosphere of the beautiful auditorium. I could feel the magic resonating from the boards beneath my feet, so I tried to capture and harness that feeling...housing it within that special place of mine. I nodded to the sound person and waited for my music to start.

* * *

ALᴇxᴇɪ

I sat with an audience of family members at The Shrine Auditorium, waiting for my niece Natalia to perform her practice solo. I turned my wrist for what felt like the hundredth time to check the hour, and then sighed when I realized only a few moments had passed. I would have preferred for Madame not to have mentioned to the dancers about how I had rented the auditorium for the day. I definitely hadn't wanted them to thank me, like some feudal lord, but no sense dwelling on what cannot be undone.

Over the years I'd been to hundreds of these performances, having raised Natalia for the past twelve years. She had come to live with me when she was eleven years old because my irresponsible sister couldn't be roused to drag herself away from her drugs long enough to care for her young daughter. She had finally succumbed to the usual outcome of hardcore drugs and had died ten years ago, wasted and alone.

Natalia had grown up a bit self-centered and entitled. I think I may have overcompensated just a bit, as I was worried she would be lost and longing for her dead mother...or rather, that had become my excuse of refrain. It was my way of deflecting responsibility for her selfish ways.

Despite having been to numerous rehearsals and performances, I loved watching ballet and wasn't too proud to admit it. The emotions the dancers evoked with their bodies and their representation of the music was what drew me in. I had fallen in love with ballet as a young man and that love had never abated, if anything it had grown stronger. So I put up with Natalia's drama, so I could enjoy something beautiful on the rare occasion.

Marcus had just finished his solo and as usual had given a powerful performance. I respected his drive and ambition, when it came to his dancing, but only that. He treated Natalia like yesterday's trash, but no matter what I said to Natalia about Marcus, she wouldn't listen. If she were my daughter, I would forbid her from seeing him. I'd tried playing that card a time or two, but to no avail. He was lucky I hadn't cut his balls off. He definitely needed to be watched, especially since he'd been spending more time with Ivan lately. God only knew what machinations drove that pairing.

Natalia took the stage and moved beautifully to her chosen music. She had really flourished under Madame's tutelage and I would expect nothing less than her to be chosen by the LA Ballet to perform with them. She and Marcus shouldn't have any issues on that front, they were both phenomenal dancers. The next dancer was taking the stage, as Natalia came to sit next to me.

"What did you think, Alexei? I think I did outstanding, and Madame thought so too. Did you see how I hit all my jumps and leaps effortlessly? I will make principal at the LA Ballet with no problem. How could they not want me? I mean really, I'm definitely better than all those other girls dancing with Madame. We're going to Circus Disco tonight to celebrate. Auditions are in two weeks, so this will be the last time to go out and have fun. I don't need any more practice, I nailed everything. Are you listening to me, Alexei? What did you think of my performance? Did you see that crazy awesome arabesque? Hello, are you even paying attention?"

"Uh huh...you looked great, Natalia, very beautiful."

A female dancer had just walked to center stage and had stood there for a moment...eyes closed, face upturned slightly, perhaps listening for something...some cue. As if hearing my thoughts, she'd nodded to the technician who started her music. Who was she? Why did she seem so familiar to me? She was tall for a dancer. She had alabaster skin, but then under the lights they all looked pale, but she glowed, like a luminescent pearl. She had dark hair, but I couldn't tell anything else. Her dancing was beauty and innocence personified. I've watched many a dancer over the years and this girl was probably one of the best dancers I had ever seen. She reminded me of someone...someone I had once loved and lost. I gasped out unintentionally and could feel Natalia's eyes upon me after my uncharacteristic outburst; no doubt her mouth was hanging open as she gaped at me.

"Who's that dancing on stage?" I asked not taking my eyes off the beauty performing, so I missed Natalia's facial expressions, but her voice had said it all.

"Ava." Disdain dripped off each syllable.

She didn't speak again after that, giving me a brief respite from her incessant chattering.

"You will introduce me to this Ava."

"Whatever." Knowing Natalia, this was accompanied by a roll of her blue eyes.

Ava finished her routine and I stood, signaling to Natalia I was ready to have my introductions made. We walked towards the side of the stage where Ava had been talking with a few of the other dancers, pulling a jacket around her shoulders. She must have sensed we were headed her way because she'd stopped talking and awaited our approach.

"Mr. Vinokourov," she said, reaching out her hand to embrace mine in greeting. "I'm Ava DeLaney. Thank you for providing us with this wonderful venue to practice in. I was quite swept away with the magical aura of the stage and the grandeur of the auditorium."

Up close she barely reached my chin and she had an ethereal, delicate quality about her. Her large silver eyes drew me in and I felt as if I were looking into a mirror. When I felt a gentle tug on my hand, I realized I hadn't let go of hers yet. I released it with a small smile of apology.

"Ms. DeLaney, you are an exquisite dancer." As we spoke my eyes roamed her face, taking in all of her features separately...large, expressive silver eyes, small upturned nose, full lips, and a wide beautiful smile, one that lit her entire face.

"I don't think I have seen a more accomplished dancer. You remind me of a dancer I had known in my youth. Grace was quite exceptional and you dance much in the way she had. I saw her perform with the New York City Ballet and I swear it was love at first sight. She stole into my heart with her first fouette."

Ava looked at me in stunned silence. Her eyes shimmered like liquid silver from the sheen of unshed tears. She'd taken a moment to collect herself, visibly gathering her composure, like the jacket she had just pulled around her shoulders. Despite her valiant attempts, a lone tear skated slowly down her cheek. Compelled by forces beyond my control, I saw my hand lift to capture that lone tear. I wiped it gently from her cheek with my thumb, as my fingers rested lightly against her delicate jaw.

"Are you talking about Grace Leclair? She...she was my mother."

❧ 6 ❧

AVA

I WAS MEETING MARCUS and some of the other dancers at Circus Disco, a club on Santa Monica Blvd. It was rather iconic LA and we thought it'd be cool to hang out there. Tonight we were celebrating the completion of our training with Madame. We ended today with our practice solos performed at The Shrine Auditorium. What an incredible experience that was.

Circus Disco was likely to be busy, but Marcus knew someone that worked the door, so getting in wouldn't be a problem. I thought it would do me some good to get out and socialize with others. My headspace was a bit off after my interaction with Mr. Vinokourov. Our conversation had kept playing through my mind and tickling my heart. It was surreal to have met someone who had actually known my mother Grace. It was an amazing happenstance, but I was having a hard time processing it.

Technically, we were all finished today and though I felt ready for the auditions, I planned to continue working with Madame over the next two weeks to perfect my solo. This past month with Marcus and Madame, for the most part, had been

wonderful. Marcus was a dynamic dancer who instilled confidence in his partner and I had felt safe and secure in his arms,
initially that is.

We had connected through our dancing, but I got the distinct impression he would have pursued something more, if I'd
been interested. He was good looking, there was no denying it
and well he knew it. But over the past several weeks I had gently,
yet repeatedly side stepped, sometimes quite literally, his attempts to take us in a direction I hadn't wanted to go. I just
wanted to be friends, but not with benefits. Over the last couple
of weeks, I had become increasingly uncomfortable and it
hadn't helped that Natalia would have happily cut my Achilles
tendon for dancing with Marcus. She was neurotically possessive, which should make for an interesting evening to say the
least, as I might be dodging roaming hands and a knife wielding
ex-girlfriend.

I took a cab to Circus Disco, even though it wasn't far from
the apartment that I shared with Willow. Speaking of that brat
Willow, she totally bailed on me. I didn't like flying solo, with no
wingman, but she had to work at the art gallery unexpectedly.
One of the models had contracted the flu or something, so Willow was filling in for her, as one of the living art models. This
would be Willow's first time participating in one of the private
art exhibits, as she usually attended to the front of the gallery
assisting the clientele. She'd been beyond excited, yet apprehensive, and had been bouncing around the apartment like a wet
poodle with a full bladder. The memory of Willow hopping
around in a crazed frenzy cracked me up so much that I had
snorted out a laugh. The cab driver gave me a dirty look through
the rear view mirror, apparently laughing out loud to oneself was
against the cab code of conduct, who knew? Whatever, that crazy
girl made me laugh and I couldn't wait to hear how her evening
had played out.

Thanks to Willow's neurosis though, I was running late. However, despite my late arrival and the line running down the street, Marcus's friend had come through and we had been able to get right in. When we walked through the club doors we were hit by the heavy beat of Panic! At The Disco's, Miss Jackson which was transitioning into Katy Perry's, Dark Horse. I grabbed Marcus by the hand, dragging him out onto the dance floor. It was packed, but I didn't care. I loved this song.

The club was fairly crowded for a Thursday night, the warm spring weather bringing people out in droves. In no time at all I had sweat running down my back, which was made worse by Marcus snugging up behind me, with his hands on my hips, swaying back and forth. I pulled my long hair forward, over my right shoulder to get it out of the way. It hung down to my waist and I was quite certain by the end of the night it would look as if a family of rats had taken up residence. I should've worn it up like always, but Willow had been quite insistent that, "I absolutely had to wear it down." I'd even let her dress me. Oh well, what were friends for, at least she'd dressed me in something I actually liked.

I was wearing a '50s inspired outfit consisting of a white business shirt with a pointed collar and sleeves rolled to mid-forearm. This had been tucked into a flared, black pleated skirt that hit mid-thigh. We'd paired the whole ensemble with t-strap cherry-red patented leather heels. My makeup was old Hollywood. We used subtle eye color, but with dramatic winged eyes and red lips. I was feeling retro chic, and looked dead sexy, if I did say so myself. I snorted...I was a 'tard and knew it. I might be graceful while dancing, but I tended to be a bit clumsy in everyday life, somewhat like Jennifer Lawrence, well maybe not quite that bad. She had tripped while walking up the stairs to receive her first Oscar, falling in front of millions of people, the poor thing.

After dancing to a few more songs we headed over to the booth where our group had set up camp. Our waitress had already taken the first round of drink orders, so I made do with one of the waters having danced up quite a thirst. Glancing around the group, I recognized the dancers John and Kurt, who were friends with Marcus. Oh and there was the lovely Natalia, with the not so lovely personality. When our eyes connected she glared daggers at me, and then turned back to chat with an older guy sporting a hideous moustache and dark, slicked back hair.

Over the past four weeks I'd repeatedly tried talking with Natalia, but to no avail. I hated strife though, so I would continue in my attempts to be friendly, if not friends. Her possessiveness of Marcus was the problem. She refused to believe me when I had told her that Marcus and I were just friends; it was frustrating not to be taken at my word, as truly she could have him. When our waitress came back, Marcus ordered a beer and I ordered the house white. I wasn't a picky wine snob with a hoity-toity wine palette; hell, give me Boone's Farm and I'd be happy. As we waited, we'd chatted it up, raising our voices occasionally to be heard over the music.

We finished our drinks and hit the dance floor again. We had been dancing for some time, when Marcus left to order more drinks from the bar. I stayed on the floor dancing to Jason Duerlo's, Talk Dirty. Several other people joined our dance group, mixing and matching with people that I knew and those I didn't. I was having fun, meeting new people and getting to know the other dancers better. I danced with Kurt, who was just as 'handsy' as his best friend Marcus. I swear, these guys thought they could just touch you, whenever and wherever. When I stepped back to put a bit of space between us, I bumped into someone behind me. I turned to look over my shoulder just as John stepped up placing his hands on my hips, sandwiching me between himself and Kurt. We danced that way for a while, but when I started to feel like tonight's dinner special I executed a graceful exit, stage left.

I managed to make my way back to our table without tripping over anyone, rather noteworthy and I thought I might have to jot that down in my journal. I was smiling to myself when I sat down at our booth. I risked starting World War III by asking Natalia if she knew whether or not the white wine was mine. She stared at me for so long before answering, that I grew uncomfortable under her scrutiny. When finally she did answer me, it was with an overly bright smile that didn't reach her eyes, as she said, "Marcus dropped the wine off for you before hitting the restroom." Progress...surely not and definitely not after that eerie stare down, it must be the alcohol.

I picked up the glass of wine and sipped it slowly, the fruitiness of the last glass missing from this one. It wasn't bad, I thought and shrugged to myself. It just wasn't as good as the previous glass; maybe it was a different brand. Everyone from our party was gravitating back to the table, finishing their drinks and ordering more and chatting happily with everyone. Marcus, John, and Kurt were sitting next to one another laughing and carrying on. The three guys that Natalia had been chatting with earlier were back as well.

I glanced about the table at the six guys, they were all so different looking, but the lot of them together was a sight to behold. Their hair color ranged from the pale blonde that Marcus had to black. They were all taller than my five foot eight inches and were fit, though some more muscular than others. They were about my age or a few years older. It was amusing to watch the giggling drunk girls from the surrounding tables unabashedly checking the guys out and boldly asking them to dance. I sipped my wine and watched as they flitted about like manic hummingbirds, attempting to catch their notice. Alcohol and conversation flowed freely about the table, as we laughed and chatted about random things. I participated when I had something to add; otherwise, I just enjoyed the atmosphere.

Marcus and John were chatting about some club they'd gone to last weekend, but the music seemed to be playing directly into my head, loud and painfully, so I was having a hard time understanding their distorted voices. Halos were winking around the lights surrounding the dance floor and blinking my eyes hadn't cleared the haziness. I looked at my wine glass, as I put it down on the table before me, noticing it was only half gone. Shaking my head, I picked up my water glass and chugged it in three swallows. Marcus looked at me with a raised brow, and I waved my hand with the universal, yup all's good. I was squirming in my seat restlessly, wanting to dance or go do something else. I didn't know what I needed, but I had to get up and decided to hit the restroom.

As I stood to go, I grabbed the table to keep myself upright, as the room was spinning like a tilt-a-wheel. I rarely drank, but one and a half glasses of wine did not a drunk Ava make. I closed my eyes briefly, only to snap them right back open, as it had only intensified the room spinning about me. While trying to focus, I noticed that Natalia was leading Marcus by the hand, out to the dance floor. Kurt and John followed behind them, leaving me alone with Natalia's non-ballet friends and the creepy moustache guy. I turned to leave for the restroom, but the dark haired guy had grabbed my hand and led me out onto the dance floor. His two buddies were on either side of me and the four of us were dancing on the opposite side of the floor from Marcus and Natalia. Mr. Creepy Moustache guy was still at the table watching me rather intently.

Despite not being ballet dancers from Madame's, all three guys were excellent dancers, though extremely provocative. I felt overwhelmed and uncomfortable with their attentiveness, but yet I felt really good too...loose and limber. The beat flowed through me, like it often did when I got lost in the music. The dark haired guy behind me had started grinding his hardened cock against my ass, his hands rough on my hips. I felt a sudden sharp, painful sensation at my right hip. I turned to look at what had poked me, when the dark haired guy behind me took my hand turning me to face him. My vision was fuzzy around the edges and I squinted at the overly bright lights.

My dark haired dance partner looked me over, searching my face, my eyes, looking for what I couldn't have said, but when he seemed satisfied, he said, "I'm sorry I hurt you baby, my keys were in my front pocket and I keep a church key on my keychain." I must have looked perplexed, because he further explained that a church key was used to open cans and bottles. Well, he had been rather up close and personal with my ass. I shook my head again, though I needed to stop doing that. You'd think I'd have learned by now that it didn't help in the least.

One of the other guys, a tall blonde, handed me a glass of water which I'd taken with a lopsided grin of appreciation. I drank the entire glass, feeling beyond parched, moaning as the cool wetness slid down my throat. I felt a blush creeping over my chest and neck at having moaned out loud, but I couldn't seem to make myself care. We walked back to our table, though I think I may have stumbled a bit along the way. So much for having a graceful night. Once we arrived, I announced with an uncharacteristic slur that I had to use the restroom, and then blushed hotly, feeling completely drunk. Natalia decided she needed to freshen up and came with me. I know, I know...apparently despite the adversarial nature of our relationship, girls pairing up to go to the restroom really was a universal truth. We managed to make it there and back without killing one another, and neither had I fallen into the toilet, though it was a near thing, definitely news worthy on both counts.

The only person remaining at our table when we arrived was Marcus. I decided this was a perfect time to head home, and besides I didn't feel right. I'd have to remember that Circus Disco's white wine packed a punch, as I felt decidedly drunk, despite having had less than two glasses. Cheap date, am I? Lordy, now I was channeling Yoda. That was the deciding factor, I was out. I said goodbye to Marcus who kissed me on the lips, lingering much too long. He wanted to take me home and tried to persuade me into agreeing. Uh...no way, Mr. Hands, I'll take a cab.

Oh God, did I say that out loud? I watched his face closely, though I felt my eyes crossing as I tried to focus. Nope he looked the same; I must have just thought it then, phew! I turned to say goodbye to Natalia, who was staring at me so intently, that it had creeped me out a little. Hey, I hadn't kissed him back! I said a quick bye and stumbled towards the front to catch a cab.

There was a long line of people waiting to hail a cab, so I walked a little ways down the sidewalk to bring up the rear. As I stood there waiting for my turn, my arms and legs felt numb, my head fuzzy, and my vision blurred. I looked down at my purse, fumbling to open it, wanting my cell phone. The line was moving forward, but I didn't notice, as I was still focused on my purse. I couldn't seem to keep ahold of my cell phone, as it kept slipping from my clumsy fingers.

I heard a car stop to my left and smiled drunkenly when I saw a cab idling next to the curb. I moved forward in what felt like slow motion, opening the door and tumbling not so gracefully onto a seat smelling of stale smoke and sweat. As I tried to sit up and close the door behind me, someone entered the cab with me, though I couldn't focus on their distorted face. I felt a sharp pain in my right arm and tried to soothe the sting, but my movements weren't coordinated. When I attempted to speak, everything had closed in, funneling to a single pinprick of light that blinked out, taking me with it.

❧ 7 ❧

sage

"READ 'EM AND weep bitches...full house, aces high! You boys are no match for the man on fire."

With a quick flick of my wrist, I threw my final hand onto the table with a flourish. Grinning like a fool I swept the pot of chips into my growing pile, over two hundred bucks. Moans of disgust could be heard around the table.

"Fuck me running, don't you ever lose, Sage," Carter grumped while worrying his vertical labret, the piercing in his bottom lip. Carter James was my best friend and owner of L'Inked Tattoo Studio where we held our monthly Friday night card games.

"Not if I can help it. Why play if it's not to win." I smirked, Carter knew I was competitive, but liked to win, fair and square.

Twins, Corbin and Shane Johnson, had taken off after we'd cleaned up the pizza and beer mess. Carter and I went to the corner of the studio, where there was a black leather couch and a TV mounted on the wall. Grabbing the remote off the table, I turned on the TV, which was a rebroadcast of the CBS Evening News.

Good evening, Pat Harvey reporting.

Tonight's lead story, once again finds media darling Alexei Vinokourov most recently seen walking the red carpet at the Oscar's, front and center in a new investigation. Sources inside the LAPD and the DA's office confirm an investigation is underway to connect Mr. Vinokourov to an alleged network trafficking small arms, humans, and drugs. Five years ago, Mr. Vinokourov had been investigated in relation to the brutal murder of then Deputy DA Tomi Delacourt's family. DDA Delacourt had come home to find her husband hanging from the banister, brutally eviscerated and her toddler daughter upstairs...dead. Three men making up the security detail guarding the family had also been murdered. DDA Delacourt went missing from protective custody a few days later and has not been heard from since. No charges were ever filed in the multiple homicides. The investigation of Mr. Vinokourov had been shelved at that time.

In other news, the growing trend of young women missing, in and around LA, has not abated. Over the past few days, the LAPD has confirmed another four young women have been reported missing by family and/or friends. However, sources inside the LAPD would not comment as to what, if anything, was being done to protect the women of LA. There's also an alarming increase in abductions around large sporting events that this station has recently uncovered. When asked specifically about this trend of missing persons leading up to national sporting events, such as the Super Bowl, they declined to offer a comment. We will continue to bring you, our viewers here at CBS, the latest information on this ongoing, exclusive investigation.

In local art news, for you aspiring prima-ballerinas out there, don't forget the auditions for the Los Angeles Ballet are in a few weeks. On the CBS website you will find a link for information pertaining to the audition process. Good Luck to all of those auditioning.

Have a Great weekend Los Angeles. This is Pat Harvey for CBS Evening News, signing off.

I hadn't heard about these latest girls that were missing, but Monday's were when I checked in and was updated by Lieutenant Clarke with any new developments. But, as I listened to Pat Harvey recount the story from five years ago, my jaw grew tighter and my gut churned with anger, to the point of nausea.

Tomi remained missing and was presumed to be dead, just like her family. At one time Tomi and I had been lovers, before she married for money and prestige, hoping to advance her career. We had parted amicably, but had lost touch, mainly due to my undercover assignments. However, Tomi had reached out to my grandfather before she'd disappeared, wanting to get a message to me. I'd been deep under at the time and hadn't received the message. Not only had my grandfather died unexpectedly while I was undercover, but Tomi had gone missing and whatever she had wanted to tell me was gone with her. I'd found a note from Tomi in my grandfather's desk stating there was a package she had wanted me to look after. I had never found the package and had no idea as to what that package might have been. Frustrated and grieving, I'd gone back to my assignment, which was where I'd been for the past six years.

Last year, after the death of his only daughter, the LAPD Captain in charge of investigating the Vinokourov organization for human trafficking, recruited me to infiltrate migrant sex clubs operating in the Los Angeles area. Clubs that were thought to be run by Vinokourov. He was suspected of killing the Captain's daughter in retaliation for the new LAPD investigation. The organization was allegedly drugging and abducting men and women to traffic through his clubs. Once there, those abducted were forced into prostitution and later sold through the blackmarket sex trade.

Some of these clubs were garnering horrific reputations. Where nothing was off limits and these men and women were being abused in the most heinous of ways. The more extreme clubs often encouraged the abuse of their slaves, as they were often referred to.

With the introduction and glorification of bondage and punishment by mainstream media and some well-known novels, clubs specializing in bondage and submission were popping up faster than they could be closed. These clubs bared little resemblance to what the lifestyle was really about or how the people involved truly interacted or behaved. This last year of trolling through these gutter clubs had been an exercise in, fifty ways to fuck up my life.

With the abundance of these bondage-type novels, there had been an influx of adults wanting to experiment with bondage. Vinokourov recognized this growing trend and found a way to capitalize on this desire by forming a network of migrant sex clubs. They were attracting a wide variety of people wanting to play at sex. Luckily for these unsuspecting adults, most clubs weren't trafficking slaves and were plain old sex clubs. However, these average, uninformed people were playing at a lifestyle that they knew nothing about and had no idea what they were doing. For example, they had no technical training in rope-play, therefore there had been a corresponding rise in ER admissions, mostly related to injuries sustained while attempting bondage games or the overzealous administration of punishments. No safety measures were being instituted, no safe-words utilized; they were playing at things they knew nothing about.

It would be funny, if it weren't so sad. Though, some nights I worked hard to suppress my laughter and failed miserably, as I shook my head in disbelief at the stupidity of people. If nothing else, their antics provided comic relief for my growing discontent. But, the darkness dogging my heels with the depravation at some of these clubs was becoming hard to ignore.

Case in point, tomorrow I was hitting a new underground sex club in West LA. It wasn't clear if this new club was associated with Vinokourov or not, but there was only one way to find out; attend and participate as the member they all thought I was. Over the past year, I had ingratiated myself so thoroughly into the scene, that the players were treating me as one of their exclusive club members.

"Yo Carter, I'm out. I'll swing by tomorrow night after the club."

"Try not to spank too many asses tomorrow night." Carter gave me a knowing nod and smiled. Stupid fucker, good thing he was like a brother to me or I would have wrestled his scrappy-ass to the floor right then, forcing submission MMA style. Probably should have anyway, that would've helped release some tension.

I hopped into the Stang, my restored, but not stock 1965 cherry-red Mustang Raceback and had taken off towards my home in Laurel Canyon. I gripped the steering wheel, brooding over my current assignment. Carter was the only one who knew I was undercover and how much I was hating it. He gave me grief to lighten my mood, which had been caustic at best. But damn it all, I was done with this crap.

This assignment was wearing on me. I was done having to watch people have sex. Done with watching men and women abusing one another, in an attempt to find what they think they need. A need that would remain forever out of reach, considering they didn't know what they wanted for themselves, first and foremost.

What these people sought, but didn't recognize, was the surrender of their trust to another for the attainment of a deeper intimacy. That was the missing piece that often sent people looking elsewhere for answers, like through these clubs. I hungered for that connection too...a living, breathing entity formed when two people came together in perfect harmony, one the extension and fulfillment of the other. I don't feel that can be attained without the combination of two souls, perfectly matched and attuned; and it wouldn't be found here in this hell.

Driving west on Melrose, I turned the Stang north onto N. Crescent Heights Blvd. Cool spring air flowed through my opened windows, blowing my longish dark hair into my right eye. By the time I crossed W. Sunset Blvd I'd relaxed into my seat and my left hand rested indolently on the wheel. My watch bezel was glinting in the streetlights and the radio was playing jazz soothingly through the speakers, tempering my mood.

The corner of my mouth kicked up; apparently Carter had hijacked my preset radio stations...again. He was quite the prankster and loved to change the settings on my stereo to random stations.

My all-time favorite radio station prank was when they had all been set to Radio Disney. That particular time, I'd had a date in my car with me. We'd been heading down the Pacific Coast Highway towards Laguna Beach. My date had reached over and turned the radio on. Carter had put the volume on high, so the speakers started bleating out Hannah Montana. God that had been hideous, especially at that volume. But, more so because visions of a stick-like Miley Cyrus, twerking Robin Thicke, and humping a foam finger had been looping around my head on repeat. Once you see it, you can't un-see it. There was no rinse and repeat button to scrub the vision clean.

Smiling at Carter's intuitiveness, I enjoyed the soothing, mellow jazz that was his attempt at taming the discontent that had been growing inside me. Pulling into my circle drive a couple miles up Laurel Canyon Blvd, I sat in my car and enjoyed the night view of downtown LA.

Tonight, I was meeting with that Russian guy I'd been pandering to for months now. He was on our shortlist of players, mainly for the reputation he'd attained with his overzealous punishments and extreme bondage. He definitely seemed low-rung to me, but if he could get me into Vinokourov's world...I'd take it. The number of missing women was escalating and needed to be stopped.

❧ 8 ❧

NATALIA

"**R**AT BASTARD!" I screamed through clenched teeth while slamming my hand against the steering wheel.

I just knew it! He had to be cheating on me again, though I'd naively thought we'd worked things out. He'd been sniffing around Ava from the moment she'd pranced into Madame's and now there was someone else? I wanted to hate Ava, I really did, but she'd been so nice to me even when I'd been downright hateful. For the most part I had tried to ignore her, so I wouldn't have to be mean. It drove me crazy that Marcus wanted her, but then he always wanted something or someone.

Yesterday before our solos, we'd fought over Marcus wanting my help to get Ava drunk. He was hoping with her intoxicated she'd be more willing to go home with him. He'd said, "If I could just have her once, then I could fuck her right out of my head and be done with this obsession." Does he think I'm stupid? I know how he operates. Thursday after she spoke with my uncle Alexei, who'd acted completely out of character, I'd been sure to invite Ava to our after party at Club Disco...just as Marcus had demanded.

Ava had ruined his carefully laid plans for the evening by leaving and going home in a cab. Her solo departure had prevented Marcus from getting his way, which was never a good thing I've discovered. So here I was on a Saturday night following his cheating ass around LA, waiting for the opportunity to catch him in the act once and for all.

After what had seemed like endless driving, Marcus had finally pulled into the driveway of a craftsmen style home. The neighborhood was nestled within an affluent area on the outskirts of Pasadena. Praying he didn't recognize my car, I drove on by and parked down the street and around the corner. Walking slowly back towards the house, I wondered how and why Marcus would be in such an area, unless some socialite was slumming it. He was beautiful and all that, but when it came right down to it, money was what mattered most, especially to the women living in these houses.

There were several cars parked around the house and I recognized a black one as Ivan the creeper's. He worked with my uncle and I had known him for years, not that I liked him or chatted with him much. Last night he had crashed our party at Circus Disco, sitting at our table like he had every right to be there. I can't figure out how he had even known we would be there. And why was it every guy I knew stared at Ava so covetously. I didn't get it. I had checked her out trying to see what the attraction was, but I couldn't see it and for God's sake she had huge fucking lips. Whatever!

I was getting pissed off all over again. I wanted to walk up to the house and boldly ring the doorbell and bang on the front door, just to see the look on their faces. The thought of Marcus and Ivan, along with whoever else was in that house, laughing in my face stopped me from storming the front stoop. Instead, I snuck around the back of the house hoping to find a door unlocked and got lucky, or so I had thought. Stepping quietly inside the house, I stood in what seemed to be a mud room just off the kitchen. I was shaking my head at the stupidity, given we lived in drought-ridden LA, when I heard the voice of a distressed woman cry out in pain.

My night's mission to catch Marcus suddenly seemed childish and I wanted to leave before someone discovered me cowering in this stupid mud room. I turned to do just that, when I heard another cry of pain. Looking out the back of the house, then over my shoulder towards the kitchen, I sighed and turned back around to go see what was going on.

Shaking and scared, I walked quietly towards where I thought I'd heard the woman's cry of pain, as well as the distinct tenor of male voices. Whipping my head back and forth, I prayed no one would catch me sneaking about. I looked around the corner from where I stood, seeing an empty hallway with lots of closed doors. My heart was racing, knowing that without a doubt, whatever I sought would be at the end of that hallway, behind the very last door.

I looked around once more before moving quickly towards the door in question. Holding my breath, I peeked through the crack where the door met the frame and quickly covered my mouth before a startled gasp could escape. I stood frozen, blinking my unbelieving eyes, hoping the vision before me would disappear between one blink and the next. I felt sick with dread and remorse when nothing had changed.

"Have you guys been at it the whole time I was gone? Jesus Ivan, did you at least give her some water? When was the last time you gave her a dose of the drugs? We don't want her remembering." Marcus asked, while unbuttoning his shirt and kicking his shoes into the corner.

"We gave her more drugs about thirty minutes ago and she had more than enough water with that. The video is done so who fucking cares. I'll be taking her to the Club later anyway," Ivan said as he stepped away from the girl.

She was blindfolded with her arms bound behind her back. Her widespread knees and chest were resting on a padded bench. Her face was turned away from the door, so I couldn't see who she was. I watched in horror as Marcus walked up behind the girl and slammed his cock deep into her with one brutal thrust. She cried out in pain with the force of his attack. Grabbing a fistful of her hair to aid in his thrusting, her head was yanked back, giving me a glimpse of her face, a rigid mask of pain.

"I don't think I will ever get enough of this one. I might decide to keep her and to hell with the club. That's it, baby, you know you love it. You've cum repeatedly for me, for us, haven't you? Can't deny the evidence trickling down your thighs. Oh and I will make you cum again and again, don't you doubt it. I'm hardly done with you."

I thought I would throw up right there and forced myself to swallow the vomit coating my throat. How long had they been raping her? I turned from the scene unable to watch the brutality of Marcus raping Ava. Nostrils flaring, I attempted to control the nausea and rapidity of my breathing, knowing if I didn't they would give me away. It was so over with Marcus. There would be no reconciling after his obvious infidelity, no matter how much he begged and apologized.

"Ivan, get me a beer?"

"Get your own damn beer."

"Busy here."

"Ingrate."

Shit! Turning fully around, I frantically looked for a place to hide. I opened a door to what turned out to be a linen closet. Seeing no other options, I crawled in under the bottom shelf curling into a fetal position to fit. Hooking my fingers under the door, I pulled it silently shut just before Ivan walked past me. Resting my forehead on the carpet, I turned my head towards the door so I could watch for shadows underneath. I was afraid to blink for fear I might miss something or be discovered.

I must have fallen asleep because I opened my eyes after what seemed like hours of being stuck in the damned closet with the cloying scent of Snuggle Bear fabric softener. Unable to escape, I'd been forced to listen to their endless assault on Ava; over and over again they'd raped her. The deafening quiet had pulled me from my listless stupor. I heard the faint sound of footsteps leaving, a door shutting, then the unmistakable voices of Ivan and Marcus talking close to my closet hell.

"Okay, so while she's recuperating for the next round, let's go get something to eat. I don't know about you, Ivan, but I've worked up quite an appetite," Marcus said while zipping his pants from the sounds of it.

"Let's go to Bistro 45, off Colorado on Mentor. I'm in the mood for Simon's Scottish salmon."

"I don't care where we go Ivan, as long as you're buying, but I'm driving. I'd rather be dead than caught driving around in your POS black car. Hey, what do you think about keeping this one for ourselves. I'm no where near being done with her and you seemed to be enjoying her assets too."

"No, we have tonight and that's final. We already have a buyer for her at the club and he's expecting delivery tonight. Besides, we tried that last year and again about a month ago and neither ended well, did they, Marcus?"

I'd never heard Ivan so commanding. Usually he was placating and sounded rather stupid, like he'd only just disembarked from mother Russia. This Ivan made my hair stand on end and break into a cold sweat. While this Marcus made me feel dirty. Dirty and used, a cheap whore to the stranger he was.

I had to get out of here. I was hungry and my legs had long since gone numb from being cramped in the closet for so long. I heard the door slam behind them, cutting off their arguing voices as

Marcus was still trying to make a case for keeping Ava to themselves. I waited a bit longer before opening the door with slow deliberation. I heard the other guys leave earlier or I thought I had, so I checked down the hallway left and right to be sure. When I felt safe, I crawled out of my closet hell.

Slow to stand, pins and needles were attacking my legs as I unfurled from my fetal position from under the bottom shelf of the closet. I shook out my legs and my cramped back, and then stretched my stiff neck left and right. I had to get out of here before Marcus and Ivan came back. I started down the hallway with that intention in mind, when I heard Ava moan from the bedroom where I had first seen her. I kept walking down the hall, ignoring her and her pitiful mewling; I didn't want to become involved in this. As I rounded the corner back towards the mud room, I stopped and sighed. No matter how much I wanted to walk out the door and leave Ava and all her problems behind me, I couldn't do it.

I turned around and walked quickly back towards her room with decisive determination. When I opened the door, I found Ava on the bed, naked and hands bound to one of the posts. I wasn't sure how I was going to get her away before someone came back. She was going to have to help me if she wanted out, or I'd just turn and leave for real, that's all there was to it.

I searched the drawers for something, anything she could wear, finding a shirt and some running shorts. My hands were shaking so bad that I dropped the clothes twice on my way over to the bed.

I stood looking down upon Ava and felt a wave of pity, she was looking pretty rough. I untied her wrists and went about putting the clothes on her as if she were a helpless toddler sound asleep. By the time I was done wrangling Ava into the clothes I'd found, I was dripping with sweat and out of breath and frustrated that she remained oblivious.

"Ava...Ava," shaking her shoulders, and with my mouth next to her ear I yelled her name as quietly as possible.

"Ava, come on you have to wake up. Ava, please, I want to get you out of here." Her lashes fluttered a little and she rolled her head back and forth, but wasn't waking up. Seeing no other options, I pulled my arm back and smacked her across the face.

"Please...please no more." Her pleading tone brought me to my knees. What have I done?

"Ava, we are getting you out of here. No more I promise. Let's go right now! Get up, you have to help me. Let's go right now or I swear I'll leave you here, I've had enough."

She was finally able to sit with my considerable help, though she was listing back and forth. After multiple failed and aborted attempts, we managed to get her off the bed and onto wobbling legs. Placing my shoulder under her arm, we stumbled down the hall and out the back door, like two sailors after a weekend bender. When I saw lights coming down the street I hid us behind some bushes until they passed and then we made our way to my car. I shoved Ava into the passenger seat and buckled her in, then ran around to my side of the car and took off back towards Hollywood.

When we were closer to where I thought Ava lived, I stopped by an alley just off Melrose and helped her out. While I may have wanted her free from the hell she'd been trapped in, that didn't mean I wanted to be involved. So I decided to leave her in the alley and she could make her way home from here without too much trouble.

"I'm going to drop you off here Ava. I know you live close by, so just walk home, okay?" As I gave her these instructions, I led her to the end of the alley, out of sight from the street. As I turned to leave, I saw Ava had already fallen over onto the dirty pavement and I was plagued by indecision. Self-preservation ultimately won out and I left her there. She'd be all right I told myself. She was at the back of the alley, hidden from view. She'd be safe there...yup she'd be fine. Mmmhmm, just fine.

What was I going to do about Marcus and Ivan? Nothing, that's what. I'd just pretend I didn't know anything about them having had Ava. That'd be for the best...for all involved. I'd just act ignorant to the whole damned drama, shouldn't be too hard.

❧ 9 ❧

sage

Present Day

W HAT THE FUCK!
I opened the door, thinking the shadow was a homeless person and had planned to offer some pizza leftover from last night. I hadn't expected pinwheeling arms and legs.

I heard a startled, "Oomph," as I thrust my arms forward and lunged to catch the falling girl. I landed hard against the floor, but managed to keep her cradled against my chest, hopefully sparing her from injury. At the sound of a long, slow inhalation I looked down, checking to see if she was catching her breath from the fall or was in pain.

Her skin appeared unnaturally pale and her full lips colorless, though chapped and raw at the corners. Her long brunette hair hung over my arm, spilling onto the floor in a tangled puddle. As I checked her over, she snuggled in closer, turning her face up towards mine. Dark lashes framed beautiful, liquid silver eyes. Eyes that were bloodshot and clouded with pain, silently pleading for help. A moment was all we had, before her eyes fluttered shut and her body went limp. I placed my hand above her mouth, feeling for the warm exhale of breath and I sighed in relief when a soft puff of air caressed my palm. The pulse in her neck was beating rapidly, but fuck...so was mine.

"Carter, Carter...CARTER."

"Geez, Sage, keep your fucking panties on. I'm right here...." His voice trailed off when he saw me sitting on the floor cradling the unconscious girl.

"What the hell! Where did sleeping beauty come from?"

"Don't stand there gawking you idiot...call 911." Turning back, I contemplated sleeping beauty, thinking that was the perfect name for her.

"They said they'd be here quick like. The station house is just down the street." He thrust his hands into his pockets, pacing back and forth, worrying his labret.

"Grab a blanket from the back, she might be in shock...her hands are like ice," I was holding her left hand, when Carter came back in and placed the blanket over her.

"Go out front Carter so the paramedics know where we are." I directed him, never taking my eyes off her ethereal face.

I heard several sirens coming. I would bet LAPD was tagging along as well. She was breathing in soft, shallow pants and her pulse still fluttered frantically. I hooked a chair with my booted foot, dragging it over to us and propped first one of her legs and then the other up onto the chair. I noticed dark bruises ringing each of her delicate ankles, looking suspiciously like ligature marks. I picked up one of her hands and noticed the same bruising around each wrist. Some fucker had abused this beautiful, delicate girl. Rage flashed through me quickly and I snapped my jaw closed, tight and quick, nearly biting my tongue in the process.

Squealing breaks and screeching tires announced the arrival of the ambulance and LAPD. Harsh voices and equipment echoed loudly. Booted feet slapped against the dew dampened pavement, as LA paramedics and LAPD rushed through the doorway. The paramedic dropped his rescue bag next to us and began a quick head to toe assessment of sleeping beauty while throwing questions at me. The LAPD beat officer decided to start hitting me with questions too. One after the other, in rapid fire they drilled me. One of them was about to be handed their ass, 'cause the need to vent my spleen and release some tension rode me hard. Since Mr. Paramedic was tending to sleeping beauty, tag Mr. Officer, you're it.

"Officer...Shut the hell up. Let's attend to sleeping beauty first, and then I'll answer your questions." I glared at the LAPD officer through slitted eyes, making sure my point was made and received.

Once that beatdown was over, it took a second for me to realize the paramedic was talking to someone through his mic, saying, "...She's unconscious, quite possibly drugged, dehydrated, heart rate is elevated and thready at 130, blood pressure low at 75/40, skin is pale and clammy, pupils dilated." He stopped briefly, listening to someone through the ear piece tucked into his left ear.

"An IV has already been started, normal saline wide open. Heads up for the trauma/rape team, rape is highly suspected. Apparent ligature marks on bilateral wrists and ankles and faint bruising around her neck." While he listed the more obvious transgressions against her, he stared into my eyes assessing my reaction. I looked down at her delicate neck and saw the faint bruising circling it. When I looked up and into the questioning eyes of the paramedic, whatever he must have seen in mine had him nodding his head as he finished with his report. With no way to vent the rage and helplessness that was pouring through me, at her obvious abuse, I could only imagine the fury that would have been glowing within my blue eyes.

"En route with Jane Doe to Cedars-Sinai, ETA 5 minutes. Unit 517 out." Once the paramedic finished his update to the hospital, he asked, "Is there anything you can tell me that might help with her treatment?"

"She was leaning against the front door, but I could only see her shadow. Thought she might be a vagrant. I opened the door and she literally fell into my arms. She was briefly conscious, initially shaking like maybe jonesing for some crack. She looked used and abused." I stated through clenched teeth because that was exactly what had went down. "After she looked up at me, she promptly passed out."

Mr. Officer took that moment to jump in with his questions. I guess he'd been patient enough. So while they loaded beauty onto the gurney I answered what I could, which wasn't much.

"My name is Sage Cartier. I was here visiting my friend Carter James, who owns L'Inked Tattoo Studio. Got here around 9 pm and sleeping beauty arrived around 1:30 am. Called 911 around 1:33 am. Don't know anything else."

"That's all you've got?" asked the LAPD officer with blatant irritation.

"Yup, that's all I've got."

"I'll take down your info and if I have any further questions, I'll be in contact."

"Sounds good. I'm going to the hospital too, in that ambulance like it or not. She's alone and until we know where her family is, I will be her family." As I stared down the officer and the paramedic tipped his head at me in the universal, 'let's go' head nod. Completely not protocol, but fuck it. Rules were sometimes bent, oftentimes broken.

"Carter, I'm headed with them, catch you later my man. I'll grab the Stang tomorrow. Watch over my baby."

Stepping out front, I hopped in the back of the rig, where they had already loaded beauty. I sat on the bench along her left side, picking up her hand. I gently caressed the back, my huge mitt dwarfing hers. I'm not sure what it was about this girl that tied me into knots. Probably the situation, but I couldn't stand to see a woman hurt, let alone one so obviously abused.

"I'm Brian Patton," the paramedic said, as he continued working to stabilize her, but she had yet to rouse. Her heart rate had decreased, while her blood pressure had increased, both of which were positive signs the paramedic told me. About half way to Cedars-Sinai her hand moved a little and her respirations picked up. Brian looked at her face expectantly. Her lashes fluttered and her eyes opened to reveal liquid silver shimmering in confusion.

"What's your name?" Brian asked.

At first she looked at us with utter incomprehension, blinking a few times as she tried to clear the cobwebs. Her tongue peeked out swiping moisture along her plump, but chapped bottom lip and haltingly whispered her name. A name that would be etched upon my heart and soul forever.

"Ava," she said with a hoarse whisper, "Ava DeLaney."

With that, she closed her eyes and gripped my hand tight, yet brief. It seemed exhaustion pulled her under this time Brian assured me.

At the hospital everything was bright, loud, and ran at warp speed. We were hustled through the ER doors from the ambulance bay, down a hallway past admitting and directly into a trauma bay. Ava, I loved the sound of her name as it rolled around the confines of my head, had awoken again when we arrived at the hospital.

Brian was giving report to the Registered Nurse, an attractive red-head who was writing everything down on an admissions record. Three other nurses, who wore gloves, gowns, masks, and blue caps that covered their hair, were attaching Ava to various monitors. Careful not to touch her too much, as they were clearly attempting to preserve any evidence collected. They still spoke to Ava with a gentle, but reassuring tone.

I waited for someone to kick me out, but Ava still had a death grip on my hand. The LAPD officer from L'Inked stood outside the trauma bay door, talking with another officer. Ava squeezed my hand, so I turned my head back to her, eyebrow cocked in inquiry. She searched my face, and probably found me lacking, as I'm sure I was looking a bit rough. I hadn't shaved in days and my longish hair was a mess from having repeatedly ran my left hand through it in agitation. She finished her inspection, which had felt much like a caress upon my bare skin, and so I squeezed her hand hoping to offer some sort of comfort.

She looked into my eyes and whispered, "Who are you?"

At first the question seemed odd to me, how could she not know? But then, how could she? I swallowed trying to wet my dry throat and croaked a husky, "Sage Cartier."

Ava nodded, and then turned back to the nurses caring for her.

❦ 10 ❧

AVA

TURNED MY FACE away from Sage, focusing on the wall where an old clock was loudly ticking away the seconds of my life. How many had I missed? How many had been stolen, never to be reclaimed? The red-haired nurse came over and began talking to me. I could hear her but I wasn't tracking what she said; nothing was penetrating the cold numbness I was wrapped in.

My mind was drifting off again when I felt a gentle hand upon my cheek. I turned towards Sage, who was cradling my face like delicate blown glass about to shatter. His beautiful eyes were looking at me with a tenderness that I honestly couldn't comprehend. I didn't know Sage, but I couldn't deny that I felt drawn to him, which was probably due to the drugs I had been given.

"Ava, the nurse needs to collect some blood. Then they'll be starting your exam in a few minutes, when the doctor arrives." He said with sadness resonating through his husky voice. I didn't understand that, nor did I understand the sudden flash of anger that replaced the shadows lingering in his electric blue eyes.

I turned to the nurse who'd been patiently waiting for me to get my shit together and nodded my consent. Sage was still holding my hand and I gave it a tight squeeze. The nurse had already gathered all of the necessities to take a blood sample. Placing a tourniquet around my arm, she swabbed my antecubital space, which is that crease at my elbow, with an alcohol pad. Still wrapped in numbness as I was, I barely flinched when the needle pierced my vein. She withdrew multiple vials of blood, and I saw a rainbow collection of colored tops...blue, green, purple, and red. For some reason, this had a small smile pulling at the corners of my mouth because clarently several quarts of blood were required for all of the tests ordered. A small bubble of normalcy floated through my consciousness, as I thought of my friends young son blending the two words clearly and apparently, to make his own perfect word...clarently. I used it all of the time. As the nurse taped a cotton ball over the puncture site, a petite Asian woman wearing hospital scrubs and a lab coat walked in.

"Ms. DeLaney, my name is Dr. Sabella Wong. I'm going to be performing a forensics exam on you, but first I wanted to ask you some questions." I liked that she was direct, but soft spoken. I felt a small measure of comfort in that. However, I didn't like the look that she was giving Sage. He responded by standing up and giving my hand a squeeze. Oh hell no! I was having none of that and wouldn't let go.

"Please don't make Sage leave." I hated the pleading tone in my raspy voice.

"I'm sorry, but it's protocol. I have to ask you some difficult questions, Ms. DeLaney, and I have to perform a very intimate exam. It would be best for Mr. Cartier to step out into the hallway. He may return as soon as we are finished."

Sage lifted his hand and caressed it gently down the side of my face. "I will be right outside the door, Beauty. I won't be far." He gently pried my fingers from his colorless hand, blanched from how hard I'd been gripping it.

"Sage, please don't leave. Please don't leave me." I was sobbing at this point, going from numb to overly emotional in a single breath. I felt raw and exposed, knowing that for whatever reason, only Sage could hold my edges together and keep me from bleeding out.

"Stay, please stay," I begged in a broken whisper. I turned towards Dr. Wong, imploring her with my eyes. Couldn't she see I felt like I was dying? I closed my eyes and took a deep breath, trying to gain some semblance of control. Nothing in my life would ever be the same. Everything was different. I was different and could feel the strangeness trying to break through the cold surrounding me. At the sound of whispering I opened my eyes to see Sage talking to Dr. Wong. She was nodding her head, with a look of surprise upon her face. Sage turned around and walked back to me. He sat, picked up my hand again and just like that, all was right with my world. Well not really, but Sage was able to stay and that was a start.

"Okay, Ava, let's get started. I'm going to record my questions and your answers. Would that be all right with you?"

I nodded my head in consent.

"I'm sorry, Ava, but would you please verbalize your consent for the recorded record?"

I said yes aloud for the record, but the emotion and enormity of that simple answer was evident in the rasp of my raw throat.

"For the record, would you please state your name and that you are consenting to be examined and treated?" I did as she asked.

"Very well, then let's begin. Now, Ava, I'm going to be asking you some questions while performing your exam." She gave me a reassuring smile, hoping I'm sure that the diversion of questions would distract me from the poking and prodding. The red-haired nurse, whose name I couldn't seem to remember, brought over a standing screen and placed it between Sage and I.

"There's an opening, here in the middle of the material," she said as she showed us. "This will allow you to continue holding Sage's hand, but will afford you some privacy during the more delicate parts of the exam."

I nodded, acknowledging her kind gesture with the screen. "I'm so sorry, but I can't remember your name."

"No worries, it's Aubrey," with a small reassuring smile she turned and walked over to Dr. Wong.

Dr. Wong started with some simple questions: age, birthdate, height, and weight. Was I current on all of my immunizations? When was my last tetanus shot? Was I currently taking any medications? All the while, she and Aubrey had been scrapping under my nails, including the hand held by Sage. Next, they had me slip off the t-shirt and running shorts I was wearing, neither of which I had ever seen before. These were placed into an evidence bag and I was left wearing a thin, white sheet. Putting my hand through the screen again, I blindly searched for Sage's hand. He captured mine gently, soothing my wrist with his thumb. The questions continued: relevant medical history, recent illnesses, past surgical history, if any.

"Ava, when was the first day of your last menstrual cycle?" Dr. Wong asked me, her gaze steady, giving nothing away.

"Well....I don't have periods. I've always been irregular, so a few years ago my doctor gave me a shot to stop them altogether. She'd said because my body fat was so low from dancing, that my cycle would remain erratic and that the shot would help."

More to herself than to me, she muttered, "That's good."

Shaking my head at all the fuss, I realized that up until this point the exam hadn't been too bad, just some questions and nail scrapings. Aubrey snipped a piece of my hair, placing it into another evidence bag and after sealing it shut, she grabbed a special swab stick, saying, "Can you open your mouth for me, Ava? I need to swab the inside of your cheeks?"

Confused, I didn't respond at first, until it dawned on me as to why. Although I opened my mouth slowly, the movement had still aggravated my sore jaw and cracked lips. But Aubrey managed to swab my inner cheeks separately, despite my limitations.

"What day is it, Ava?" Dr. Wong inquired when Aubrey had finished.

"Huh? Trick question, right? To see if I have a head injury or something? It's Thursday night, Friday morning?" I answered, coming out more as a question than as a statement.

Dr. Wong gazed at me sympathetically. "Actually," she paused for a moment, as if allowing me time to accept the inevitable, then continued, "It's Sunday morning, Ava."

My stomach dropped and a hummingbird tried to escape from inside my chest. I was about to lose my shit for real and if Sage hadn't been holding my hand, I think I would have fallen to pieces. Oh...My...GOD! I started shaking. I'd lost days, literal fucking days of my life were gone. Grabbing my head with my right hand, hazy memories pounded away at my skull, only to dance away, like manic bumble bees stinging when I got too close.

"The last thing I remember was getting ready with my roommate Willow on Thursday night. I had planned to meet with some of the other dancers from Madame's Dance Studio at Circus Disco. We were celebrating the completion of weeks of ballet training in preparation for the auditions with the LA Ballet. Why...why can't I remember anything else?" The confusion and the blank space in my memory were freaking me out and I started hyperventilating.

Dr. Wong explained that whatever combination of drugs I'd been given, had probably caused retrograde amnesia. The amnesia making me forget the past few days, including the events leading up to when the drugs were administered. Retrograde amnesia, may or may not be permanent she had informed me. Her explanation didn't make me feel any better.

"Whatever drugs you were given or least what type, should be revealed in the blood we've already collected and the urine we will collect once we are finished here."

Dr. Wong stepped away, leaving me with my senses reeling and endless questions as to where I'd been. She came back carrying a special ultraviolet light called a Woods Lamp, she explained. After releasing Sage's hand, they had me stand at the side of the exam table. I was standing on an evidence sheet that had been placed onto the floor. They put it there to collect any evidence that should happen to fall off me, that way it would still be collected and processed.

I was unsteady on my feet, naked and shivering, but I managed to stay standing while waiting for the next exam. Aubrey turned off the overhead lights, just as Dr. Wong turned on the Woods Lamp. Everything white was glowing. Dr. Wong ran the lamp along the front and back of me, verbally noting for Aubrey and the record anything she found that should be documented. The lamp illuminated various things that were invisible to the naked eye, she explained to me when I asked what they were looking for. When she finished, the lights were turned back on and I was asked to sit back down on the exam table. They looked over my skin again and noted the ligature marks on my wrists and ankles, as well as the bruising on my neck and buttocks. They remarked on how chapped my lips were and the cracks that were in the corners of my mouth. Next, they assessed my breasts, specifically my nipples, which were red, distended, and very bruised. They burned and ached beyond imagining. Good Lord, what had been done to me and why?

Aubrey brought over a little metal stand that contained various instruments, slides, fixatives, and a lubricating jelly. Dr. Wong sat on a rolling chair and asked me to scoot to the end of the bed, placing my feet in the padded stirrups. I did as she asked, then reached back through the screen to hold onto Sage for dear life. He'd been so quiet through the entire exam, but I could feel his comforting presence despite his silence. A bright light, clipped to the metal stand, was aimed at my lady bits, illuminating her and all of her bald, naked glory.

"Okay, Ava, I'm going to do a visual exam of your genitals, externally then internally. I will explain everything as we progress, that way you won't be alarmed. I want you to tell me if you experience any discomfort or pain." I agreed and she got started, telling me where she planned to touch, but more disconcerting, telling me what she found during her exam.

"Outer and inner labia are bruised and swollen. I'm going to touch you now, and spread you apart gently. Clitoris is extremely swollen with a raw, chaffed appearance." She gently ran a lubricated thumb across my clitoris, and my butt clenched and jumped a little off the exam table. A moan of pain, and to my mortification pleasure, escaped my mouth. I managed to stifle my sobs, but tears of pain and frustration leaked from the corners of my eyes. I could feel a trickle of arousal slide down the crack of my butt, forming a little wet spot under me. I was beyond mortified. How could I find that stimulating when I'd been so obviously abused?

"I suspect you were given some kind of sexual stimulant Ava. The drug will control your body, making it respond whether you want it to or not." It didn't make me feel better, but I understood what she was saying.

"I'm going to put a speculum in now and use a special scope that will allow me to check your vaginal walls and cervix for any bruising or lacerations." I felt the warm slide of metal followed by the ratcheting clicks of the speculum being engaged.

"There appears to be extensive vaginal bruising, including the cervix, which is swollen. There's a large tear where the hymen would have been located. Were you a virgin, Ava?" With the incredulous tone she had used to ask the question, you'd think I was some sort of mythical creature that played with faeries and rode unicorns. Though she probably hadn't meant to sound so unbelieving.

Sage gripped my hand tighter, the only sign of emotion he had expressed so far, but that little gesture broke my reserve. I started sobbing uncontrollably, shoulders shaking and tears flowing unchecked. I whispered to Dr. Wong, "Yes...and someone stole it from me."

"What was that, Ava?"

"Yes, Dr. Wong, I was a virgin before all this was done to me. Not only did they steal two plus days of my life, but they stole my virginity. My virginity. Mine! My gift...Damn it! I wanted my first time to be with the man I loved." My voice trailed off, getting smaller. "The man I would have given my heart and soul to, but they took that from me and it's not fair."

Sage dropped my hand suddenly, the abruptness scaring me. But then there he was, with his back to the doctor and his bright blue eyes fixed upon my face. He sat down next to me on the exam table and somehow managed to pull me into his arms without disturbing Dr. Wong's exam.

"Shhhh, it's okay, Beauty, don't cry. What happened doesn't count." Sage leaned over me, kissing my forehead with a light press of his lips, and then I felt his cheek pressed to the top of my head.

"Your first time can still be with the man you love and if he's truly worthy of you, he will know it for the gift that it is. That special moment will be yours and his. No one can take that from you. It will still be your gift, Ava, to give in love." His voice was low and husky, wrapping around me, just like his arms. I could stay just like this forever, getting lost in the sound of his voice and the comfort of his arms. Well, maybe not just like this. I'd prefer to have some clothes on. Oh and nothing says, "Hey, I'm Hot," like having a doctor hovering between your opened legs and a speculum shoved into your vagina.

"Are we almost done? I mean, every girl dreams of being the life of the party and all, but I think I've had about as much fun as I can handle." I whispered against Sage's chest. My voice cracked at the end of the sentence, raspy from the rawness of my throat and the need to suppress these futile tears. Everything about my body was raw...inside and out...my mind, my emotions...my heart and soul were raw and bleeding. I felt a breath away from shattering into a million little pieces. I think Sage may have shot the good doctor a look of reproach while my eyes were closed, because she cleared her throat and give a little sniff before speaking again.

"Ava, we are indeed almost finished. Are you settled enough for me to continue with the exam? With Mr. Cartier on this side of the barrier?"

"Yes, but may we please be done soon."

"All right then. I am going to do several vaginal swabs and a curetting, which is a scrapping of sorts. We need the specimens to run multiple laboratory tests. These tests are to rule out any venereal diseases, cultures for potential infections and tests to assess for any DNA matter that doesn't belong to you, Ava." As she explained all this, Aubrey handed her some instruments. The samples were collected, put in their proper containers, and then placed into sealed evidence bags to be sent for processing in whatever method was required.

"I'm going to exam your rectum now, Ava."

Sage hugged me tighter. I felt his jaw clenching against the top of my head, where he'd been resting it. Really, was nothing on my body left sacred? I felt her spread my cheeks gently apart, yet it was still uncomfortable. And apparently no, nothing had been left untouched. She informed me that I'm slightly red and have a few small tears, but nothing major.

"By the feel and look of things, some kind of anal lubricant was used, thank God for small mercies."

"I'm pretty sure the mercies afforded weren't for me, Dr. Wong."

She inserted a lubricated finger into my rectum, assessing for internal damage. A small whimper escaped. It was definitely un-comfortable, bordering on painful. Just as I was about to tell her to stop, she withdrew her finger.

"There is definitely some damage to your rectum, Ava, but thankfully none of the tears are through the rectal mucosa. No further intervention will be necessary. However, you'll need a stool softener for the next week or so, but other than that, your rectum should heal with no problems. Additionally, I'm prescribing a fourteen day course of antibiotics."

As she was explaining this, Aubrey covered my legs and placed them back on the exam table. If I hadn't felt raped before, because I couldn't remember what had happened, I was feeling it now. My every nook and cranny had been poked and prodded. I had been exposed and examined under the bright lights...leaving me nowhere to hide and no way to ignore what was done to me. I had been violated and in the most heinous of ways, there was no escaping it and no way to recover from it. How was I supposed to reconcile who I was before, with who I was now?

I didn't want to be this Ava, victim Ava. I wanted to go back to ballet Ava, virgin Ava, waiting for her one true love Ava. This Ava was gonna suck! Aubrey brought some hospital scrubs for me to wear, but I felt so dirty, I wanted to scrub my skin clean first and told her so.

"I can give you a wash cloth and a towel, the restroom is through the door over there," she tells me, pointing to the corner of the room. "However, there is only a toilet and a sink in there, I'm sorry to say."

At this point, I'd have used toilet water to bathe. But hey, warm running water was even better. I could at least clean the lubricant off. Sage helped me to the bathroom and I handed Aubrey the sheet I'd been wrapped in. She would add it to the growing collection of evidence to be catalogued and processed. Thank God there was no mirror, as I wasn't sure I could have handled looking at myself too closely in the bright light. I don't think I would have liked what I saw.

I used the toilet first and it had burned far more than I had anticipated. Plus, lucky person that I was, I had the distinct pleasure of trying to pee into the cute little specimen cup that Aubrey had left for me. Taking short panting breaths, I focused on the task, instead of the pain, just so that I could empty my full bladder. Good Lord! I washed up and put the scrubs on. Wanting my hair off my neck and out the way, I tied it up into a sloppy bun by twisting it around upon itself.

Stepping out of the restroom, I noticed the exam room was empty, except for Sage. He was leaning against the wall, talking on his cell phone in a low voice. He must have sensed I was watching him because he turned and looked at me. Rage and pain were competing emotions on his face and in his eyes, before they were quickly replaced by alarm and concern. Before I knew it, Sage was holding me cradled against his chest and I was shaking again.

"You overdid it. You were swaying on your feet Ava, like a sapling in Santa Ana winds. Luckily, I have quick reflexes or you would have ended up on the floor again."

He sounded almost angry with his gentle reprimand. I chanced a peek up at him, his face giving nothing away. His eyes were glowing hot and bright, the blue electric in their intensity and they were focused completely on me. Our little interlude was interrupted by the clearing of Dr. Wong's throat. We broke apart, though Sage kept his arm around me, probably concerned I would pass out again.

"Ava, why don't you sit over here in this chair? You look about ready to drop and we can't have that. We need to go over what will happen next and your discharge instructions." Dr. Wong sat and I joined her, sitting in the chair she had recommended. Sage decided to remain standing, but positioned himself behind my chair with a gentle, but supportive hand upon my shoulder.

"First off, Ava, is it acceptable to you that I speak freely in front of Mr. Cartier? I would be happy to ask him to wait outside while we finish our discussions."

Oh, the good doctor was exercising a little muscle. I raised my brow at her though. I mean hadn't the horse already left the barn? Hadn't the boat already sailed? Hadn't the cherry already been popped? 'Too soon?' I thought to myself. But, I had no more secrets left, no mysteries to uncover. Sage probably knew more about me than my best friend Willow. Oh Willow, I wanted my best friend more than anything right now. She was going to absolutely freak out! If she tried to feel guilty about going to work...well, Ava just might have to cut a bitch.

"Really, Dr. Wong, thank you, but we are long past the time for privacy. I appreciate your concern, but Sage is a huge comfort to me. He's already heard and seen all the nastiness done to me. I'm just thankful he can stand to touch me, when I can't stand the thought of my own skin resting against my muscles and my bones. I feel utterly disgusting, dirty beyond comprehension. So if it's all the same to you, I'd like to finish this up. I want a scalding hot shower and a gallon of soap in the worst possible way."

"Very well then, Ava. All the evidence we've collected will follow strict protocols implemented in cases such as yours, thereby preserving the chain of custody. This was done to protect you and the evidence collected. In the event the evidence collected is required in the prosecution of the guilty party, we want no questions as to the validity. We want the person responsible to be held accountable and we don't want any loopholes getting in the way of justice."

She went on to tell me in more detail that they will be checking for infection, venereal disease, any sexually transmitted diseases, including hepatitis, and of course for pregnancy. Though with the shot, I should be protected, and she confirms this.

"I could offer you the morning after pill, Ava. However, at this point I'm afraid plan B wouldn't help you because too much time has passed."

My knee started bouncing up and down, mirroring the rise in my anger. Whoever had done this, had not only raped me, but had ripped the virginity from my body, hurting me in ways that I had yet to comprehend or even imagine. I was only just realizing they may have left behind some wonderful little presents too. Presents that I couldn't stamp with return to sender or re-gift and send to someone else. The longer I thought about all the potential scenarios, the more pissed off I became, but I would rather be mad and angry as hell, than sad and defeated.

"I want you to take the antibiotics for the next fourteen days as prescribed. I want you to take the stool softener I mentioned earlier, for a few weeks and you should be careful with your diet; be sure to get plenty of fiber and drink lots of water. You don't want to get constipated and strain to have a bowel movement."

Ugh...maybe we could have kept that potential difficulty a secret from Sage. Discussing the rape was easier than this, maybe this one thing could have remained a mystery between us. I looked at Sage over my shoulder, offering a self-effacing smile and a shrug that said, 'well we could have done without that little tidbit being aired, all public like.'

"I want you to follow up with Aubrey in two weeks. She's a nurse practitioner trained specifically in sexual assault cases and is a certified Sexual Assault Nurse Examiner (SANE). She will have your lab results and can do another exam to be sure that you are healing properly. I will leave you the names of some well respected crisis counselors, should you like to talk to someone about how you are feeling and coping. Do you have any questions for me, Ava?"

I sat there for a moment trying to think of important questions. I'm sure tomorrow, when I've had more time to process things, I will have a million and one questions, but right now...not so much.

"Thank you, Dr. Wong, for your care and gentleness during the exam. I don't imagine it was any easier performing the exam than it was receiving it. But you made it as tolerable as could be expected."

She nodded her head to me and then glanced to Sage before she turned to leave. At the door, she turned back and let us know that a different LAPD Officer would be in to take a final statement from me.

A few minutes later the LAPD officer sauntered in, preening like a peacock with its chest puffed out. Something about his demeanor made my skin crawl and I was immediately on edge. Sage must have felt me stiffen because he stepped behind me, placing both hands on my shoulders. I felt simultaneously comforted and protected.

I waited for Officer Peacock to introduce himself and begin his questioning, but apparently he wasn't quite ready to start. First, he needed to do a very thorough visual examination, I would assume, by the way he looked me up and down. I watched his face as he did so and if the sneer on his thin mouth was anything to go by, he found me rather lacking. I swear I could hear Sage grinding his teeth and a low growl in his throat. I shifted to look at him, but he kept me in place with a firm, but gentle hold on my shoulders.

"Officer!" Sage barked at the cop. He looked up at Sage and whatever he found on Sage's face had him straightening and clearing his throat.

"Yes, well...my name is Officer Todd. I am with LAPD's Robbery-Homicide Division, Special Assault Section (SAS). I have some questions for you, Ms. DeLaney." Looking up at Sage, he asked, "And you are Sage Cartier, the one who found Ms. DeLaney at L'Inked Tattoo Studio on Melrose?" I felt Sage nod his head in confirmation. Officer Todd continued, though returning his gaze to me. "It is to my understanding that before Mr. Cartier found you at the studio, you two had never met before. Would that be a true statement, Ms. DeLaney?"

"Yes." My voice was soft, but hoarse from crying and the abuse I had suffered to my throat.

"Just as I had expected. Mr. Cartier you'll have to step outside while I question the witness regarding the events of the past several days."

I may have only just met Sage, but I knew without a doubt that Sage would not be budging one inch from behind me. Officer Peacock could just go fuck himself. Sage confirmed this with a simple, but emphatic, "No." Officer Peacock was so taken aback by the force of Sage's answer that he quite literally stepped backwards.

"I think Ms. DeLaney has been through enough already, don't you Officer Todd? She has no memory of the kidnapping, nor of the rape that she suffered at the hands of that sadistic mother fucker. Her last memory was of being in her apartment with her roommate Willow early Thursday evening. She vaguely remembers waking in the alley, but her first clear memory was of falling into my arms at L'Inked. So unless you have something else to ask or to add, Ms. DeLaney has been released and would like to go home now. So why don't you leave your card and if she thinks of something else, she can contact your department." But not you was implied.

"No evidence was found in the alley or the surrounding area. We suspect you were transported from somewhere else and dumped there. Then you made your way down the street to L'Inked Tattoo Studio."

Really Sherlock, you figured that out all by yourself? Officer Peacock wasn't the brightest bird in the flock. I shook my head at his stupidity.

"We were unable to find your wallet or purse. But I did contact your roommate, a Ms. Willow Sinclair. She's been updated that you were found safe and unharmed."

I jumped out of my seat so fast, I almost fell over. I stalked towards Officer Todd who, by divine happenstance was shorter than me. When I was standing directly in front of him, I had the distinct pleasure of looking down at him.

"Really, Officer Todd. You call what I have suffered as, "unharmed?" Are you insensitive or just merely stupid? If you would but open your eyes and look at me, you would clearly see a girl who has been abused and grievously so. Have you taken the time to speak with Dr. Wong about the injuries I sustained? What I've suffered? How dare you stand there judging me as if I were a whore trolling Sunset Blvd. Fuck! You!"

I was shaking with rage. Did he think that I had somehow brought this upon myself? That I deserved it? Did I? Had I been leading someone on, being a cock-tease? Had I wanted to go with this person? Had I actually liked it, enjoyed it? I grabbed at my head, as the pain brought me to the floor and I curled into a fetal position, deaf and blind as to what was going on around me. Until I felt someone lifting me and I struggled to get away. The musky scent of Sage wrapped about me, like a warm blanket and I settled right in. He walked us across the room and sat in a chair, cradling me against his chest again.

As I was coming back to my senses, I heard him speaking softly to me, "Come back to me, Ava. I've got you now. Come on, Beauty, come back, honey. I won't let anyone hurt you." Each statement was punctuated with a small kiss to my eyelids, the tip of my nose, my cheeks, the corner of my mouth and ever so gently along my chapped lips. Then so softly I had to strain to hear him, Sage whispered against my mouth, "I would kiss away every hurt you have suffered, taking the pain into myself. I would use my body to protect and to serve yours. I would show you what it was to be properly loved, if you would but trust me with your body. Come back to me, Beauty. Don't leave me here, alone and lonely, not when I've just found you."

Sage kissed gently down my face, capturing my tears. Opening my eyes, all I saw was Sage and that was all I needed. His eyes were shimmering as he looked down upon me. "Welcome back. You had me worried."

When he ran his left hand through his already messy hair, I noticed his knuckles were reddened. I asked him what had happened after I collapsed to the floor. Evidently, when Officer Todd and his condescending attitude had pushed me too far, Sage had pushed him quite literally, with a fist to his jaw. Then he had thrown him out of the room, stating his Lieutenant would be hearing from Sage.

"The good doctor Wong was going to sedate you, but I wouldn't let her. I hope you don't mind that I intervened. I didn't think you'd want to be under the influence of drugs again."

"Thank you, Sage. I would not have wanted to be sedated, I've definitely lost enough already, including time. I really do want to go home now."

"My friend Carter, the one who owns the tattoo studio you stumbled upon, brought my car over. I can drive you home, if that is all right with you?"

I was still cradled in his arms and though I didn't want to leave the comfort they afforded me, but I wanted to leave the hospital more. I moved to sit up and Sage helped me to stand. I felt a little more in control while standing on my own two feet and I finally answered Sage. "Yes Sage, it's more than all right with me. But, dear God, if you don't mind, let's hurry before someone else comes along to block my escape from the insane asylum."

"All right, Beauty, let's go before the little men with white coats come to take us both away." He smiled a lopsided grin at me that had a little dimple winking in his left cheek. How could I have missed that? Sage removed his leather jacket and held it out for me, and I placed my arms into the sleeves. It was still warm from his body and I pulled it closer trying to inconspicuously inhale some of the heavenly Sageness embedded in the collar. He ushered me out of the exam room with a gentle hand to my lower back and took us back down the corridor towards the ER entrance. We stepped into the cool morning air and crossed the parking lot to where his car was supposed be parked and waiting.

We approached an older car that had been beautifully restored and I have no doubt it belonged to Sage. I thought it might be a Mustang, but hey, I'm a girl and cars aren't really my thing. I do love my powder blue VW bug though. I looked to him for confirmation and he nodded with a beautiful smile that completely transformed his face. His dark hair was hanging in disarray across his forehead and I was momentarily struck dumb. I quite literally stopped in my tracks, jaw hanging open and just stared. At this point, I was kind of jealous of his car. He must love that car a lot, to smile so beautifully at its mention. I could only hope and pray that one day someone would smile like that at me.

"She's a beauty, isn't she? I restored her with my grandfather years ago. I'd wanted a few modern conveniences though, so I can't say she's stocked to original. But I don't care, I love her anyway."

Sage opened the passenger door for me and I slid onto the cool leather seats. He shut my door softly, and then went to his side and got in. Giving me a quick once over before he started the engine and then we were off.

⊰ 11 ⊱

sage

A S WE DROVE away from the hospital, I was ready to commit murder and to hell with my career. Ava was quiet, gazing out the window and I couldn't possibly imagine what she must be feeling as she relived and processed the events of the last few hours. Those events were currently ripping through my mind and soul, causing me to grip the steering wheel tight enough it creaked in protest.

Ava had been drugged and violated by this unknown person for days. As if that weren't enough, she'd consented to a forensics exam, in essence being violated all over again. Intellectually, I knew that wasn't true, she'd been treated with the utmost respect and care, but I hated that she'd been subjected to the process at all. She was quite the scrappy little thing however, impressing me with how she'd handled herself with the good doctor, but especially with Officer Todd. First thing Monday his Lieutenant would be hearing from mine. His behavior had been despicable at best and there had better be some sort of disciplinary action implemented.

What was I going to do about Ava? She represented a multitude of complications and an array of answers all rolled into one beautiful conundrum. Lieutenant Clarke would not be happy about my bringing a potential witness home. No matter how many ways I tried to explain the situation, any defense attorney would have whatever information that Ava provided us discredited, stating collusion with the prosecution. It didn't matter that I was worried about her safety or that in all good conscious I couldn't just drop her off at her home and drive away knowing she could be in danger. Added to that was the fact that I was currently working an undercover assignment and by stepping out of character, I could ruin and undermine the persona I had spent the last year developing.

In truth, there was nothing to be done about Ava. I couldn't change who I was, even though, at times, I had to pretend to be someone else. I was taking her to my home in Laurel Canyon and I'd deal with the fallout later. Decision made, I relaxed my grip on the steering wheel as a sense of calm descended over me.

"Sage, where are we going? This isn't the way to my apartment?"

My calm evaporated with the sound of fear lacing her raspy voice and dancing in her beautiful silver eyes. I was worried she was going to fall out of the damned door, with the way she was pushing herself away from me and up against it. Shit, I'd locked it, hadn't I?

"Ava, I realize you don't know me, but you've trusted me all night, don't stop now. Trust yourself. Know that I wouldn't do anything to harm you. I don't think you should go home. You should call your roommate, Willow, right?" She slowly nodded her head. "I think you should tell Willow to stay at a friend's house for a few days. We don't know who did this to you or why. For all we know that person could have your address and could be planning to take you again. Perhaps even your roommate. I want you safe and I'm sure you want her to be safe too."

She still looked fearful, but that was slowly morphing into anger...good. I'd hoped bringing Willow's safety into the mix would help her to trust me and illustrate the importance of staying away from her apartment for now. I wasn't ready to let her go just yet anyway. I reached my hand out, giving her the option to embrace it or not.

"Ava, I can't imagine how hard it must be for you to trust right now and especially not a stranger. You must be wondering if you had trusted the wrong person and ended up in that dirty alley. Take a leap of faith with me, Ava. I'm one of the good guys. I will keep you safe, Beauty. Trust in that, if nothing else."

I waited as she searched my face for hidden motives and half-truths, but I was being as transparent as I could be. I couldn't tell her I was a detective with the LAPD, that part I had to keep hidden. My heart leapt at the trust she afforded me when she placed her delicate hand into mine. That took an incredible amount of courage and faith on her part, especially after all that she'd been through. One day I hoped to show her that trusting me was the right thing to do. I continued holding her hand, gently rubbing her wrist as we drove to my home in the canyon. Pulling into the circle driveway, I shut off the engine and we both stared out the windshield, taking in the early morning view. I turned to look at Ava, who was still looking out over LA.

"It's a beautiful view, Sage, and I'm happy to find it so," she said with a small, sad smile.

I agreed that the view was indeed beautiful, but what I didn't say, was that I found her more so. "Let's get you inside so you can get cleaned up. I'll give you a tour of the house later," I told her as we walked through the front door. I disarmed and promptly reset the alarm system, that way she'd feel a small measure of comfort in the safety the system provided. I pointed out a few things as we made our way to the back of the house and the master bathroom.

I had renovated the entire house after my grandparents left it to me. They had lived here for over twenty years, so the house had needed a little lovin' and updating. I'd always enjoyed working with my hands and loved the process of bringing each room up-to-date and back to life. The master bath was especially nice, sporting a deep jetted tube and a tiled walk-in shower with dual shower heads. The former was why I had brought Ava to the master suite. I thought she might enjoy a long soak in a bubble bath, but she had surprised me stating she would rather have a shower. I showed her where everything was located.

When I turned to hand Ava her towel and wash cloth, she was staring at herself in the mirror, a look of horror and disgust upon her face. A lone tear was traveling down the side of her face. I couldn't stand to see her pain and stepped forward to offer her comfort, my hand rising to cradle her face. But as I approached she stepped back, holding her hand up to me, palm out. I stopped, dropping my hand to my side.

"Don't, Sage. I'm afraid if you touch me right now, I'll break." She took a deep, shuddering breath. "You have been so supportive and to a complete stranger, but please...don't touch me right now." The last came out as a whispered sob. I could see she was barely holding herself together, trying hard to be strong and brave. She was trembling again and it took all my formidable strength to stay put, allowing her the space she needed to regroup.

"All right, Ava. I'll go into the bedroom and sit on the bed, but I'm leaving the door cracked. Call out if you need me, otherwise I'll leave you to your privacy." Walking away from Ava just then was probably one the hardest things I'd ever done in my life. So much had been taken from her and right now she needed to feel like she was in control, but that didn't make it any easier.

I stepped into the master bedroom, which I had decorated in soft grey tones and headed straight for the small liquor cabinet I kept near the corner fireplace. I didn't care that it was early in the morning, a couple fingers worth of scotch sounded really good about now. I sat on the edge of the bed with my head hanging forward and held the tumbler loose in my left hand.

I was exhausted from my night at the club, even though I had ended the night early. Whenever I had to pander to that Russian dumb ass, low-rung, bottom feeder, it drained the life from me. He was utterly ridiculous. I would laugh at his antics, if I didn't fear he would take his inadequacies out on someone else. That guy needed his ass kicked, in the worst possible way.

This undercover assignment was killing me. I hated the scum I had to associate with. The kind of people that could have easily been involved in what happened to Ava. They were scumbags...peddlers of flesh and sex. It sickened me the amount of people I saw being forced into prostitution and felt helpless to stop it. I took another swallow of the scotch trying to wash the bitter taste from my mouth, but to no avail.

From where I sat, I could hear Ava as she moved around my bathroom and when the water to the shower had come on. I thought back to earlier this morning, when Ava had literally fallen into my arms and into my life. I was having a hard time reconciling the fact that we'd only just met. What I was feeling wasn't shiny and new. It was raw and gritty, dark and possessive. I wanted to mark her as mine, but she had enough physical marks already and I couldn't begin to imagine the psychological ones. But, having her here with me, in my home and in my shower, was lighting me up and pushing all my buttons. I mean shit; I might as well just piss a circle around her and call it a day...that was how possessive I was feeling. I had always been dominating and decisive, even during my early teens when I was experimenting with sex for the first time. I knew what I liked, what I wanted, and how I was going to get it.

My feelings for Ava were conflicted. I wanted to make her submit, yet I wanted to pamper and hold her. I wanted my scent all over her and in her. I wanted to fuck her so hard and so deep that every molecule that fucker had left behind was replaced with mine and mine alone. Yet I wanted to make love to her softly, sweetly, showing her how beautiful it could be, especially when done in love. I wanted to take away all her pains and carry all her burdens because it was my right to do so. However, it wasn't my right, not yet at least, but I planned to make it so. I knew my own mind and what I wanted. And I had no doubt I wanted and needed Ava...today, tomorrow, and every day thereafter.

During the exam at the hospital, I had held onto Ava's hand hoping my presence would comfort her. Dr. Wong had clinically catalogued every one of Ava's injuries and it had taken all of my control not to react to the descriptions. But when she had described how Ava's delicate tissues were bruised and swollen, her virginity ripped from her body, anger had flashed hot on her behalf, causing my hand to close in reflex. That brief show of emotion had broken Ava's reserve wide open. I had ran to the other side of the barrier to hold her together. Not wanting to add to her discomfort, I had focused on her eyes, capturing her gaze and offering her the comfort of mine. My vivid imagination had painted a picture of what the damage to her body must have looked like.

Just then Ava cried out in pain and I was in the bathroom before I even registered what I was doing. As I stood at the shower entrance looking in at her, I realized my imagination had paled in comparison to reality. Numerous bruises littered her pale skin, a stark testament to what she had suffered. She had her eyes tightly closed as water cascaded over her head and down her body. The water ran gently off the tips of her bruised nipples. Competing emotions were raging inside me just then. I wanted to pound someone into the dirt, retribution handed out with brutal force. Yet stronger than that was the need to kiss and lave her using my mouth to ease her pain. I stepped into the shower after yanking off my shirt and throwing it onto the tiled floor.

"What is it Ava? What's wrong, Beauty?"

Her eyes snapped open to angry little slits. I had expected her to cover herself, but she didn't. Despite her bravado, the pain in her wounded eyes pulled me forward and feeling no reason to check the impulse, I moved to comfort her. She raised her hand, stopping me yet again, a disturbing trend that was chaffing against my nature.

"Talk to me, Ava." My hands were twitching at my sides, aching with the need to hold and comfort her, especially when I saw that she was trembling. A combination of pain, shock, and righteous anger I'm sure.

"Look at me Sage. Look at what that sick fuck did to my body."

I kept my gaze upon her face, stepping forward slowly, but inextricably.

"I said...Look At Me, Sage," she said with desperate anger and a sweeping gesture down the front of her body. My eyes followed her graceful hand, but at a more leisurely pace.

"I'm so dirty, Sage. I want to scrub every inch of my skin raw, but I can't because it already is," she said with a broken confessional like whisper.

At this point, any pretense at being in control of my emotions, had long since frayed beyond my reach. As I stepped closer to Ava, I knew I was crowding her, almost touching her, but I couldn't stop myself. The turbulence swirling through the silver depths of her eyes was pulling me under, her pain so clearly evident. I was literally vibrating with the need to take her into my arms and comfort her. I wanted, no I needed to kiss her chapped lips, caress her bruised body, and alleviate her pain.

I was cradling her head gently in my hands, between one breath and the next, with no memory of moving. I kissed the top of her head and the corner of her mouth, while reaching blindly behind her to increase the water temperature. I was hoping between the hot water and my body heat that she would warm-up and stop trembling.

"How can you stand to touch me? I can barely stand to be in my own tainted, defiled skin. I feel so fucking dirty, Sage. How will I ever be clean again?" She was resting her forehead against my chest, sobbing quietly, and repeating herself.

How would I convince this beautiful woman that she was special, not tainted, used, or dirty? Actions, not words, I thought to myself. Her courageous spirit was shining through, like a beacon I couldn't deny. Everything about her spoke to me and in a language only my heart and my soul could decipher. Our connection could never be duplicated; there was no way I would be letting her go.

"Let's get you cleaned up, Beauty." Reaching for my sandal-wood shampoo, I poured a generous amount into the palm of my hand and worked it into a lather. I loved the idea of her smelling like my shampoo and soap, probably more than I should. I turned Ava sideways to the shower head, wanting to keep her warm, but out of the stinging stream of water.

Her back was to me when I lathered the shampoo into her hair and gently massaged her scalp. Running my hands down the length of her thick hair, it surprised me how when wet it reached to the bottom of her butt. I tried to remain clinical, but it was hard not to notice she had a tight, delicately muscled ballet butt. Something about the body of a dancer had always lit me up. Long, toned, flexible muscles, moving with fluidity and grace, yet powerful and strong. The erection, that I'd been trying not to sport, was very interested in what was literally right in front of us. I swept her hair up to give it a good lather, noticing as I did, all the bruising on her butt and that promptly took care of said erection.

To say I was feeling a bit homicidal would have been a gross understatement. I could have quite happily killed the person responsible for hurting Ava and with my bare hands. I was afraid that if Ava knew or even sensed the depths of my possessiveness, she would be running as fast as she could away from me and the darkness staining my soul.

By the time I finished washing and conditioning Ava's hair, she was swaying on her feet. Between the events of the last few days, the warm humid air, and my relaxing ministrations, the poor thing had to be beyond exhausted.

I grabbed my sandalwood soap and lathered up my hands. I had planned to use a wash cloth, but decided it would have been too abrasive to her abused skin. Plus, how could I deny myself the chance to touch and caress Ava, learning her beautiful body through gentle touches. I draped her long hair over her shoulder, so when I washed her back her hair wouldn't get soapy again.

Mindful of her multiple bruises, I slid my soapy hands down the slender column of her neck gently washing her skin as I went. Next my hands traveled to the delicate curve of her shoulders and after soaping my hands again, I washed her arms and her hands. Then I slid down her beautiful back and sides before turning her. She placed her hands on the wall in front of her at my direction which allowed her to support herself while bending her slightly at the waist.

Careful not to hurt her, I gently washed her hips and noticed the finger imprints left by the bruising grip of her sadistic rapist. My hands trembled with rage at the abuse she had suffered. So I took extra care to be gentle as I washed her beautiful butt, running my left hand between the tight globes, cleansing away the lubrication and oil left behind. Ava took a sharp breath in and I heard her breath quicken.

"I'm sorry, Ava. I didn't mean to cause you more pain." Pulling her right arm up and over her head, she placed it against the wall at a ninety degree angle. Then leaned forward putting her forehead against her arm, as if resting.

Ava cleared her throat before speaking and I noticed the muscles of her back were quivering. "It wasn't painful, Sage, just an...unexpected sensation."

"Okay, Ava, but let me know if I hurt you," I said, then continued on, washing the back of her legs before turning her fully around and positioning her so her back rested against the warm shower wall. Uninhibited, she stood before me with her arms hanging loose at her sides. I ran my soapy hands lightly over her chest and delicate breasts, but I let the soap run over her abraised nipples instead of washing the painful skin.

Ava was flushed from the shower, lending her otherwise pale skin a delicate pink hue. Her eyes were closed preventing me from examining their depths for clues, as to what she was feeling, or thinking in this moment. I made my way down to her stomach and her hips, gliding my soapy hands along the way. Kneeling in front of Ava, I was finally able to see the damage done to the delicate tissues between her legs and nearly came undone.

Controlling my temper had never been a problem before, but with Ava, my emotions seemed to be running near the surface and riding me hard. I took a deep breath and exhaled slowly. I ran my soapy hands ever so softly across her swollen clitoris, abused labia, and down to the entrance to her vagina. I noticed, as I finished gently cleansing the rest of her, that the bruising stood out in stark relief against her waxed skin.

I turned her towards the water, rinsing the soap away, and then guided her to lean back against the shower wall again. I'd been fighting the urge to place my lips upon her and I couldn't resist anymore. I knew I should be worried about whatever diseases that prick might have left behind, but I couldn't make myself care enough to stop. So when I looked up at Ava to see how she was doing, she was gazing down at me with her silver eyes slumberous and passion filled, clearly on the same page.

Leaning forward I placed open mouthed kisses along her bruised left hip, trailing my wet lips across her stomach to her other hip, stopping briefly to kiss and tongue her navel. Her legs were quivering, so she placed her hands on my head for support. I continued to kiss and lave her, wanting to heal her pains with my mouth. I worked my way closer to where I was dying to be. When I gently parted her I could see that she was even more red and distended, flushed with arousal.

I didn't want to cause her more pain, but I absolutely had to taste her. I looked up at her, assessing her response, as I gently placed a reverent kiss upon her clitoris. She pulsed under the soft press of my lips and I took a shuddering breath in, as her hips jerked forward involuntarily. She gripped my hair tight, pulling me deeper into her, though I don't think she realized she was doing it. I was only too happy to oblige, placing more open mouthed, gently sucking kisses, on and around, her clitoris. I flattened my tongue, dragging it from her clit to her weeping entrance and back again, repeating the process over and over, until Ava came on my tongue. A flavor I would forever be addicted to.

I sat her down on the shower seat and walked forward on my knees, nestling myself between her opened thighs. I barely noticed that my jeans were soaking wet and clinging like shrink wrap to my erection...the hungry bastard...tight and constrictive.

I placed my hands on either side of her face, using my thumb to raise her chin. I wanted to gaze into her eyes, as she gazed into mine. I loved that despite what she had been through, she could still look at me with passion filled eyes. Her pain and trauma receding to the background for a brief respite.

Leaning forward, I ran my tongue along the seam of her slightly parted lips, letting her taste her own uniqueness. I pulled her bottom lip into my mouth with a gentle sucking motion, careful of her chapped lips. She opened to me and I had to restrain myself from diving in and plundering her mouth. I was so aroused, I was afraid I would inadvertently hurt her. I had never felt this hard in my life. My cock was ready to explode. I could feel little pulses of cum leaking out with the involuntary flexing of my hips.

With my breath heaving in and out, I pulled away from the haven her mouth represented. Resting my forehead against hers, I tried to calm my racing heart and slow the swaying of my hips, before I came in pants like a green, fourteen-year-old virgin. I was still flexing my ass, I couldn't seem to control it, but luckily I wasn't near Ava's more delicate bits or she'd run screaming for sure. Once I calmed a bit, I placed a gentle kiss upon her forehead and looked deep into her eyes.

"Let's get you rinsed off one more time, dried off, and dressed so you can get some sleep." I said, as I assisted her to stand, placing her back under the stream of water for a minute. After I wrapped a fluffy white towel around her body and another around her hair, I led her into the bedroom.

"I'll be right back, I'm just going to get cleaned up too. I placed lotion and a brush on the nightstand if you want to use them."

I headed back to the shower to strip out of my wet jeans, which was easier said than done. A huge sigh of relief escaped me; damn did it feel good to relieve the strangulation on my engorged cock. I couldn't resist stroking him from root to tip for a moment, just long enough to pacify his need for touch, or so I thought. With each strong pull, I had to stifle the moans that were creeping up my throat, not wanting to upset Ava with my quick ministrations.

My left hand was gripping my cock tighter, my hips were flexing again with each pull, and cum was dripping over my fist, increasing the sensitivity to each stroke. I was biting my lip so hard, I tasted blood in my mouth, but I didn't care. I was so lost in my head, envisioning all the things I had just done to Ava, and all the things I was dying to do. I felt animalistic in my need for her. I wanted to erase that sadist from her body and thinking of all the ways I could do that, got me closer, a few more pulls and I'd be off.

"Sage?" I froze at the sound of Ava's voice coming from behind me.

Turning slowly towards Ava, I searched her face and her eyes for any sign of disgust or distress, but all I saw was inquisitiveness. I was still biting my bottom lip, puffy from my continued abuse. My hand was still wrapped around my cock, which had jumped at the sound of Ava's voice.

I stared into her eyes, testing her resolve. The darkness in me wanting to seek out the weaknesses in her, wanting to exploit those things that would amp her up and bring her to the brink and hold her there. I continued stroking my cock, far too gone to stop, though I probably should have. I watched her, as she watched me, which pushed some major buttons. Her eyes were hooded, but shining with passion and they followed the movement of my hand, as I stroked up and down. With my bottom lip still caught between my teeth, I took my thumb and smoothed the side of it over the head of my cock, slippery from the warm cum and beyond sensitive at this point. I stifled a moan, not wanting to run her off with my aggressiveness. Still wrapped in her towel, she walked closer, stopping directly in front of me.

"Don't hide from me, Sage. We are beyond that I think. Be yourself. I want to hear you, please don't hold back," Ava said, as she ran her thumb along my bottom lip, gently prying it from between my teeth. It felt swollen from where I had bitten the hell out of it.

Ava leaned forward placing a small, but brief kiss against my abused lip, then stepped back a pace or two. But not too far away. So that when I slid my thumb over the tip of my cock again I could easily reach out to her, glossing her bottom lip with my essence. Her tongue peeked out, the tip collecting every drop, and dragging it back into her mouth. A shudder ran through me, because let's face it, that was fucking hot. My grip tightened, as I was closing in on the finish. My heart rate increased, my chest was heaving, and moan after each moan escaped unheeded. My left forearm was taut, my bicep bulging, and I reached out with my right hand bracing it against the shower wall. My head kicked back, as my stroking picked up speed, and I was moaning low and rumbly. I was holding off, extending this moment with Ava as long as I could, just in case I didn't get a repeat.

I felt Ava walk up behind me, snugging her naked front to my back, her pelvis resting against my flexing ass. Her arms snaked around my waist and rested on my tight abdomen. I felt her place a hot, open-mouthed kiss between my shoulder blades, her wet lips and tongue dragging across my skin.

And. That. Was. All. It. Took.

I exploded with the most intense orgasm of my thirty years, moaning out Ava's name. I was still stroking my cock, though my pace had slowed to a gentle drag up and down, enjoying the intensity. I took a deep breath in and out, trying to regulate my breathing and decrease my heart rate. I turned towards Ava pulling her into my arms.

"I should probably apologize, but insincerity isn't my thing. That was by far, one of the most intense orgasms I have ever experienced. I won't say I'm sorry that happened because I most definitely am not. Thank you, Ava. That was, quite simply, incredible." I leaned down and gently kissed her lips. "Let's get you ready for bed. I know you have to be exhausted."

She stepped out of the shower and I ran some water washing my mess down the drain. I handed Ava a new toothbrush my grandfather must have bought and some toothpaste. Stepping into the bedroom, I found Ava an old USC Trojans t-shirt and some boxers to wear and I put on some boxers myself, though I generally slept naked.

"Do you need to dry your hair before bed?" I asked, handing her the clothes.

"No, I'll just braid it. I'm far too tired to fuss with it right now."

I led her back into the master bedroom, pulling down the gray comforter on the far side of the bed, furthest from the door. Ava climbed in and I tucked the covers in around her. Leaning down, I kissed her gently on the lips.

"I'll be in the bedroom next to you, Beauty, call out if you need me and I'll come right in, I'm a light sleeper. The house alarm is set, you're safe here, so please don't worry." I was near the bedroom door when I heard Ava call out.

"Sage...please, just lay in here with me. Hold me so that I can sleep." I couldn't resist her plea and honestly I didn't even try.

I had put her on the far side of the bed, so that I was closest to the door. If someone were to get past my security system, they would have to go through me, to get to her. And I could guarantee, no one was getting to Ava again, no one but me that is. I snuggled in behind Ava, pulling her back to my front. Her curves and hollows, fitting perfectly to my hollows and curves, as if we were custom made one for the other.

"Sage," Ava said softly, her voice drifting into sleep, "thank you for caring for me in the shower."

Thinking that was all she had to say, I answered, "You're welcome, Beauty."

"But, Sage, I especially wanted to thank you...for giving me a beautiful memory to focus upon instead of the nightmares that were plaguing my imagination."

I placed a kiss upon her shoulder and felt her relax into sleep, soft puffs of breath signaling she was out. As I drifted off, Ava safe in my arms, I thought how profoundly my life had just changed. Ava may think I had saved her, but in reality she had saved me by falling into my arms and giving me renewed purpose. I had felt my soul withering away this past year, as it hid from the dark stain invading me with every club door I walked through. Ava was just the light I needed to find my way out of the dark. As sleep finally took me under, my last thought was I could love Ava forever, with no trouble at all.

❦{ 12 }❧

AVA

"A VA?" WILLOW KNOCKED softly on my door. "Ava, please come to lunch with me. You can't stay in your bedroom forever. Come on, honey, we can go to The Pie Hole, it's your favorite."

I could hear Willow outside my bedroom. She probably had her ear pressed against my door, listening for proof of life. When not dancing, I stayed in my room, not wanting to talk to anyone in general, but specifically not about what had happened. I knew she felt guilty about going to work that night, which was ridiculous, she'd had no choice.

"Ava, I really need some retail therapy. Come on sweetness, I'm buying."

Quickly opening the door, hoping to catch Willow off guard, she tumbled into my room, landing on her ass. She glared up at me, a look of surprise upon her face and retribution in her eyes. Shocked at having succeeded so beautifully, I bent over laughing. My tears of laughter quickly morphing into tears of frustration and sadness. I had barely smiled, much less laughed since the rape. So my sudden outburst felt beyond foreign and incredibly awkward.

It had only been a couple of days since I'd been back home from Sage's. Logically, I knew I needed more time to process what had happened to me, but I had jumped right back into life, wanting things to go back to the way they were. I hated being this sad and miserable person. It felt like this oily substance was invading my mind and body, tainting my soul with its very presence. No matter how hard I tried to move on, it clung to me tenaciously. I wasn't coping with the unknowns at all, especially when my imagination kept trying to fill in the blanks. The fact that I may never know who had done this to me or why, was a bitter pill to swallow.

"Come here, you," Willow said from the floor, opening her arms for me. I got down on the floor with her and laid my head in her lap, wrapping my arms around her waist. She stroked my hair away from my face, soothing my nerves. I felt myself relaxing under her comforting touch, tensing only briefly when the bruising around my neck was revealed and she gasped out loud. But, before I could say a word she gently brushed her hesitant fingers over them, acknowledging their presence, without making a big fuss.

"I don't know who I am anymore, Willow. I feel like the Ava I was and have always been is lost and I don't know where to find her. I'm disconnected from my dancing, like there's a barrier of some sort preventing me from reaching that place inside my head, where the magic and creativity occurs. I know you understand what I mean, as you go there too when playing the violin. Yesterday at the studio, Madame said my dancing looked flat, like it was missing something. I wanted to scream at her that she was right. My freaking virginity was missing, stolen from my unknowing and unwilling body!"

I was sobbing uncontrollably now. Ballet had always been my life, my ambition. It defined who I was, what I wanted to be, and if I didn't have that then it felt like I had nothing. I'd been patiently waiting for my chance. I had willingly sacrificed and delayed my dreams, only to have some unknown person rip them right from my grasp. It wasn't fair, but then life wasn't fair, and I knew that all too well. Maybe I should just give up dancing for now and maybe forever.

"I'm so sorry, honey, if I had come with you..." Willow said, sobbing along with me, "...none of this would have happened. I'm so sorry, Ava, it's all my fault. I let you down...my best friend."

"Willow, stop it! First of all it's no one's fault, least of all yours or mine. Shit happens; I'll eventually get over it. But as of right now, you will quit blaming yourself, I won't have it. Tell me about your Thursday night at work, 'cause I'm tired of it being all about Ava. I want to hear about Willow." I gave her a small, sad smile as I sat up, wiping my cheeks with the ratty hem of the USC t-shirt that Sage had given me to wear.

Willow and I sat facing one another on my bedroom floor, lunch forgotten as we got back to the business of friendship as opposed to the business of keeping me from drowning in a pool of shame and sorrow.

"Do you remember that I was going to work in one of the private rooms, as part of the living art exhibit, because one of the girls had the flu?" I nodded my head. "Well um, I didn't know, that um, this particular exhibit was done, well..."

"Out with it, quit stalling. It can't be that bad."

"...completely naked. I was kneeling on a white pedestal, with my butt resting on my heels and a blue satin ribbon tied loosely around my wrists, which were held behind my back. I was told to sit just so, with my chest upright, no slouching, and eyes trained on the floor no matter what I heard." Willow had somehow managed to spew all of that in one long breath.

"Good Lord, Willow. Did they force you? Do we need to go report this?" I grabbed her hands in distress.

"Oh God, no, I'm so sorry I scared you. I wasn't forced to participate, Ava," she said and then swallowed audibly. "I volunteered actually. Oh honey, it felt so naughty to be naked and on display, especially with people walking about me fully clothed. I felt like a Venus de Milo statue, beautiful, but untouchable. The exhibit had only lasted about an hour, but it had felt like forever since I was kneeling on my knees the entire time. Yet it had flown by, especially with how worked up I had felt. Eventually, I could tell people were leaving by the way a gentle hush had fallen over the room. I heard a door snick closed, then a deadbolt sliding home, and figured I was alone. That is, until I heard a whispered command from behind me...a deep, resonant voice telling me to remain still. Damn near scared the piss right out of me, I thought I was alone."

"I probably would have peed myself, right then and there."

"I know, right? So there I was, all alone, and as naked as the day I was born, sitting on a pedestal with my hands behind my back. 'Mr. I have a really lovely voice' was standing just behind me. You would think I would have been dying to turn around to look at him and I won't deny it, I had been beyond curious. But, what I had wanted most, Ava, was to please him by following his instructions, rather than turning around to take a peek at him. His presence, his aura if you will, overtook the room and oddly enough, I was simultaneously comforted and disconcerted. I know it sounds hopelessly untutored and naive, but he had me at, 'remain still.' Something about the dominance in his voice had made me want to do as he asked. It felt instinctual, Ava. I didn't even question it at the time, but how was he was able to reach these emotions inside me that I had never felt before? Because now that he had, they were awakened and alive, and vibrating with the need to make him happy. I don't really understand any of it, especially not how he made me feel what I did."

She took a deep breath, looking away from me. I could see something was clearly bothering her. When she turned to look at me, tears were running down her cheeks. Guilt and remorse were competing within her beautiful eyes, but pain was the most prevalent. I gathered her into my arms wanting to comfort her. It was so much easier to give comfort than receive it.

"Ava, I'm so sorry. If I hadn't stayed after the exhibit was over, I would have realized that you weren't home and reported it sooner. Maybe whoever had you, wouldn't have kept you for so long. It's all my fault, I should have come home." Willow scooted away from me, out of my arms. "Don't comfort me, damn it, I don't deserve it."

"Listen up, you. I'll say it again, but for the very last time, Willow." I scowled at her for good measure." It. Was. Not. Your. Fault! Got it? Not your fault, Willow, nor mine. Now, if you will, I want to hear what happened with Mr. Commanding and his lovely voice."

Willow sat there contemplating whether or not she would fess up to whatever had happened. It was all right there on her face. I wonder if she realized she was emotionally transparent? I bet Mr. Lovely and commanding had been all over that. Poor Willow wouldn't be able to hide what she was thinking or feeling. What an enticement, to any man.

Willow took a deep breath and plunged right in. "So I was sitting on the pedestal, butt resting on my heels, and hands behind my back. He was standing right behind me, so I still had no idea what he looked like, but damn, did he ever smell wonderful."

At this she closed her eyes and shrugged her shoulders slightly, moaning a little as she did so, all with the sweetest little smile. It was if she were enveloped in his unique scent just then, in truth. It was funny how the heart and mind could conjure sensations and feelings from our senses, and pull them from our memories to live again.

"He stepped behind me and pressed against my naked back. I could feel the fine, soft weave of whatever he was wearing. A dove grey suit jacket, I later discovered. He gently pressed tight against me, leaning slightly to the right and he asked me what my name was. I told him and then he asked my age. Twenty-five, I said. After that, things became interesting because he told me to call him Sir. I was not to speak unless asked a specific question, so I remained silent and waited, anticipation bubbling in my veins. He had asked one final question. Was this my first time participating in the private rooms as a living art exhibit, to which I replied...Yes, Sir."

"I swear it sounded like he mumbled it would be my last," she said and shrugged her right shoulder. "I'm not sure. Finally, he said if I did as commanded, I would be rewarded. He backed that comment up with a soft, wet kiss to a spot right behind my ear. My stomach was quivering, like restless butterflies about to take flight, from one simple kiss. A kiss that would have brought me to my knees, had I not been sitting on them already."

"Wow, just wow," I managed to reply, despite my jaw hanging open and practically touching the floor.

"Yeah, wow perfectly sums it up. I'm not going into the details right now. Honestly, I'm still processing what happened later that night, and what those things say about me, and what I thought I knew about myself. I will tell you this, before we left the gallery that night, he had brought me to the brink of orgasm numerous times. He wouldn't let me go over, holding me right on the edge. It was beyond frustrating, yet wickedly provocative. Now, that's enough about that. Let's go to lunch. I'm hungry and you're too skinny."

"All right, Willow, let's go eat, but I'm calling Sage so we can all get together later. You guys need to meet him and I need to see him. Let's meet down at the Santa Monica Pier, it'll be the perfect place. I'll call Sage, while you call Mason and Daniel. Tell them two hours from now, okay? And bring your violin, won't you?"

❧ 13 ❧

AVA

ILOVED SPRINGTIME IN California, a time of birth and renewal. When the air was perfumed with the heady fragrance of orange blossoms. Their sweet scent was reminiscent of my childhood, evoking such wonderful memories. I hoped by going to the beach with my friends today that I might capture a sense of that renewal heavy in the air. Perhaps, I might even find solace in the warm coastal breeze. Realistically, it was probably too much to hope that the breeze would cleanse me of the stain of rape. That tenacious darkness was still clinging to my soul and raping me of my joy. No, I think it might actually take the entire ocean to feel clean again.

While talking to Willow earlier, I realized that I needed to be with my friends instead of alone. I didn't want to wear 'lost and vulnerable' anymore, but it felt like hope had forsaken me, leaving me to drown in this wretched darkness. I prayed that they could pull me from the swirling chaos of my mind.

Willow and I had each made our phone calls...so Sage, Mason, and Daniel were meeting us at the Santa Monica Pier, by the iconic

Route 66 sign. Willow had brought her violin and Daniel was bringing his guitar, knowing it would soothe me. I prayed that seeing Sage would help and not be too awkward. I couldn't get him out of my mind. He pulled me in and despite being a virtual stranger, he made me feel safe and protected. We barely knew each other, but tell that to my heart because it didn't seem to feel that way.

I parked McCoy and we walked towards the pier along the strand, a paved pathway where people could walk, run, skate, or bike. I could see Mason and Daniel hanging out near the Route 66 sign, but I didn't see Sage yet. I searched the crowd and spotted him walking towards us from the opposite direction.

He didn't see me, so I took the time to drink in all that was Sage. His dark hair was messy, which must be normal for him because I'd only ever seen it in disarray. He had on faded jeans, with a threadbare hole mid-thigh and a baby blue t-shirt. Oh my word! He was wearing flip-flops and had masculine, yet beautiful feet. I hadn't seen Sage since he had brought me home Monday. I wasn't sure how to act. We'd argued a bit about my leaving his home because he hadn't wanted me to leave yet, fearing for my safety. But, I had needed my own space to regroup and process all that had happened. Plus, I hadn't wanted to miss my ballet training with Madame, though in retrospect, perhaps I should have taken some time off.

Sage had definitely seen me now. He was walking straight towards me, looking directly into my eyes. When he was closer, I ran towards him, jumping into his arms. I wrapped my legs around his waist and clung to him like a demented monkey. I felt like crying. How could I have missed this, missed him so much already! But I did, I truly did. I put my face to his neck, smelling the uniqueness that was Sage and pressed a kiss to his neck.

"Hey, Beauty, I've missed you too." I kept my face buried in his neck. "Ava, look at me please," he said while giving my butt a little squeeze with his hands.

I looked up at him through my lashes, feeling a bit shy. He placed a soft gentle kiss upon my lips, then my cheek, my neck, over the bruising still lingering there and back to my lips for a deeper kiss.

"Hi, you," he said, after reluctantly pulling his lips away.

"Hi," I said breathlessly. "I should probably get down. I need to introduce you to my gawking friends, otherwise known as the peanut gallery, but I like being right here in your arms," I whispered the last little bit into his ear.

Sage opened his arms and I slid down his body onto my feet. I turned towards my friends, who were probably wondering if I were a bit touched in the head by now. I wasn't one to go about jumping into the arms of men I barely knew. They would just have to learn that Sage was different. "All right you goons, get over here and meet Sage."

Willow, my newest friend, was the first to approach.

"This is Willow Sinclair, my roommate. Willow, this is Sage Cartier."

"It's so nice to meet you. Ava mentioned you stayed with her at the hospital. Thank you, Sage, for being there for her. As Ava's family, we appreciate you stepping in for us." She had taken both his hands in her hers, giving them a squeeze.

"And these two guys, trying to act all aloof and badass, have been my best friends since childhood. The taller one is Mason Alexander and standing next to him, is his trusty sidekick, Daniel Creighton." No one said a word, as the three of them were having a pissing contest and staring the other side down. They each wanted the opposition to break first. I scowled at them. If it weren't so frustrating, I'd be laughing at their idiotic posturing. "Seriously you guys, knock it off."

"Sage," Daniel said first, while hooking his thumb over at Mason, "my neanderthal friend and I would like to thank you for caring for our Ava. She's like a sister to us. We've been friends, family really, since Ava was about three. So thank you for caring for her." Always the negotiator, Daniel stepped forward briefly shaking Sage's hand. Daniel was just too beautiful for words. Light brown hair streaked with blonde, changeable hazel eyes, and about six foot tall, which was a few inches shorter than Mason and Sage. He was leaner than Sage, but still had great muscles. Girls loved him, especially when he broke out the guitar and sang. His voice reminded me of Jared Leto, strong but with a great husky rasp. I loved listening to him and he had brought his guitar, knowing I would want him to sing for me.

Then there were two. Sage and Mason continued taking each other's measure, neither wanting to break first. Without a doubt however, I knew who wouldn't break.

"Thank you," Mason said, stepping forward to shake Sage's hand. They were both tall, but that was where the similarities had ended. Sage was well muscled, but lean, whereas Mason was thickly muscled from playing college football at USC. Mason had blonde hair and warm light brown eyes, and Sage was all dark and brooding with bright blue eyes. They both projected an aura of control and dominance, so this posturing wasn't surprising, but it had better stop and soon because I wouldn't tolerate it for much longer.

"Let's go to Soda Jerks, we can get some ice cream or a milkshake, then sit and people watch for a bit," said my peace maker Daniel.

We walked over, placed our orders, then sat and waited. I was sitting on Sage's knee, wrapped in his arms, feeling safe for the first time in days. We weren't really talking, just watching random things, oddly comfortable in our silence. Mason was sitting on the tabletop next to us watching Daniel, who had gone to retrieve our orders and was walking back with a tray full of yumminess.

After handing everyone their orders, Daniel knelt on the bench. He was resting on his knees with his butt on his heels, right next to Mason's feet, like always. They were such good friends and had pretty much been inseparable since elementary school. I could feel Sage watching them too. Mason leaned down to say something to Daniel, which had him turning his face up, listening intently to whatever Mason was saying. Daniel smiled, then turned away to look out over the water. Mason continued looking at Daniel for a moment, before turning to look out over the water too.

"How long have Mason and Daniel been a couple?" Sage asked quietly, after watching them interact for a while. "The love they have for each other is refreshing to see. Must be hard for Mason though, going into professional football, but being dominant will help with any possible locker room drama. I'm sure he's worried about the NFL Draft, not everyone is open-minded about male-male partnerships."

"What? No, they're not a couple Sage," I said, shaking my head at him. "No, they're just good friends, close like brothers. They have always been this way with each other. They're not gay, not that I would care, but they're just friends."

Sage was giving me look that if I were to decipher it correctly, it meant, 'You don't know what you are talking about, crazy woman. It's obvious to anyone looking.'

"My bad, I must be mistaken, you have certainly known them longer," Sage said, with a touch of, 'I know I'm right,' laced through his voice.

I looked backed over to them, thoughtful. Could I have missed them loving each other, all these years?

"Hey, you guys, let's walk down to the beach, closer to the water. We can spread the towels out, then Daniel and I can play some music." Willow had already started towards the water by the time she finished her sentence. Naturally, we got up and followed, like the good little ducklings she expected us to be. It was fine though, I wanted to be closer to the water anyway. Sage gathered my hand in his and we walked to where Willow was already setting up. Sage sat down first, spreading his knees apart to make room for me. I sat, leaning back against his warm chest and I was immediately enfolded into his strong arms. Putting my head back against his shoulder, I nestled in. He was rubbing his thumb gently along the bruising still visible around my wrist, like he hoped to eliminate the damage and the remaining evidence with each stroke.

Daniel and Willow were talking about what song they were going to play first. She was standing, tuning her violin, while he was sat cross-legged on the towel tuning his guitar. Mason was across from the two of them and to our right. We made a lovely little circle of friends. My two boys had been my family for years, but now I had Willow and perhaps Sage too, at least for now.

They started covering random songs and genres, playing beautifully together. They flowed seamlessly from one song to the next, like they had performed together for years. Perhaps they had, while I had been caring for Maman. Their communion was beautiful to watch and to hear. They spoke fluently one to the other, in the exquisite language of music, weaving a melodic tapestry. Willow's violin was the perfect complement to Daniel's voice and guitar, floating over and under him.

Next they played 30 Seconds to Mars, *Alibi*, which had tears slipping from my eyes. Daniel had such a wonderful, husky voice. Sage placed his hand on my cheek, turning my face up to his. I could drown in the deep ocean of blue within his eyes. He delicately wiped the tears from my cheeks and kissed my lips softly.

"This song speaks to me, Sage. Not the relationship aspect, but about falling apart and getting back up again." I was quietly sobbing at this point, so I turned in his arms, straddling his hips and hugged him tight. Daniel's voice and Willow's violin were creating an atmosphere where I felt safe to let go, purging some of the grief trapped inside. Between losing my adoptive mother and the rape, I felt like I was splintering, fracturing beyond repair. I didn't know how I was going to keep it together. How many times would I be kicked to the curb, before I stayed down, with no will to get back up?

"I don't think I can take any more Sage, I've reached capacity. I'm all alone in the world, I literally have no family. My mother and grandparents were killed in a car accident. My adoptive mother died from cancer. I don't know who the hell my father is. Then there's the rape. I mean really, what's next? How do I move on from here? God! I'm pathetic. I feel so lost, floundering on a turbulent sea and drowning, Sage. I feel like I'm drowning." I whispered through my tears, not wanting to interrupt Willow and Daniel, who were playing so beautifully.

"I won't let you drown, Beauty. If you can't find the will to get up, then I'll pick you up and I will carry you until you're ready to try again. Though, perhaps I won't let you go, once I have you."

We sat that way for some time. Sage cradled my fragile spirit in his capable hands and I poured out my grief, old and new. Behind me, Willow and Daniel continued playing and had drawn quite a crowd with their talent. People wanting to listen to the music had migrated over, close enough to listen to the music, but far enough away to be respectful of our space.

Willow sat down when Daniel started his solo. He performed James Wolpert's rendition of Jack White's, *Love Interruption*. I had heard him cover it once before, it was an angsty piece, full of longing. Wanting love to dominate and overwhelm, changing you from being without love, to having a love that consumes you completely. I had asked him once who he longed for, but he had never answered me. Now I wondered if it had been Mason all along and that left me questioning what I really knew about my two best friends.

Daniel's voice was a husky whisper at first, rich in longing, but tempered with sadness. I turned in Sage's arms so I could watch him sing and play. His head was down, looking at his guitar. When I glanced over to Mason, I was caught off guard by what I saw. Love, naked and exposed, shining from his eyes and pain etched clearly upon his face. The longing was so apparent that it nearly broke my heart to see it. He watched Daniel intently, as he sang the lyrics to the song.

Daniel finally looked up from his guitar, hazel eyes brimming with emotion as he gazed over at Mason, who had already looked away to talk to Willow. How could I have missed this? How could they not see what was so obvious? I looked back at Sage and he nodded his head in validation at the truth I had only just realized about Mason and Daniel. I was thoughtful as I continued watching Daniel, who was now chatting with Willow.

"Those lyrics, I had thought they were about some girl he had met in Palm Springs. He never really had any girlfriends and was always hanging around with me or Mason. His family would not be accepting, not at all. Maybe that's part of the reason why he doesn't say anything. Mason though, I wouldn't have guessed he loved Daniel that way, not in a million years. He has always been with this girl or that. I mean I've always thought he was a bit of a, well to put it bluntly, a slut. Do you think that was just a front, to hide what he was really feeling? Neither one apparently realizes that they love each other. Unless Mason knows, but hasn't said anything to protect him. I could definitely see him doing that. He has always protected Daniel, who had a very strict upbringing. His parents have definite ideas about what is acceptable for their eldest son."

"Well, Mason could be protecting him, but in my opinion, I don't think either one knows a damn thing. I think they are so blinded by what they think they know that they don't see what is standing right in front of them, practically waving its arms, jumping up and down."

"Daniel, Willow," Sage calling out to get their attention. "You guys were awesome. Do you ever play at local clubs? I'm no music expert, just your typical music fan, but you two could easily make a career in the music industry, I would think." Sage turned to Willow, saying, "Willow, Ava said you work at an art gallery and play with a string quartet, have you thought of doing something like Lindsey Stirling?"

"Oh, I love her, Sage. She was on one of those talent shows, but didn't do very well. The judges were rather rude I thought, but look at her now. Thank you," she said, with a shy smile.

Addressing Daniel, Sage said, "I understand that you're in law school. If you ever decided to give up your day job and pursue music, join forces with Willow here and I bet you two would be a huge success."

Before Daniel could respond, Mason interrupted, asking, "So what's your day job Sage, Ava didn't say?"

I rolled my eyes at Mason, good grief, still with all the posturing and perhaps a little frustration at his situation mixed in too.

"That's because we never got around to discussing it," Sage answered with a great deal of sarcasm. "What with Ava fainting into my arms as our introduction, an ambulance trip to the hospital, and an exam to rival the rape...Yup, all kinds of time to get down to the inane business of, hey what do you do for a living."

I turned to see Sage was seriously scowling at Mason. "Mason really, what the hell is the matter with you? Why are you being so confrontational? It doesn't matter what Sage does for a living, as long as he's not going around killing people and burying the bodies in his backyard, who cares? I really appreciate that you're trying to protect me, Mason, like the brother that you are, but quit being so confrontational. Would you please try to get along with Sage?"

"And you, mister," I said pinching Sage's bicep, "don't be looking so smug, you're just as guilty. It was an innocent enough question, no need to be all defensive about it. So what do you do, since we're talking about it?"

"First of all," Sage said, "we weren't talking about it, Mason was asking about it. But, to answer the question, I own and operate a private security business." Sage looked at over to Mason, "And with your size Mason, I could offer you a job if football doesn't pan out for you."

◆{ 14 }◆

sage

IVAN, THAT LOW-RUNG bottom feeder, had texted earlier to inform me that he was taking me to Club M, one of the more extreme underground sex clubs. I'd been trying to find this one for months now, but with the migrant activity and exclusivity of this particular club, it had proven impossible to find without help. The group we suspected of running it was highly suspicious of everyone and consequently were stingy with whom they allowed entry, especially into the more extreme clubs. I'd been working this assignment for over a year and was only just now being given access.

My first six months had been utilized gathering information, building my reputation within the sex club scene and planning, always planning on how best to bring them down. Despite how these investigations were dramatized on TV, the reality was, they weren't wrapped up into neat little bows, all within a sixty minute time slot. They took time and patience and I was seriously running short of the latter. This could be the break we needed, so I'd have to dig deep for patience, which might prove to be impossible. Ivan, that little Russian upstart and the current bane of my existence, was the reason for my dearth of patience. He was sadly mistaken however, if he thought he could possibly teach me something or hold my metaphorical reins. It wasn't going to happen, as it was only a matter of time before my threshold for bullshit was breached.

We met in downtown LA, on the fringe of The Fashion District. In this part of town, there happened to be an abundance of abandoned buildings, making it the perfect place for hosting the underground club scene. I pulled into a parking lot on the backside of one of these old buildings. Ivan, Low-rung to me, pulled in and stepped out of his ten-year-old black sedan. I was leaning against my car with my right hand tucked into my front pocket and my right foot crossed over my left, admiring the architecture. Turning towards Low-rung, I nodded in greeting, then turned back to the building, chuckling under my breath as I did so.

Jesus, he was a walking cliché for a low budget '70s porno. Tonight's exceptional ensemble came complete with tight leather pants and a green silk shirt. However, the true inspiration and highlight of my evening was the hideous porno moustache he was sporting and the slicked back hair. Shaking my head, I went back to admiring the architectural details of the historic buildings.

It saddened me that these buildings were being left to ruins and reduced to housing underground sex clubs. Workers had labored for years to bring these intricate buildings to life and here they remained, a testament to the quality of their work, yet here they were, dying a slow death. Where were the preservation societies to care for them? It was only a matter of time before they were beyond saving. As were the unfortunate souls that were trafficked through these decaying doors and housed within against their will.

We went through a darkened alley to reach a set of double doors, where we entered the back of the building. The first thing I noticed, besides the bouncer minding the entrance and it's darkened corridors, was the pervasive, moldering smell of the building. I ran my left hand along the bottom of my nose, which did nothing to help, nor did the lemon Pledge some industrious person had used in their attempts to cover the stench.

We stood inside the entrance waiting to proceed to wherever Club M was located. I took a moment to covertly scan the area, which due to the low lighting, was covered in shadows. There were three corridors off this back entrance. There was a bank of elevators straight ahead of us, but I doubt they were functional. The corridor to the left was completely dark and the one to the right, had an anemic bit of light illuminating the distant part of the hallway, our destination I would presume. I resolutely ignored the way that the thick-necked bouncer guy was staring me down, thinking he was mind fucking the shit out of me. I turned my head slightly, staring back with a look of bored indifference, always a sure way to piss off the hired muscle. He topped me by a good three inches and a solid forty, but if it came down to it, his cockiness would be to my advantage. His black sports coat and blue collared shirt did little to conceal the identifying ink on his neck, nor the weapon on his right hip.

"MO is bringing in some new videos tonight for our viewing pleasure," Low-rung said, while licking his thin upper lip and adjusting his junk yet again. I swear the guy must have, 'the herpes,' crabs, or jock itch...something, because he was pathologically ritualistic about yanking on his junk. I couldn't decide whether I should offer him an antibiotic, some powder, or the number to a shrink, so he could get help for his multiple issues. Though I feared his type of fucked up was beyond help or intervention.

Low-rung had explained how these new rape videos were being featured in a private suite, called the Luxe room. Club members could come to watch and participate in scenarios depicting rape and degradation, while the videos played along in the background. Apparently, the sadistic fucks who got off on these scenarios, could act out the scenes with one of the many sex slaves at their disposal. These slaves were either drugged to ensure participation or fearful for their lives and the possible physical retribution if they didn't. Most were being pressed into prostitution and trafficked through these clubs against their will. For this reason alone, I endured the black stain threatening to invade and corrupt my soul. With each act of sadism I witnessed, with each person lost to this heinous underworld, I could feel the stain creeping in and pushing me towards the darkness.

Down the corridor, at the door to Club M, we found a carbon copy of the bouncer from the lobby. After another stare down, he allowed us entry into the club door. We stepped into the reception area, where there was a greeter of sorts. Though I guarantee she wasn't the kind of greeter you would have ever found at your local Walmart.

She had short spiky black hair with delicate, pixie-like features and pale skin. She was wearing a wide slave collar, which was clearly straining her neck. Someone had attached a rope to the back of it and bound her arms behind her back, thrusting her breasts forward and accentuating their fullness. Rounding out her attire was a set of clover clamps. These were clamped to her nipples with a trailing chain attached to the kneeling bench between her spread knees, severely limiting her movement.

"Welcome to Club M, Sirs," she said with a low, husky voice. Her gaze was down, in what some would consider to be proper deference.

Low-rung completely ignored our greeter. "You must be feeling quite honored to be here, not everyone is allowed to attend our most exclusive clubs, Sage. Club M is unlike any other club you know, not all of them come with greeters." He threw me a smirk that I wasn't quite able to decipher, as he walked towards our greeter, unzipping his pants and pulling out his little pecker. No way, in good conscience, could I call that a cock, it was far too small.

"Give us a proper kiss," Low-rung said, while shoving his little dick into the greeter's mouth with no warning whatsoever. I shoved my hands into my pockets, checking the impulse to rip his fucking head off his shoulders. The abused greeter was barely keeping her precarious balance, her toes gripping the floor for balance. Jaw clenched, I turned away from the noxious scene and took in the room at large. I tried to ignore the grunting from Low-rung and the occasional gagging from the greeter, but I'd have to be deaf not to hear Low-rung grandstanding, like the porn star he thought he was. With the way I was clenching my jaw, my molars were sure to be ground to little nubbins by the end of the night.

For an "exclusive" club, they sure weren't very discerning about their atmosphere. Looking about the main room, I could see they had tried to dress it up a bit, by throwing some cash around. There was up-lighting in muted colors around the periphery of the room, lending a soft glow to the space, along with subtle, overhead lighting. However, nothing could be done to cover the moldy scent of decay pervasive in the air. Though the air was thick with the stench of sweat and sex, that was mingled with cheap perfume and cologne, that the combination of them all could almost cover the moldy smell. I could actually do with some of that lemon Pledge about now.

A bar had been set up in the corner to my right. These low-rent, pop-up clubs allowed alcohol and without a doubt, other drugs too. Whereas the upscale, members-only type clubs wouldn't allow you to have alcohol if you were participating on the floor. They were very rigid about impaired judgment. However, if you came as a voyeur, you were allowed two drinks, but had to stay off the main floor and were kept to the viewing platforms.

I had been on one of those platforms about a year ago, when I'd been approached about going under for my current assignment.

A Year Prior

I'd been wrapping up a case and enjoying a beer, but antsy to be finished with the club scene debauchery. Just as I had been about to leave, a gentleman about fifteen years my senior had sat down at my table. He'd positioned his chair so that his back was to the wall, yet angled so he could still watch out over the floor. Cop, without a doubt. He had compelling brown eyes, which had been framed by short brown hair, liberally threaded with grey at the temples. His no-bullshit stare had assessed me for all I was worth, no fronting and no apologies made. Feeling no need to fill the silence with inquiry, I'd let him look his fill and waited for him to finish. After a moment or two he had nodded, more to himself than to me and proceeded to tell me a story. One that would change, not only the course of my career, but the trajectory of my life.

During the Super Bowl last year, the daughter of Captain Starnes had gone missing. The evidence found on scene had pointed in the direction of suspected criminal, Alexei Vinokourov. The Captain had been in charge of a covert operation to neutralize the criminal network associated with Vinokourov. He'd long been suspected of dealing in small arms, as well as, trafficking humans and drugs. The nabbing of the daughter had been thought to be in retaliation for the newest investigation.

Five years ago, a case had been built against Vinokourov by Tomi Delacourt, a Deputy District Attorney on the rise. Unfortunately, the grand jury had dropped the charges due to a lack of relevant evidence. DDA Delacourt had gone missing from protective custody, along with crucial key evidence, a few days after her family had been murdered. Since then, Vinokourov had

topped the LA District Attorney's need to watch list. It was believed that someone within either the DA's office or the LAPD
had tipped him off again. This time taking the Captain's twenty-
three year old daughter. The Captain and the District Attorney's
office wanted to bring someone into the investigation that was
outside of the department and had no association with the previous investigation.

"And that's where you come in, Cartier. The fact that you're a
detective that has been undercover for over five years, away
from LA, makes you a prime candidate. You're an unknown. We
have detectives assigned to the overt operation that only have
information on the aboveboard investigation. We also have covert operations and those detectives know all that is going on in
the overt operations, plus the covert. However, neither of those
operational details will know about you, but you will know all
about them. Your only contact would be me. We know you're on
a well deserved break, integrating back into society and up for
promotion, from what I hear," the last was stated with a subtle
rise of his eyebrow.

"We would like you to consider going back under, working
these migrant sex clubs, utilizing your skill set to gather intel.
We know they're funneling abducted men and women through
them, now we just have to prove it. Hopefully, we can put
Vinokourov away, once and for all."

✳ ✳ ✳

That had been last year, when Lieutenant Clarke had approached me and here I was, still trolling through hell. Case in
point...Low-rung, otherwise known as, Ivan Dubrovsky, who
was tucking his junk back into his leather pants and zipping
things up. His dark hair had remained slicked back from his
widow's peak, not a hair out of place. Unbelievable! The greeter

had managed to remain upright, an amazing feat considering. While giving her a quick once over, she'd raised her green eyes to mine, but that brief look had been enough. This was no ordinary sex club and she didn't belong here, I'd have to devise a way to change that. Low-rung wanted a drink or so he imperiously informed me over his shoulder, as he strutted towards the bar.

"I'll have a Corona," I told the barkeep, placing some money on the makeshift counter. Nodding, he'd asked if I wanted a lime. "No thanks, I don't fruit my beer," I said, shaking my head. Why in the world would people want to add fruit, to an otherwise perfect beer? I would have to nurse this beer along, I couldn't afford to make any mistakes while under such close scrutiny. Control and decision-making were key.

I glanced over at Low-rung, taken aback by the clear enthrallment in his eyes, the flushing of his cheeks, and the way his mouth was hanging open, practically salivating. Turning to the direction of his gaze, I was sickened by the depravity of the scene playing out before me. The same scene that had Low-rung panting in anticipation. Off to the left of the main stage area, a club member was having a free-for-all flogging a slave. The slave had been bound, bent over a bench, with his hands tied haphazardly behind his calves, with no consideration for circulation or nerve compression. He'd been blindfolded, a dildo strapped securely into his ass, while another club member was in front, shoving his cock deep into his mouth. I turned my head away from the nauseating spectacle, downing half my beer in a single drink. Fuck! So much for not drinking, but that definitely called for several beers, only nothing would ever make that scene palatable. I had no problem with consenting adults going at it, but this was rape, plain and simple.

With my beer held loose in my hand, I left Low-rung to watch the spectacle and wandered the club restlessly. I went about assessing the club participants, those who were being used and abused, against those perpetrating the abuse. I was convinced this particular club was trafficking and by the way most of the slaves were glassy-eyed, they were being kept chemically docile.

I made my way to the back of the room, where I could see a hallway was located. Low-rung had mentioned that Luxe room and while I had no desire to breach its doors, I would do it for the sake of the investigation. There was another bouncer stationed inside the tiled hall. He acknowledged my presence with a nod, but did nothing to stop me. Halfway down the hall, one of the doors had been left open, inviting members in. The dark red door had paint peeling off in little strips, like bark from a white birch tree. There were white letters stuck to the door spelling: Luxe.

I wasn't sure what I would find when I walked through the door, but twenty or more people engaged in various sex acts, wasn't quite it, though I shouldn't have been surprised. They were watching a live re-enactment of a rape at the front of the room, while the video of the actual rape was playing at the back of the room.

Glass shattered at my feet.

The sting of glass shards peppering my leg.

The cool splash of beer was soaking through my sock and pant leg.

I had shut my eyes too late and now the damage was done. Turning from the Luxe room, I walked over the broken remnants of my beer and stepped back out into the hall, completely sickened by all that I had just seen and witnessed. Looking out over the room at large, too many eyes were focused on me, the glass shattering had garnered unwanted attention. I stared back through narrowed, searching eyes, daring anyone to say one fucking word to me, most eyes shifted away nervously. Zeroing in on Low-rung, I walked towards the little pissant with determined strides.

"I want the video playing in the Luxe room and I want it right now," I demanded in a low seething voice.

"So you enjoyed our Luxe playroom. I must say I'm quite surprised, but one never knows what hides beneath another's skin," he said with a wicked gleam in his eyes and a smirk upon his thin lips.

I wanted to grab him by his ridiculous green shirt and show him firsthand what hid beneath my skin. He wouldn't like what he found...retribution. Going with the impulse, I moved to do just that, when I felt someone approaching my back at a rapid pace. Expecting one of the many bouncer guys, I turned rapidly and found another club member instead. Though perhaps not, as he wore a distinct aura of authority and dominance.

"Ivan, why don't you be a good boy and go fetch me a scotch." Turning away in clear dismissal, the newcomer focused his hazel eyes on me.

Bring it on, I had an inferno of rage and was more than ready to vent it. That fucking video was looping around my head and I wanted to scrub my eyes with bleach. I wanted to throw up. I wanted to bang my head against the wall until the images fell out, littering the floor, like shards of glass.

"Pick a slave, do a public scene of some fashion or you'll never find entrance into the world you're seeking," the new comer said.

"The hell you say."

"Name's Trey. You have to show them what you're made of, otherwise the last year of gutter trolling will have been for not. That's why you're here, isn't it? Acceptance into Alexei's elite underworld? We've all had to play the game friend, step up or you'll be out."

"Who are you really?" I stood eye to eye with this Trey, who knew more about my business and what I'd been doing over this past year than he should. By mutual understanding, we had gravitated to a more secluded area, a priceless commodity with so many people crammed into the club. But between the two of us and the waves of 'don't fuck with me' pouring thick and heavy off of us, we weren't likely to be bothered.

"Make your point before Low-rung returns with your scotch."

"Who?"

"Ivan. I call him Low-rung 'cause he's a bottom feeder and drives me fucking crazy with his posturing and strutting about."

"Ha, I like that," he said with a small chuckle. "To answer your question, two words can sum things up nicely; undercover cop."

I was not expecting that, but didn't let it show. Lieutenant Clarke should have been the only one with knowledge, as to my assignment over the past year and what I'd been doing. I wasn't about to trust this guy, regardless of what he thinks he may know.

"Not sure where you got your information...Trey, but I'm just your average guy looking for some play, bored with the regular club scene."

"Oh tsk, tsk...you are anything but average, but we can roll that way if you want to. Take some friendly advice however, get a slave and do a scene tonight or you'll be out." Trey turned towards a surly looking Low-rung, who was holding out his drink for him.

"Ivan, perfect timing, I'm quite thirsty. Our friend here was just telling me how he's going to treat us to a scene tonight." Throwing me a devilish smirk. "Have you seen him work a slave, Ivan, it's quite something to see. You might even learn a thing or two about finesse, though I doubt you'd grasp the finer points on display."

Check and mate. I had scowled at Trey, but the fucker just smiled back. Trey had backed me into the proverbial corner and damn well he knew it too, the prick. He'd thrown down the

damned gauntlet, in front of Low-rung no less, effectively ending my choices. I had options though, despite what Trey had
thought. I could walk away and without a backwards glance.

I was beyond tired of the hell I'd been navigating. Tired of
my soul being relegated to the shadows. Tired of the darkness
that clung to me and obscured the dawn's rays, denying me their
hopeful light. My pain was nothing however, compared to what
those lost and sometimes forgotten souls had been enduring in
these torture clubs, so I'd stay the course, no matter what.

Exhaustion pulled at me. Doing a scene to impress the mass-
es, with an already abused slave, was the very last thing I wanted
to do in this moment. Releasing the breath I'd been holding, I
shook my head, knowing I had no choice. I'd do the scene however the fuck I wanted to and if they didn't like my style, well
too fucking bad I was beyond caring at this point.

I had always prided myself on having tight control over my
emotions, and in turn, my responses and corresponding actions.
Tonight I had nothing. That brief glimpse of the video playing
in the Luxe room had been enough to erode what was left of
that control. The rage and anger coursing through me bubbled
near the surface, and stuffing those emotions deep enough to
work a scene, would take far more fortitude than I possessed.

Turning from Trey and Low-rung, I walked towards the
greeter. Poor girl had been at it all night. She'd been repeatedly
abused by whomever had walked through the doors. By the
looks of things, she had absolutely no say in the matter and I
was about to add to her abuse. One more sin to have piled upon
my overflowing plate. I made a detour by the bar first, grabbing
some bottles of water and a Coke, then made my way resolutely
towards the greeter with determined strides. Decision made and
consequences accepted.

Stopping directly behind the greeter, I placed my hand gently on her shoulder, letting her know someone was there. Then

glared at the guy shafting her mouth. Smart guy that he was got the message loud and clear and so had his cock apparently...flaccid much? He pulled out of her mouth, zipped up and walked away, disgruntled to say the least.

The bouncer by the door had been watching my every move and when limp dick left, I turned and dared him to say one word. I knew he was supposed to watch over the staff and the slaves, but clearly his job didn't include making sure they weren't suffering. More like, don't take off with the merchandise, unless you're willing to pay, one way or another. We had a scene to do and bouncer guy wouldn't be stopping that. No, he wouldn't because the sex scenes were too good for business. Plus I saw Lowrung talk to one of the bouncers, who must be relaying the information to the other bouncers. Kneeling down in front of her, I unlatched the trailing chain connecting the clover clamps to the kneeling bench, taking the tension off her abused nipples.

"I'm not sure how experienced you are in nipple play, but when these clover clamps come off, the pain might be fairly overwhelming." I released one, gauging her response and then the other. A startled intake of breath and a low moan was all she allowed herself, brave girl. Before rounding to her back again, I asked in a hushed tone, "What's your name little one?"

Startled green eyes searched mine, before quickly dropping. "Lilly Blue," she said surprising me, though I'd strained to hear her words. Kneeling behind Lilly, I assessed the arm bondage she'd been placed in. These people were fucking idiots. Anyone with half a brain could see that the ropes were too tight. Between the torque they had placed on her shoulders and the tightness of the ropes, her hands had probably been numb for hours. Reaching for my pocket knife, I cut the part of the rope that was attached to her slave collar in the back.

"Lilly, it's important you remain very still, while I cut this cheap-ass rope from around your arms and hands."

We were receiving a lot of attention, but no interference, which I wouldn't have tolerated anyway. Unlatching her slave collar, I threw it as far as I could, heedless of where it landed. Her skin was chaffed from the tightness of the collar and the way the rope attached in the back had been pulling on it. Before coming around to the front, I had taken a moment to massage her arms and wrists hoping to improve circulation. Her hands had been blanched white from the constriction of the rope. I couldn't imagine how uncomfortable the pins and needles feeling was just then, as sensation crept back into her arms.

Coming around to kneel in front of Lilly Blue again, I could feel her fear thick in the space between us. Tears slid silently from the corners of her green eyes, shimmering like brilliant emeralds behind a dampened fringe of black lashes. When I assisted her to stand, it was evident by the stiffness of her legs that she'd been stuck in that position for hours on end without respite, leaving bruises upon her knees and shins. I reached for the water and the Coke that I had brought with me.

"Here," I said, handing her the bottled water, "use the water to rinse your mouth out. Then drink some, I imagine you're feeling dehydrated." She did as was asked. Though whether from instinctive compliance or from sound advice and thirst, I didn't know. Handing her the Coke next, I instructed her to have a few sips. "I'm afraid if you have too much at once, you might get nauseous from the sugar."

To this point, she had only given me her name when I'd asked for it, otherwise she hadn't spoken except at our initial greeting. "Lilly Blue, I don't require this, nor do I need it, but in case you feel as if you do, you have my permission to speak freely." She swallowed more of the Coke and looked away, not speaking at all. Whatever had brought her here and however she was kept here, she'd been conditioned to behave in a certain manner. I doubt having a conversation with a club member was something that occurred regularly, if ever. But, moments later she surprised me.

"I have never been cared for before, please do not get yourself into trouble on my behalf. They are not very nice when they perceive you have done something wrong."

I looked away momentarily to collect myself. I wanted Lilly Blue to trust me, but if she were to see what was surely brewing in my eyes, she'd be too scared to trust me. Pulling off my black t-shirt, I placed it over her head and helped her to pull her stiffened arms through. Since she was so petite, my shirt reached to her knees, but at least her body wasn't exposed anymore. I didn't care if I was shirtless, especially if it saved her from be leered at. I grabbed her hand and we made our way slowly to where the restrooms were located.

Lilly went in to use the facilities and I stood outside the door waiting, thinking we couldn't shut these clubs down fast enough. I realized that what we were doing would barely put a dent into the proliferation of human trafficking, but if we could bring down Vinokourov's organization it would neutralize a major player in the Los Angeles area. I had vowed after the Captain's daughter had been found dead that I would do whatever was necessary to bring him down. We had to protect the innocent ones, like Lilly and my Ava, from this torturous life. After seeing the video in the Luxe room earlier, I'd willingly die to stop the abuse.

I'd noticed people were still watching me and wondering what the hell I was doing with the greeter. Ivan, the low-rung little Russian prick, was glaring at me from near the door because I had essentially stolen tonight's greeter from her post. Well, too damn bad, there had been no specification as to whom I could choose. I smiled back, just to piss him off.

I had given Lilly an assessing gaze when she'd stepped out, noticing she now had a hint of rose to her pale cheeks, though barely. I needed to get down to the business at hand, but the hell of it was, I didn't want to add to her abuse. There were things I wanted to know, needed to know, but I couldn't afford for her to go on the defensive and shut down on me. I needed to be thoughtful in my word choice.

"Lilly, have you been to any other places, besides Club M?" She shook her head in response.

"There are safer ones out there, Lilly, that specialize in domination and submission. They foster an atmosphere of respect and safety, but are housed in a consensual environment. If that is what your soul has been seeking, honey, you won't find it here in a club like this. Here they play at things they know nothing about and abuse their slaves for the sake of pain and degradation. Look at how they had bound you, everything about that was wrong, Lilly Blue. You need to leave here and never return or you might find yourself permanently damaged or worse."

"I cannot leave," she said with obvious sadness and resignation.

"Have you ever participated in a scene before?"

"No. They have always assigned me to be a greeter, though the method of greeting has been varied," she said with a note of disgust.

"Since you can't leave or won't, would you consent to participating in a scene with me?" I put my hand up to stop the reply that was upon her lips.

"Before you answer, we need to discuss a few things. I will not put a collar on you again, you are not my slave, and that's not my thing. We will not be using any kind of bondage because my command alone will be enough to keep you still. I won't penetrate you, Lilly, because this scene is about you and your pleasure, which in turn, will give me pleasure." While I had laid out the scene, stripped bare, I'd catalogued her various reactions and saw that she had settled on inquisitive.

"If I trust you, will you tell me your name?"

"It's Sage and I have one last thing to tell you now because you won't be able to focus by the time I'm done with you." I backed that up with a full-wattage smile.

"I have a friend named Carter James and he will be coming for you, Lilly. So you had better reconcile yourself to the idea of being rescued from this dump because I refuse to leave you here."

Her eyes were bright with tentative hope and I'd do whatever was necessary to keep that light from diminishing from her innocent eyes. I would not lose Lilly, another innocent, like my Ava, to the machinations of these traffickers. Thankfully, Ava hadn't been able to remember any details from when she had been abducted and raped. I prayed she never did because in my mind, her ignorance was vastly preferred.

As I had schlepped through these clubs, I'd kept pushing Ava from my head, not wanting to taint her beautiful memory by the filth associated with the club's clientele. I couldn't have them both occupying the forefront of my consciousness. But tonight, my Ava was already there, front and center, brought there by one of these sadistic fucks. That brief glimpse of my Ava had gutted me on the spot and I was still sick from it. To see the evidence of her brutal rape and the glorification of her pain being broadcast to the participants of the Luxe room had left me homicidal. Realizing there had been four guys raping her and not just one, had left me sick and maddened with the need for retribution.

Gazing down at Lilly Blue, I realized I'd lost control of my emotions again, during my brief introspection, because she had fear clouding her green eyes.

"Please forgive me for frightening you, Lilly, that wasn't my intention. I was thinking about the abuse that you and the others have been suffering at the hands of these manipulative bastards.

To be honest, it takes me to a place where I hardly recognize myself through the anger. If I knew why you couldn't walk away, I would fix it for you, here and now. But, whatever the problem is, I suspect it might be bigger than what we have time for tonight."

I could see the fear was receding from her eyes as she listened attentively. "Don't forget, Carter James will be coming for you. I mean it, Lilly, you're not staying here. Carter's all tatted up, with multiple piercings, but he has a heart of gold and an artist's soul, so don't let him frighten you. He's not a part of this world at all."

"All right, Sage, I will trust you. If this Carter James should ever come to find me, I will decide at that time, whether or not, I should go with him."

Spunky, I liked that, showed they hadn't broken her spirit yet.

Reaching for her hand, we walked towards the empty stage. I directed Lilly Blue to sit in a chair, as she needed to rest and drink a bit more of the Coke. I went about arranging things upon the stage to my liking. This scene would be just the two of us and nothing more. No toys or restraints, I wouldn't be needing them. I'd found a padded table and brought it to the stage. Lilly was very petite, barely five foot tall and would fit perfectly on the shortened version of a massage table. I asked Lilly to go sit on it, while I sat in her chair, taking off my shoes and socks. Standing, I unbuttoned the top button to my slacks.

"We are going to get started in just a few minutes, Lilly, but I wanted to go over some simple instructions with you first. Everything I said earlier still holds true, no penetration and no bondage. However, I wanted to stress that if you feel uncomfortable at any time or in anyway, you are to tell me, is that clear, Lilly? I want to know what and how you are feeling. But, don't worry too much about that because I will be very attentive to your body and what story it has to tell me." I stopped for a second, letting her absorb that information and assessed her reaction. She seemed inquisitive and thankfully not at all frightened.

"We are going to use a color system during this scene, Lilly. I don't generally use one, but in this instance I think we should. They are often used at those clubs I spoke of earlier, as a way to communicate during a scene, especially when simplicity might be prudent. The colors we're going to use and their meaning will be easy to remember, as they will be familiar to you. They are set up just like a traffic light. Green will be go and means all is clear and you are doing well. Yellow will be our caution color. This is for when you are uncomfortable, unfamiliar or trying to absorb and comprehend what it is you and your body are experiencing. We might pull back or slow down, allowing you to assimilate all the sensations. Red will be stop, plain and simple. No questions as to why and no reprimands. You are in control here, Lilly, and I want you to realize that. Okay so far?"

"Yes, Sage."

"Roll over and lay face down then."

Lilly went to remove the shirt I had given her to wear before laying down. I stayed her actions, placing my hands gently upon hers. "No leave it on, Lilly, they've seen enough already and don't deserve to see any more."

Off to the side of the stage, in a ratty old basket, were multiple toys and implements that could be utilized. I wouldn't be using any of those. Lord knew what diseases might be crawling all over them. I found some packaged massage oil that was still sealed and I decided to help myself to a few of those. Pouring some of the fragrant oil into to my hands to warm it, I leaned over Lilly, saying, "Just relax and enjoy little one. I promise if you follow my instructions, you will be greatly rewarded."

Using the warmed oil, I started by massaging her right hand and arm. I took my time working on the muscles that were stiff from her greeting at the door and the prolonged bondage they had put her in. Alternating between light and deep strokes, I worked to loosen the knotted muscles. I repeated the process to the other side feeling Lilly relax under my hands. After applying more oil, I worked her arches, delicate ankles, and calves.

"Lilly, how are you doing? Are we still green?"

"Mmmhmm," came her sleepy, relaxed response.

I cleansed my hands with the Purel that had been sitting next to the basket, then poured more oil into my palms. Massaging deeply, I traveled up the back of her thighs, concentrating on her hamstrings till they began to loosen, my touch having the desired effect. I came close to touching her ass, flirting with the edge of the tight globes, but didn't go there, not yet at least.

We were drawing quite a crowd, but I paid no attention to them. Besides, they weren't truly interested in what I was doing anyway. They were all about pain and degradation, not comfort. There was nothing safe, sane or consensual about Club M. They only knew about torture and forced compliance, either through physical threats of violence, actual physical abuse or some form of chemical induced complacency. I pushed all of that from my mind for now and concentrated on Lilly.

I wanted to massage Lilly's back next, so I pulled the shirt over her head and she helped me to slide it up and over, leaving her arms in the sleeves. It was big enough on her though that it wasn't constricting and made a nice little pillow for her cheek to rest upon. I massaged her back lightly at first, then deeper, alternating the intensity and the rhythm. Trailing my hands down her back, I circled her ass, and then went back up her sides to start the whole process over again. The next trip down, I gripped her ass with my hands, pushing the halves together, then gently pulling them apart, deeply kneading each cheek. I began talking to Lilly, but just loud enough that only she would hear me.

I asked how she was feeling and she said she was relaxed and comfortable, still feeling that all was green. I explained how she was not allowed to orgasm until I told her to, that in waiting, a greater pleasure would be found. She agreed to try. Massaging her ass still, I pulled her cheeks apart again and could see the glistening evidence of her arousal, a small spot of wetness below her. Perfect, she was right where I had wanted her. When I'd had Lilly lay down on the table earlier, I'd positioned her so that her genitals would be facing the wall, where no one would be standing. These club goers didn't deserve to see that precious part of Lilly, definitely not these cretin low-life fucks.

Moving her legs apart incrementally, I made the V wider between her legs. I was lightly caressing her groin, that delicate bit of skin that connected her leg to her outer labia and made slow circles as I worked my way in.

"That's it little one, try to hold still, absorb the pleasure and let it build even higher. Now arch your back and pull your hips off the table. Yes, just like that." I praised, when she complied so readily. I continued to work towards her entrance and her flushed, swollen clitoris, but waited to go there directly. I wanted her so aroused that by merely blowing gently across her erect clitoris would be enough to send her over. I gathered some of her natural lubricant on my thumbs and massaged her perineum with increasing pressure, rimming her entrance slowly, round and round. Her body was showing me how close she was, so I backed off and slowed down.

"Are you close, Lilly?"

"I...I think so...I do not...really know," she said between panting breaths.

"Perfect, Lilly, you are doing great. Hold off on the sensation that is overwhelming you, let it build, ride the rising tide of the pleasure, but wait until I tell you it's okay to orgasm, do you understand?"

"Yes. Only when you tell me, but I do hope it will be soon."

Cheeky little thing. Carter was going to be in for a lovely surprise. I worked her up and down, then in and out of that blissful state, just short of orgasm. I could see she was straining to hold off. Her muscles quivering nonstop and her voice was lovely to hear, as she strained to hold back her throaty moans.

"Now, Lilly, I want you to give me your orgasm. Go over, now!" The command in my voice was just what she had needed to achieve her glorious orgasm. Her willingness to trust me with her safety, her body, and her pleasure had been a true gift. I continued with my gentle massaging, running my finger lightly from her entrance to her clitoris and circling it lightly with my thumb.

"Again Lilly. You can do it, one more time." Off she went for a second time. Pushing her hips gently back down onto the table, and I leaned forward I placed a gentle kiss upon her left shoulder.

"You did wonderfully, thank you for trusting me with your body and your pleasure. You were so beautiful in your surrender, Lilly."

She opened her eyes to look at me. "Thank you, Sage. I never knew it could be like that. I have never had an orgasm before, that was my first and it was beautiful." Her eyes were swimming with tears, but not in sadness, rather in joy of the moment we had just shared.

The clapping started then, like ice water thrown on our private interlude.

"Ignore them, Lilly, they're all idiots. Let's get you dressed." Standing with my back to the crowd, I protected Lilly from their eyes and helped her to fix the black t-shirt. Taking her hand, we walked back over to the bathrooms and I waited outside again.

Trey approached, giving me a nod towards the restroom. I took him up on his silent offer and I went into the restroom myself, while he watched over Lilly. When I returned, Trey was still there and Lilly Blue sat behind him in a chair eating a banana and drinking another Coke. His thoughtfulness at caring for her was greatly appreciated. She was probably still floating after our scene together and the fact she had worked all evening. Trey discreetly handed me a DVD.

"You know that won't be the only copy, but I got the only one they had. Why do you want it? It's undoubtedly already in circulation elsewhere."

I shook my head. "Thanks for helping with Lilly."

"That was an impressive scene to watch. It was like you were dancing with her, changing the rhythm and intensity. I know you didn't notice the reaction of the room because you were completely focused on her, but they were spellbound. Not only did you command her, but the room as well."

"I don't give a flying fuck about impressing these people." Well, that wasn't entirely true. "My focus was on giving to Lilly, since everything has been taken from her by force. She deserved to have pleasure with no expectations."

"Oh I agree with you there. We'll see each other again I'm sure, so until then," and with that Trey walked away.

Leaning against the wall with my head back, I viewed the room at large and one person in particular. Best to go on the offensive.

"Daniel, what in the hell are you doing here?"

"I could ask you the same thing, Sage, but after watching you on that stage working that greeter girl over, it's pretty obvious what you're doing. Mind telling me why?"

"I do mind. Again, why are you here, Daniel?"

"Does Ava know you're into this lifestyle? How could you cheat on her?" His voice was indignant and accusatory.

"Leave Ava out of this. Why are you here, Daniel? I won't ask you again."

"I heard some guys talking about Club M, so thought I'd come check it out. See what things were like."

"You don't want any part of this scene, trust me. Go home, Daniel, you won't find what you're looking for here. You need to leave before it's too late to leave. You have no idea what you're messing with."

"You have no idea what I'm looking for. No idea what I want."

"Don't I?"

"No, you couldn't possibly know anything about who or what I want."

"Are you always this argumentative?"

"I love to argue, what can I say, hazards of law school."

"Seriously, go home, Daniel. Save your pent up desire, your longing, and share it with the one person who holds your heart. You know you won't find that person here. What you will find here however, is a hollow, pale imitation of what you could have, if you just had the balls to reach for it."

"That's low."

"Just callin' it, like I see it."

"I'm leaving because you are right in that one thing, I don't want any part of this scene or the people who are involved in it. Seems to me, it's rife with cheaters and abusers. But hey, just callin' it, like I see it." With that he walked away and I hoped like hell, he walked out of the club doors too.

Pulling my cell out, I dialed Carter.

"L'Inked Tattoo Studio."

"Carter, it's Sage. I'm going to text you an addy. I need you come and pick someone up for me. Her name is Lilly Blue. She's at Club M and in some kind of trouble. She might actually resist you, but take her anyway, she doesn't belong here."

"All right, mate, I'll have one of the guys tend the shop for me and I'll be on my way. What's she look like?"

"She's tiny, short black hair, green eyes and will be wearing my black t-shirt."

"I'm on it."

"And Carter, she's special, so treat her as such, ya feel me?"

"Ya, I feel ya."

"Later."

"Later."

❧ 15 ❧

Ivan and Marcus

"WELL, THAT WAS unfortunate," Ivan said deadpan, after the newest rape video ended because the victim had died during the scene.

"I guess we can add it to the collection of snuff videos for special showings. However, Marcus, I am not well pleased. You've been drugging these silly coeds for well over a year now and yet you still haven't figured out the dosing? What are we to do with this one? Hmmm, please tell me because we can't keep shoving them into random dumpsters in and around LA. Eventually, they are going to be seen mixed in with the trash." Ivan's accent was more pronounced the angrier he became. "And furthermore, Marcus, you cannot lose them either."

"It's not my fault, in either case, so fuck off. I can't help the fact that she was more sensitive to the dosing. Though this time, it had more to do with *your* new agent from Russia sampling the goods and his overzealous breath play. I mean really, how do you expect to keep our numbers up for shipment if you let *your new agent* choke them to death?"

"You'd do well to remember I only act subservient, I won't tolerate your posturing and disrespect. You were in that room with *my* agent and *you* should have intervened. This will not happen again, will it, Marcus? You can be replaced just as easily as the stock. Now, remember March Madness starts next week and it appears all is progressing for the acquisition of more stock. However, with the increased influx of tourists and fans, the clubs will be busier, so we need to increase our supply of merchandise. You and your boys need to up your quotas, there will be a higher demand for female slaves, plus we have a shipment going out that needs more variety. The chaos of the basketball tournament will help, be sure to capitalize on that. Now leave...your presence is annoying me. Oh and Marcus? Send me that greeter...Lilly is her name."

❧ 16 ❧

ALEXEI

LAST FRIDAY, I had come to the office with the introduction to Ava DeLaney still fresh in my mind and had charged Ivan with the task of having her investigated. I had wanted to know more about the dancer, but too much time had passed since then and my patience had come to an end. I had phoned Ivan first thing this morning, informing him he had exactly fifteen minutes, not one minute more, and that report had better be in my hands. Hearing a knock at my door, I glanced at my watch, three minutes to spare, the lucky bastard. I would have rather ripped his fool head off, truth be told.

"Enter." I stood by the window, looking out and cringed at the tone of impatience that had bled into my voice. As the door had opened, I turned to see Ivan walking in. He was sporting his usual slicked back hair, leather pants, and that ridiculous moustache he was so proud of. I didn't understand his fascination with the hideous thing and I had wanted to tell him that the '70s had called and wanted their porno 'stache back.

"I've waited long enough, Ivan, what do we know?"

"Last week on Friday morning, Ms. Ava DeLaney was report-
ed missing by her roommate, a Ms. Willow Sinclair. When Ms.
Sinclair came home early in the morning, she had noticed that
Ms. DeLaney wasn't there, which was highly unusual according
to the roommate. Ms. Sinclair had last seen Ms. DeLaney on
Thursday evening, before she had gone off to work and Ms.
DeLaney had left to meet friends at Circus Disco."

Ivan paused and looked over the notes he held tight in his
hand.

"Ms. DeLaney didn't turn up again until early Sunday morning. She had stumbled into L'Inked Tattoo Studio, with no
memory of where she had been...or what had happened to her."

Ivan stopped his report again, to collect his thoughts presumably, not really the brightest of my people, but we'd been
together since the very beginning.

"Do not make me ask for the details again, Ivan," I said with
quiet deliberation and narrowed eyes. He pulled at his shirt collar, looking decidedly uncomfortable, his Adam's apple bobbing
up and down nervously.

"LAPD was called to L'Inked Tattoo Studio," he said after
clearing his throat noisily and fidgeting from foot to foot, "as
was an ambulance. She had passed out, so the owner of the studio, one Carter James, had called 911 for assistance."

He paused yet again and I waited, patience frayed to the point
of breaking. What in the world is the matter with the guy? Just as I
was about to unleash my frustrations, he resumed his report.

"The ambulance took her to Cedars-Sinai, where she was
treated by a Dr. Sabella Wong, head of the Rape Response
Team."

After hearing the word rape, everything else was lost to a
vortex of indistinguishable noise. Reaching out my hand blindly
for support, it landed with a slap against the cool glass of the
window pane.

"Place the report on my desk and leave," I told Ivan with icy precision, not bothering to turn around. Once I heard the door shut and knew that I was alone, I dropped to my knees. I have not known such pain and anguish, since losing my Grace and had never thought to taste its unique, bitter flavor again. But knowing the child, *my own* child, that was conceived in love and only recently found, had been so brutally mistreated was enough to slay me to the bone. I sat slumped on my knees, head tipped back, looking up at the blue sky through the window. "WHY!" I cried out in despair, asking no one in particular and expecting no answer in return.

Twenty-three years ago

I was meeting Grace at her SoHo apartment for a relaxing dinner at home. She was eight months along now. She had a small baby bump on her lovely ballet frame and was beyond beautiful in my eyes. She would say she was fat and awkward, while I would say that she glowed with motherhood. I loved that she was having our child and a baby girl, if the tests were to be believed.

I was still looking for a way to extricate myself from the underworld in which I had become trapped. It was hard, if not impossible, to find a way out once they had their hooks into you. When coming to visit Grace, I always took extra precautions, careful that I hadn't been followed. The truth was, they would use Grace and my love for her, as a means to control me and make me their puppet.

"My love." I had pulled Grace into my arms the minute I entered her apartment. Our little baby bump made for a bit of maneuvering, but the feel of Grace, safe and secure in my arms was indescribable. I gently kissed the top of her head, her forehead, and the corner of her lips, before delving into her mouth. It felt like home, to be in her loving arms and I proceeded to kiss

her, as if she were the very breath in my lungs. Slowly, yet reluctantly, I pulled away from her mouth and held her in comfortable
silence. Looking down into her beautiful blue eyes, I was humbled by the faith, adoration, and love shining in them, whether I
was deserving of it or not. Taking a step backwards, I dropped to
my knees in front of Grace, much to her astonishment.

"Alexei, what in the world are you doing? Get up from there,
silly." Grace was giggling and trying to pull me up, but I wasn't
having it.

"In a moment, love, I want to have a chat with my Ava."
Kneeling before my two girls, I was overwhelmed by the love I
felt for the two of them.

I placed my hands reverently on Grace's abdomen; my Ava
was kicking her feet at me in greeting. She loved when I chatted
with her and would kick and move about, sometimes kicking
Grace a good one. That always earned me a stern look for getting Ava all worked up. Grace lifted her shirt and I placed a kiss
on her beautiful, naked abdomen. Speaking softly to Ava, I caressed the skin stretched tight over my growing baby girl.

"I love you so much, my Ava. I can't wait to meet you in a few
weeks. I'm hoping you look just like your exceptional mother
and not your neanderthal father. I will always love you and I will
protect you and your mother with my very life. Keep growing
and thriving my little angel." I kissed Grace's abdomen one
more time, then stood and swept her into my arms, this time for
a longer, deeper kiss.

"What can I do to help with dinner?" I asked, directing
Grace to sit on the couch. She was in incredible shape, but tired
easily this late in the pregnancy.

"It's in the oven and ready to eat whenever we are, Alexei. I
decided to order delivery from that little Italian place we love so
much. There's some wine decanted on the counter for us to
have. Would you please pour me a small glass." She said with a

look that dared me to tell her no. Ha, as if I could deny her anything and poured her a small glass of the red and a larger one for myself.

Wine glasses in hand, I went back to where Grace was resting on the couch. I placed the glass of wine next to her and I took the opportunity to kiss her lips again. Then, I sat on the couch, turned Grace sideways, and pulled her feet into my lap. I took a few sips of the red wine, savoring its mellow flavor and I rested my gaze upon Grace and couldn't look away. I reached blindly for the lotion on the table beside me, warmed some in my hands, and I began massaging her feet. I watched her relax under the soothing strokes, her blue eyes drifting into slumber and within moments, my beautiful girl was fast asleep. I continued massaging, though gradually slowed my movements, until they had stopped altogether.

My eyes traveled over her endearing features and I thought to myself, how the hell did this gutter rat from Russia get so damned lucky? I wouldn't question it, but I needed to find a way to leave my current situation within the Russian underworld. As a youngster, fresh from mother Russia, I'd had nothing and no one to rely upon. I had my strength and if I were being honest, my very agile mind. The combination had taken me far within the organization, but this life was not the one I had wanted when defecting to the US, nor was it what I had aspired to be. I wanted to be a legitimate businessman and I could envision all the ways to achieve that end. I had been working quietly towards this goal for several years. I was ready to make a break, but I feared the organization would not be receptive to my breaking free of the brotherhood, as it were.

I watched my beautiful girl, sleeping the sleep of the innocent and I thought about how I had never slept as such. I felt tainted by those around me, tainted by association. A sense of dread overcame me, as I thought of all the ways the brotherhood could make my life a living hell. I wouldn't do anything to jeopardize my Grace, or my Ava, and I would walk away to keep them safe.

Three years later

I was in Southern California checking out the sex clubs and the potential for human trafficking in Los Angeles. Maxim, head of the brotherhood, as I had dubbed the organization years ago, had sent me here to look into the potential for expansion. He had been wanting to expand to the West Coast for years, especially being a hotbed for inequity and depravity. So here I found myself, thousands of miles away from my Grace and Ava, walking through multiple levels of hell. My heart had sunk when Maxim had asked, or rather ordered me, to go to LA.

Apparently, I was just the man to bring this project to fruition. He'd merely wanted to keep me under his thumb and in his control, beholden to the brotherhood. I felt my chances for escape had long since slipped through my fingers. He knew I had been drifting away, searching for a way out. I'd been keeping my distance from my Grace and Ava, hoping no one would realize they were mine. I ached for them endlessly. Little Ava was such a beautiful child; she looked like her mother, but had inherited my silver eyes. She was sweetly precocious and inquisitive. I loved that little girl and her mother something fierce and I couldn't believe they were mine.

I'd been in LA for a little over a week now and I had been dying to get home. I'd done everything required by Maxim and we could indeed run a huge profit by expanding to the West Coast, LA specifically. I was scheduled to travel back to New York tonight, having made the necessary contacts within the sex industry. I felt dirty, the darkness of the underworld clung to my very pores. I felt as if I needed to shower repeatedly, scrubbing my skin of the filth. I didn't want to take this home to my Grace and Ava. I was slowly dying inside and only my beautiful girls were keeping me sane.

The phone fell to the floor with a clatter unnoticed, my fingers having gone instantaneously numb. I stood for a moment, staring at the wall in my kitchen. I really needed to repaint that wall, there were little scuff marks everywhere. I had only just arrived from LA, stopping by the house to shower, before going to see Grace and Ava. The phone had been ringing when I'd walked in, which was weird, since I had my cell phone with me. Where were my keys? I needed my keys. I had to drive somewhere. I think I needed to go somewhere. I couldn't think. What was I doing? Why was I crying? I felt tears, wet upon my cheeks. What's going on? I said aloud, wiping the wetness from my face. Looking around in confusion, I saw the phone was lying on the floor.

"Hello," I said, after putting the phone to my ear.

"Alexei?" Ivan was saying over and over through the line.

"Ivan?" Shaking my head in confusion.

"Did you not hear a word I said? Grace and her parents are dead. Dead, Alexei, killed a few hours ago in a car accident. Alexei? Alexei?"

"I heard you, Ivan. Thank you for informing me. I will see you at the office tomorrow. Bye."

I could hear my name being called, as I'd hung up the phone. I dropped hard to my knees on the wood floor not even registering the pain. Head hanging loose on my neck, disbelieving. No, it can't be true. My Grace can't be gone. No, it's a lie. She can't be dead.

No, no, no, Noooo! I screamed to the ceiling, praying it wasn't true. I didn't recognize my own voice, as I whispered brokenly, Oh God, please don't let it be true. Not my beautiful Grace...my heart...my soul...my reason for breathing...oh God. No.

A few hours later I had found myself downtown at the coroner's office, gazing upon the beautiful, yet pale face of my Grace. Once I had regained my composure, I had called Ivan back to have it arranged so that I could see her. I wouldn't be able to accept the truth of her being gone, until I had seen her for myself. Even then, only my head would ever accept this reality, not my heart, no never my heart.

Looking down upon my love, I waited for her blue eyes to flicker open, but they didn't. I found myself holding my breath, hoping that she would breathe for me, but when she didn't and I died a little more inside. I couldn't stand to see her vibrance gone, her spark for life missing. How, dear Lord, how do I go on? Where do I go from here? I had to find my Ava, where could she be? Who would have her? Our beautiful child, my only connection left to Grace.

When I left the coroner's office, I had left my heart behind with Grace. Stepping outside, I wondered how the sun could possibly be shining, when I was in such a dark place. I felt like a vampire might, relegated to the darkness and ready to burst into flames in the light of day. I was feeling decidedly numb, but not so lost in my head that I didn't realize I was being followed. I had thought to just play along, feign stupidity, as I really wasn't in the mood for a confrontation.

I continued walking down the street and my tail had kept pace. Up the street and around the corner, I ducked into an alley and waited, deciding to force an encounter. I wanted to be done with this nonsense and if blood were to be shed, then all the better, as I'd rather be with my Grace anyway. I didn't have to wait long, as a man in his early fifties came into the alley with me. I continued to lean against the brick wall, arms crossed at my chest. There would be no stopping whatever was about to go down.

"Alexei Vinokourov, we've been watching you for some time now. I'm Bradley, Sean Bradley," he stated while reaching out his empty hand to shake mine.

Hmmm...not what I had been expecting.

"I have some information I'd like to share with you, regarding Grace Leclair."

Now he had my undivided attention. Straightening from the wall, I shook his hand and I stood directly in front of this Bradley, waiting.

"We've been watching you for some time. Following your movements. We know about your recent trip to LA for Maxim. We also know of your disillusionment, your quiet efforts to escape Maxim's yoke. Just as we know about your efforts to rescue some of the young women you've found trapped within the sex trade."

My head was reeling, but I didn't let that show. How could this, 'we' know of my efforts? I had been very careful about secreting the women away. I didn't say anything, but rather continued waiting Bradley out, as he was taking a breath to continue anyway.

"We know about Grace and Ava, though you have been very good at keeping them hidden."

Bradley stopped talking and looked around before staring directly into my eyes saying, "What we know that you do not, Alexei, is the fact that someone inside Maxim's organization, at his direction, killed Grace and her parents. It was not an accident as you were led to believe."

The numbness that I'd been immersed in was swiftly replaced by a raging inferno of emotions. A conflagration of incapacitating pain and anger, both competing for supremacy, had been sparked by his devastating words. I had heard the term, 'seeing red,' but hadn't understood until just that moment, what it felt like. I was lost in a maelstrom until Bradley hit my jaw with a resounding thud, snapping me from the mental chaos.

"Are you with me now? They made it look like an accident, but it wasn't. We had a guy watching Grace. She and her parents were on their way to a girlfriend's house, where Ava had been playing. They were deliberately run off the road. Our man could do nothing to stop what happened, it was so unexpected. He rendered aid at the scene, Alexei, but to no avail."

I honestly didn't know how to react to that. I wanted to commit murder and I was more than ready to hunt down the fucker that had taken my beloved away from me. I needed to cut the head off of the proverbial snake...Maxim. However, Bradley stopped me in my tracks with one simple question.

"If I could guarantee you Maxim and no jail time, would you consider working for us?" He held up his hand to prevent me from answering, as if I would need to even think about that question. I would take whatever was offered to see him dead. Hell, I would sell my very soul to avenge my Grace.

"We have also taken the liberty to hide Ava from those who would seek to do her harm." With that final statement, it didn't matter what I would or would not have done because I would do anything for my Ava.

❧ 17 ❧

AVA

HOW I'D MANAGED to arrive at Mason and Daniel's without causing an accident was beyond me. By the grace of God I'd made it though because I had been on auto-pilot the entire trip from Sage's house. Flinging McCoy's door open, I fell out landing hard on the driveway. I skinned my knees and palms when my feet had become tangled in my haste to get into the house. I pounded on the front door when I reached it and rang the doorbell incessantly, like an obnoxious ding-dong ditcher.

"Ava, what the fuck?" Mason said, as he opened the door for me.

"Mason..." Stumbling through the door and into Mason, I pushed off him, making my way through the house towards the bathroom.

"I think he may have followed me here. Don't let him in, Mason. Don't let him find me."

"Who? Don't let who in?" he asked, after shutting the front door and followed after me.

"I saw it. Oh God! How could they do that to me?" I pulled my top over my head, dropping it along the way to the bathroom, nearly running into the wall. Vaguely, I heard Mason asking me questions, but all my attention was focused on my mental land-scape. Where I watched Sage, watching a video of me...bound and helpless, raped by four guys, not just one.

"But why? Why would he have that?"

"What did you see, Ava? Who had what? Ava, you're not making any sense."

"Sage...It was Sage," I cried out.

By the time I reached Mason's bathroom, I was down to my bra and undies. Slamming the door behind me, I barely made it to the toilet, when the retching started and I could hardly catch my breath with the force of it. I could hear Mason outside the bath-room door wanting to storm in, but I was preoccupied with the porcelain god I was hugging and didn't care. Once the retching had stopped, I flushed the toilet and sat up, swiping the back of my hand across my mouth. Once in the shower, I turned on the water and blindly reached for the soap, scrubbing at my body, over and over again, while the icy water pelted my skin. I just wanted to feel clean and pure again. Opening my mouth to the icy water, I rinsed out the aftertaste of vomit. I found myself on the floor, in the cor-ner of the shower, when my legs would no longer support me. Wrapping my arms around my knees, I rested my forehead on them and I sobbed for all that was lost.

✳ ✳ ✳

sage

"Mason! Daniel! I know Ava's in there," I said, pounding on the front door. "Open the damned door." I paced back and forth waiting for them to open it. I turned around to look at a car passing by with a noisy muffler and ran my hand impatiently through my hair.

"Sage."

Turning at the sound of my name. I was caught off guard as Mason's fist collided with my jaw. Luckily, I had pulled my head back just enough to decrease the heat of his punch; otherwise I might be sporting a broken jaw about now. I seriously wanted to rub at my jaw, but wouldn't give him the satisfaction of knowing it hurt like a bitch.

"That one was free. I deserved it for unintentionally hurting Ava, but the next one won't be. So you had better think hard before trying that again. You might be younger and in shape after the NFL Combine, but I will take you down, Mason, don't doubt it."

"You're welcome to try. I protect what's mine, especially Ava."

"Really? Is that why I saw Daniel scoping out the action at one of the more extreme sex clubs downtown? What's he looking for, Mason? Could it be that elusive missing piece? The one he obviously longs for? Was he looking for the person that would make him feel complete? Wouldn't know anything about that, would you, Mason?" Staring at Mason, I caught a brief glimpse of confusion, surprise, and finally disbelief, before he shut down, hiding behind his mask of anger.

"You're so oblivious as to what's right under your nose, Mason, you're going to miss your chance. Pull your head out of your ass, before it's too late. I'm done wasting my time with you. I'm going in to talk to Ava...to explain, so you had better step the fuck out of my way. Now." And with that, I pushed my way through the door that was Mason, to follow the trail of Ava's clothes. What in the hell? I opened the bathroom door, but I didn't see Ava, even though I could hear the shower running and assumed she was in there. Opening the shower door, I found her on the floor. She was in the corner, hugging her knees, and with her face buried in her arms.

"Ava? Ava, let me explain, it's not what you're thinking. Look at me, Beauty." I reached in and turned off the water, which was freezing cold. Grabbing a towel from the linen cabinet, I stepped into the shower and wrapped the towel around her.

"Ava, come on, honey. Let's get you out of the shower and warmed up."

Looking up at me, she had tears and water running down her pale cheeks. The anguish in her beautiful eyes was more than I could stand and had my stomach dropping because I was the one that had put the devastation in them. I stood with her cradled in my arms and I walked out of the bathroom. Mason was with Daniel, who had just arrived home. They were standing in the living room having a heated discussion by the look of things. They turned to look at me in surprise, when they heard the door slam against the wall.

"Do you have a spare bedroom or someplace where I can get her warmed up? I found her on the shower floor, under a spray of icy cold water." I spat that statement at Mason and well he knew it, since he turned his face away from us.

"Down the hall, last door on the right, it's the spare bedroom," Daniel told me, head swinging back and forth between Mason and I.

I turned away. I had pushed those two enough; hopefully they would work their shit out. Closing the door behind us, I sat on the bed with Ava cradled against my chest. Tilting her chin up to look at me, I grazed her cool lips with the warmth of my mouth, hoping to infuse her with some of my heat.

"You shouldn't have run from me, Ava. It guts me to know you think so little of me. I wish you would have had faith in me...faith that I would have had a valid explanation for having that video. But you ran before I could explain." I kissed her a few more times, but she wasn't responding and I was worried about her state of mind. After drying her with the towel, I stood to pull the covers back and laid her down. I stripped to my skin and climbed in beside her, gathering her into my arms. I was hoping the skin-to-skin contact would increase her body temp and pull her from her stupor.

"Come on, Beauty, you're stronger than this. Talk to me, or better yet, listen. Let me explain what's going on and if you still don't want me here, I will turn away and leave. Though, you should know if I do, I'll be leaving my heart here with you because you own every inch of it. If I can't have you, then my heart's useless to me. A hollowed out organ, collapsing upon itself without your radiance to fill it with sunshine. I know I should have told you long before now what I am, but I couldn't." I felt her stiffen in my arms, ready to bolt out the other side of the bed.

"Oh no you don't," I said, tightly hugging her back to my front. "You're going to let me explain." I huffed out a large sigh. I was about to break some serious rules.

"Why do you call me Beauty?"

"Well, that was kind of random," I chuckled, "especially when I was about to break some serious rules for you. But to answer your question, it started with you stumbling into Carter James' studio and falling into my arms. We'd had that moment of connection when our eyes had met for that brief second, then you had passed out, pulling your fainting goat routine." I pinched her side when she huffed at me.

"Carter had walked in seconds later, saw you laying in my arms and he had asked where sleeping beauty had come from. So it was Carter who dubbed you sleeping beauty, but from that point on, you had become Beauty to me. I had wanted to be your prince charming, albeit a dark and unworthy one, but the one whose kisses would awaken you. All I could think about was how much I had wanted to place soft, gentle kisses on your abused lips, healing them. How if I were to place kisses on your eyelids, you would open those beautiful eyes for me, so I could fall deeper under your spell. I had wanted to be your protector, your healer, your slayer of dragons, even then. I had simply wanted to be yours, wanting to claim you and have you claim me. It was instinctual, visceral, and what had formed when our eyes had connected. Your obvious pain and abuse had called to the protector in me, but it was that brief glimpse of your open soul, reaching out to me, that had me snared and honestly...I'm happy to have been caught." I ended the explanation by turning her in my arms and kissing her gently upon her lips and eyelids, just like I had wanted to that night at the studio. But, she deserved an explanation as to what I had been up to, even though I shouldn't be sharing classified information.

"I've been undercover with the LAPD for the last six years, though exclusively in LA for the past year. I've been infiltrating underground, migrant sex clubs owned and operated by a group dealing in the human trafficking of men and women. Many of those abducted are drugged and forced into prostitution, forced to participate at these clubs as slaves, and later sold on the black market."

Ava was listening intently, paying close attention to my face and eyes, while I appreciated her attentiveness, I wasn't sure I wanted her looking too deep into my darkness.

"Why haven't you said anything to me? After all this time and you've said nothing." The disappointment in her voice made me feel unworthy.

"I'm technically not supposed to be telling you now. It's against the rules, especially since I'm undercover. I could be jeopardizing, not only my life, but the lives of the other detectives and that's unacceptable to me, which is why I haven't said anything. But, I couldn't have you thinking I was some kind of perverted monster, who got off on watching the love of his life raped by four sadistic mother fuckers. Assholes that I would like to kill with my bare...fucking...hands." I was vibrating with anger and remorse by the end of that little outburst. I had probably scared the piss right out of her.

Ava rested her hand over my heart, placing a small kiss upon my lips. "Just tell me Sage, tell me how and why you have a video of my rape. Help me to understand why I shouldn't get up and walk away. And, be warned Sage, if I decide to walk, you won't be stopping me."

I probably shouldn't tell her how cute I thought she was, when she was angry and assertive. No, definitely not. I would respect whatever decision she made though, even if it wasn't the outcome I hoped for.

"Recently, I was at Club M, one of the more extreme sex clubs, when I came across this video of you playing in the Luxe room. I managed to acquire the only copy they had." I wouldn't tell her that additional copies were probably floating around the other clubs. "I brought the video home and was watching it for the first time today. I was hoping I might be able to identify anything about the room you were in, or the men that had held you captive. Because, I can promise you here and now Ava, I will not rest until they are found and dealt with. Ava, I'm beyond sorry that you saw any portion of that video. I didn't want you to know that the damned thing existed."

"You have to stop treating me like I'm about to break, Sage, even though I feel like I will at times. I was coming to see you because at the audition..."

"Wait...wait a minute. How did the audition go? Did you blow them away?"

"No, it was terrible, Sage. The solo, which I performed first, was incredible. I had felt wonderful, light on my feet, my turns fluid, my jumps and leaps, effortless. I was truly proud of how I had danced. Then came the partnered routine, which I performed with Marcus. Something about him lately, I can't explain it. He makes my skin crawl. So we were about to start the routine, when he leans forward and whispers into my ear, 'Make sure you submit to me, Ava. Let go, baby, like you have before or I'll make you. Don't ruin this for me or for yourself.' Then the music started and less than a minute into the routine, I froze. Little snippets of the rape were playing through my head, though it was like they were being played through a dirty, unfocused lens. I remembered someone calling me baby, over and over, so when Marcus had said that, it must have triggered some buried memory. Though, it was more an impression of things, rather than any actual knowledge of them."

"And you came to me, to tell me you'd had this memory...this breakthrough and there I was, watching that damned video. I am so sorry, Ava." I took the opportunity to place a reverent kiss upon her soft, plump lips, a silent apology for the unintentional hurt I had caused her.

"I hope that you can forgive me one day. I would never intentionally cause you harm. You own me, Ava, you truly do. I don't know how it happened, how you got to me so quickly, but you did. I love you, Beauty, with every ounce of my damaged heart and soul."

Well, I hadn't meant to say all that, but it was a simple fact and I couldn't take it back, not that I wanted to anyway. As my words poured out from the hidden depths within my soul, the look on her face and in her eyes became my salvation, my redemption. I saw my heart and soul shining brightly in her eyes, held safe in her keeping.

I couldn't hold back anymore and crushed my mouth to hers. Thrusting my tongue into her mouth, I tasted the unique essence that was Ava. Leaning over her, I tried to slow down, but couldn't. I wanted to drink her down, in large greedy gulps. Though this was not the place I would have chosen for our first time, sometimes the time and place chooses you, who was I to argue with fate? I sprinkled kisses across her eyes, her nose, and I made my way back to her mouth, sipping of her essence. I needed to have her within me and me within her. Sucking her plump bottom lip into my mouth, I nibbled at it gently with my teeth, then soothed the small hurt with my tongue.

"Talk to me, Ava. Are you with me? Should I stop?"

Instead of answering me with words, she pushed me onto my back and straddled my hips. Leaning down she ravished my lips, kissing me deeply. Okay then, I was most definitely up for some more of that. I kissed her back, letting go of my prized control. Ava pulled away to sit up, her groin nestled snuggly against mine.

"I'm all in, Sage. Every bit of me, is all in with you. From the beginning you have held my hand, been my rock, my savior, my knight in shining armor. You have been selfless and giving, protective and caring. If you're a dark knight, a tarnished prince charming, then that is exactly what I want. How could I possibly want for more? I'm with you Sage, I am most definitely...with...you."

I pulled Ava back down to my mouth, devouring her lips again. I couldn't get enough of her. She was everything I had ever wanted, longed for and didn't deserve, but I was taking her anyway. She wanted me and that was enough. I sat her up, bending my knees, so that her back was resting against them. I pulled the extra pillow under my head, so I was propped up a bit. My eyes caressed her face and my hands followed right behind, trailing lightly along the side of her face. She turned her head, kissing my inner wrists directly over my pounding pulse, sending shivers over my heated skin. The look in her eyes, with the hot press of her lips, was all love and longing, destiny and desire. My hands made their way down the slender column of her throat, my thumbs caressing her pulse point, which matched my racing rhythm, beat for beat, in syncopation.

"I love watching you respond to my touch, Ava, it's so beautiful."

I cupped her breasts in my hands, squeezing them together slightly and I plucked at her nipples, rolling them between my thumbs and fingers. I leaned forward soothing them with the flat of my tongue and pulling one and then the other, into my mouth, suckling with increasing pressure. I let the last one go with an audible pop. Laying back, I positioned her legs so that her knees were spread wide and her feet were tucked into my sides.

"Perfect."

"Sage..." Ava gasped, breathing heavier, her desire evident with every sigh and gasp. Her pale skin glowed with the blush of her arousal.

My hands traveled slowly down her sides, over her hips and down her long slender legs and back again. I was moving towards her center, where I was dying to be. I could see the evidence of her excitement glistening beautifully at her entrance. I gathered her arousal with my thumb and circled her clit, causing her hips to buck against my taut abdomen.

"God, Ava, I could explode just watching you. Run your hands up your sides, Ava. Yes, that's it. Now cup your breasts, squeeze them a little. Good." Grabbing her hands, I sucked on her thumbs and fingers, wetting them liberally. "Now pinch and roll your nipples, pluck at them."

I continued circling her clit, dipping down to rim her opening with my finger occasionally. Her head was tipped back, her bottom lip captured between her teeth and her beautiful hair was pooling around us, tickling my engorged cock. I placed one finger into her snug entrance, working it in and out slowly, while I continued to run my thumb in circles around her distended clit. My hips gave a jerk, my cock leaking liberally with my increasing excitement. I wanted to flip her over and pound into her so hard, that I could feel my muscles twitching to comply. I slipped in a second finger, increasing the pace.

"Sage, I'm almost there, you have to slow down," Ava moaned the last bit out.

"Oh no, we can't have that. You will not orgasm until I tell you, Ava. I want you to be in a frenzy and then I still won't let you orgasm. You...will...hold...back." I punctuated each word, by adding a third finger and slamming them all home, over and over again, until I felt she was about to explode onto my hand and I backed off. She looked down at me, her eyes brimming with her arousal.

"Please, Sage, I'm so close," she moaned, while riding my fingers, her arousal dripping onto my hand. I pulled my fingers out of Ava and licked her juices off each one, enjoying her unique flavor. I ran my left thumb along her bottom lip, letting her taste her own uniqueness, then reached for my wallet on the nightstand, grabbed a condom, reached around Ava and suited up.

"Lean down here and kiss me," I said while pulling her to me, her legs moving with the change in position to straddle my hips. We kissed deeply, our tongues dueling, sipping of each other. I broke the kiss, placing a few small kisses on her lips, then grabbed her hips and repositioned her right where I wanted her, straddling my face.

"Hold on to the headboard for balance...yes, just like that. You may not orgasm until I say so, Ava. I mean it, not until I give you permission." I emphasized that command with a little pinch to her delectable ass. I had thought to keep this side of myself from Ava, but she wouldn't have it. If the brave girl was all in, then I would be all in with her. I had been wanting to taste her again since that morning in my shower. I'd had some wicked fantasies about that and more. I loved how she was all waxed, smooth against my lips and tongue, which I put to good use, kissing and teasing her clit and her entrance. I sucked her clit between my lips, then ran the flat of my tongue from her entrance to her clit and back, then fucked her with my tongue, while her hips were grinding into my face. It was heaven, but she was really close and I planned to be in her, before I allowed her to finally go over. Placing a soft, opened mouth kiss on her clit, I moved her down my body to position her over my straining cock.

"I love you, Ava, please don't ever doubt how much you mean to me. I'm all yours, if you'll have me." With that, I aligned my cock with her saturated entrance and plunged deep into her, shouting out her name. I held her hips firm in my grip, keeping her snugged tight to my pelvis, allowing Ava time to adjust to my size. I moved her legs then, to wrap around my hips and started a gentle thrusting, a slow glide forwards and back. I worked her up slowly, since she had been on the precipice multiple times. I could feel tiny ripples along her channel, signaling to me that she was getting close and quicker than expected. I sat up, wrapping my arms around her, slowing us down again and kissing her with all of the love and passion I was feeling, putting it all into that one kiss, to convey to her how much she meant to me.

I positioned her on her back, with me still nestled between her legs, which were now hugging my chest. Picking up the pace, I began to thrust deeper and harder into her core. I could feel myself growing thicker with my arousal and slowed the pace, but not the intensity, wanting this to last forever. I reached for her hands, wanting to be connected and I leaned down to kiss her soft lips, just as she told me....

"I love you, Sage," and that was all it took for me.

"Let go, Ava, I've got you."

I continued a gentle slid in and out, her orgasm rippling along my cock, tempting me into mine. I held off though, slowing to a stop deep inside her. I held her tight while she rode the crest of her orgasm. Kissing her eyes, her lips, and her mouth I traveled down to her vulnerable and exposed throat sucking over her pulse. I wanted to mark her as mine. I refrained, but barely. Looking down at Ava, she had tears dripping over her temples, a silent testament to her emotions. I captured them with my mouth and returned them to hers, my lips wet from her beautiful tears and kissed her deeply.

"What is it, Ava? Have I been too rough? Did I hurt you?"

"It was beautiful, Sage...I...I never expected it to be so...magical, so beautiful."

"Then hold on, Beauty, 'cause there's more." And with that I gathered her legs around my elbows, shifting them high and wide. All control was lost as I plunged my cock in rapid and deep, to then withdraw slowly, dragging out to the tip. By the time she was about to go over again, my hips had lost all finesse and rhythm. Just as I was about to orgasm with her, I put her legs down, cradled her in my arms and seated myself as deep as I could go...holding still.

"I love you, Ava...I simply love you with everything I am."

Kissing her sweetly on her lips, hands held, we gazed into each other's eyes, baring our open and naked souls. Held connected in every way possible, we went over together, experiencing the most profound, beautiful moment of my entire life. Ava pulled her right hand free, caressing the side of my face, her thumb gathering the tears I hadn't realized were coursing down my cheeks.

"I love you," she said turning to kiss my arm beside her face.

I dropped my forehead to hers, humbled by her love and forgiving nature. I was amazed by the fact she could see past my darkness to see me. She had become my reason for breathing, for living. I would protect and love her with everything that I had. I would give her up and forfeit my life for hers, if that was what she needed, because without her, I was nothing...forever lost to the darkness, searching for my light, my love, my true north. I had found that in Ava and I wouldn't let her go without a fight.

⇥ 18 ⇤

Daniel

"WHAT'S GOING ON with you and Sage? And, what the hell happened to your throwing hand?"

Mason was staring out the front window when I started asking him questions. He turned his head slowly back around, but didn't look at me, rather gazed down the hallway to where Sage and Ava had just disappeared. So I was unprepared for the look on his face and in his eyes when he turned back around and focused intently on me with his light brown eyes.

"Daniel, do you have something to tell me?" he asked quietly.

"No, not that I'm aware of. What's wrong with Ava? Why was Sage carrying her? What's going on?"

"Ava came barreling in the front door crying, fairly incomprehensible, then disappeared into the bathroom. Shortly after she arrived, Sage showed up. I sucker punched the fucker. He deserved it for making Ava cry. After that, we had a very interesting conversation. Are you sure you don't have something to tell me? Sage said he ran into you the other night."

Shit! Well, I hadn't meant for anyone to find out about that, especially not Mason. I took a deep breath, thinking quickly. I had no desire to address that issue now, if ever. Before I could think of a plausible explanation, Mason started talking again.

"Daniel, I can see the wheels turning in that analytical brain of yours. Put the brakes on, it's not going to work. I know you were at Club M. A sex club and an extreme one, if I were to believe what Sage told me. Really, Daniel? What were you thinking? Why the fuck would you go to a place like that? You hardly date as it is. Have you been hiding things from me? We've been friends forever and you should know by now that you can tell me anything. I would never judge you."

I turned from his scrutiny, shoving my hands into my pockets to hide their shaking and I closed my eyes. Exhaling the breath I had been holding, I couldn't do this right now. I shook my head; there was no way I could just throw it all out there. I had kept these feelings suppressed for too long. I wasn't sure I could even reach them...to present them naked and vulnerable at Mason's feet. What if I was spurned or rejected, losing my best friend in the process? No, I couldn't do it. What I felt was beautiful, not wrong as some would say, no....no I won't share; my soul would whither and die without his friendship. I started for the front door, needing to escape the pain that had been tearing me apart for years. "I gotta go, I'll talk to you later. Tell Ava I'll call her." I was practically running for the door, which of course was closed, delaying my escape.

"Daniel...wait."

Mason's voice was soft, but carried a note of uncertainty I had never heard before. I stopped at the front door, but didn't turn around. I couldn't look at him right now; too much of what I was feeling was sure to be written plainly upon my face. I rested my head against the door. Fuck, I felt like I was dying. I was panting in an attempt to control the pain in my heart, the churning in my gut, and the loneliness that had been eating me alive for years. I could hear Mason moving around, perhaps walking closer to where I was, but I couldn't tell over my panting breaths. I tried to slow my breathing down. I held my breath for a moment and that was when Mason walked up right behind me. I could feel the heat radiating from him, and then his chest was grazing my back, he was that close. My breath gushed rapidly from my lips and my heart nearly exploded from my chest. What the fuck was he doing? Didn't he know how much this was torturing me? No..he couldn't possibly know. I'd been hiding it for too long.

"Daniel," he said, his warm breath caressing my neck and causing an uncontrollable quivering of my muscles and an instant erection. "I think we have a few things we need to discuss before you run away. And you were running, I have no doubt about that. The question is why or rather from whom? Who were you running from, Daniel, me or yourself? Now, I'm going to ask you again, was there something you wanted to tell me?"

I swallowed roughly, having no spit left in my mouth from hyperventilating, though my tongue tried to wet my dry lips. I shook my head no, not trusting myself to speak. I couldn't admit how I felt. I would save us both the embarrassing fallout of that little ditty.

"Well now, that's unfortunate. I had hoped for more from you, Daniel, but since you've apparently lost your ability to speak," he gave a low, playful chuckle at that, "I suppose I can do the talking for now. So, listen up, Daniel, because I have quite a few things to say to you."

He stepped closer, if that was even possible and pressed his muscled chest flat against my back. The heat rolling off him was incendiary and I felt as if I would combust into flames right there, pressed up against the door. His feet bracketed mine and he had placed his hands on either side of the door, above my head. I was very much hemmed in, which gave me an oddly excited, apprehensive feeling that had my cock jumping and my butt clenching. Oh God!

"Put your hands at your sides, resting them against your thighs, palm down and don't move them. Do it now."

I readily complied with the command in his voice. My hands were trembling, but he wouldn't see that, besides, I had them pressed hard against my legs.

"I'm very disappointed in you Daniel."

I had attempted to whip around and glare at him for that ridiculous statement. But, he'd easily prevented that by pressing harder into me, causing my head to turn to the right side.

"So much time," he whispered against my cheek, "so much time wasted."

And with that statement, he nearly shocked me to death my placing a very simple kiss, a light buzzing of his lips, right behind my ear. Oh fuck! I was panting again. My head was a mess, to say nothing of what my emotions were doing. Pick one emotion and I was feeling it...elated, scared to death, aroused, cautious...confused.

"Why, Daniel? Why wouldn't you say anything? All this time we could have been something very different. Could have been something so profoundly beautiful. All this time!" He stepped away and I was instantly bereft. I didn't know what to do or how to handle accepting something I had never thought I would have. How do I go from longing for Mason my entire life, to having my dreams come true in a single heartbeat? I couldn't deal with the confusion. I was floundering and yet, unless I was completely mistaken, Mason had made the shift, almost seamlessly.

"Turn around, Daniel, back against the door and keep your hands at your sides."

I did as he commanded. I had never seen Mason this way and wasn't sure how to handle that either. Something was shifting between us, but I couldn't define it, nor put it into words. I could feel him staring at me, but I couldn't bring myself to look at him. It would hurt too much if I was wrong and he wasn't feeling all that I was.

"Raise your eyes and look at me, Daniel."

It took a minute or two, before I had the nerve to face my best friend. When I finally looked up, looking over his face as a whole, his bottom lip looked red and puffy, like he had been biting it. Red was flagging his broad cheekbones, flushed as they were with emotion. However, what finally caught and held my attention, was the naked emotion pouring from his beautiful brown eyes. I was captured and couldn't look away, not that I had wanted to anyway.

"Why did it take Sage, a virtual stranger, to recognize what was glaringly obvious? How could we have we missed this?" he asked, then tucked his bottom lip behind his top teeth, biting it...fuck...no wonder it was puffy and red.

"I don't know, Mason, but please...please stop biting your lip," I practically begged, all restraint gone in the presence of my overwhelming arousal and love for this man. The man whom I had loved for my entire life.

"Show me how much you want me, want us, right now," he commanded, so I jumped on that before he could change his mind. I reached for him, eager to get my hands on Mason, only to have him step back.

"I said, keep your hands at your sides. No touching, not right now. Lean back against the door," he said, and again he placed his hands above my head on either side, leaning forward slightly.

"Now show me, Daniel, show me with our first kiss, how much you want me...us."

He leaned forward, aligning our mouths for the very first time. My heart was pounding out of my chest and I was literally trembling, trying to hold still and not pull him clumsily to me.

When Mason was but a breath away, I leaned forward to close the distance between us. I placed a gentle kiss upon his abused bottom lip and I sucked the plumpness into my mouth, and I was hit with my first taste of Mason. I nearly came like a teen-aged virgin boy, instead of the twenty-three year old virgin that I was. My arms drifted up of their own volition and Mason, curse his ass, stepped away again.

"Lips only, Daniel. Put it all into your kiss, convince me, show me."

He stepped up again, closer this time. His left forearm was resting against the door, a little above my head and his right arm was at his side. Leaning forward, our chests were touching and when our lips were aligned again, I wasted no time getting at him and dug right in. With the first tentative touch of my tongue to his, I nearly exploded in truth. I was overwhelmed with all that I was feeling and experiencing, getting a little lost in my own head. Mason was having none of that and he took over the kiss.

His right hand came up, palming the back of my head, fingers gripping my hair tight and I happily followed to wherever he wanted to go. He took the kiss deeper, more aggressive, yet tender and emotional as well. It was all poured out into this one passionate kiss. Years of longing added an edge of desperation to our kiss, like what was happening could vanish, as if it never was, and all go back to a life of desolation.

Our tongues tangled, his teeth nipped at my lips, little pains that were soothed with his tongue and sucking kisses. I had never in my life been kissed like this. Fuck...the passion and the emotion, what a difference they made. Mason moved away from my mouth, the hand in my hair pulling, maneuvering my head back and to the side, exposing my throat to his hungry mouth.

He was biting and sucking down the column of my throat, surely leaving marks. I didn't care, mark me as yours, today and

every day, I'd wear them proudly. He was at the juncture between my neck and collar bone, that meaty bit of flesh there,
when his teeth clamped down on me hard. I moaned out loudly
and came on the spot, unable to hold back the pleasure of that
bite and the boiling cauldron of emotions that he'd been controlling. I could feel the warmth of my cum sliding down my
thigh, cooling as it went.

"Liked that did ya?" Mason said with a huge shit eating grin.
"Well, we'll have to work on your control and permission to
cum, but that's a discussion for later." With that bald statement,
he kissed me deeply once more, and then stepped away, when he
heard the door to the spare bedroom open.

19

sage

LIEUTENANT CLARKE HAD texted earlier this morning, there was to be a special meeting at the Captain's office at 0900. I had meant to be there earlier, but had been reluctant to leave Ava's warm side. I could easily become accustomed to falling asleep every night with her wrapped safely in my arms. I could dream of her through the night, awakening come the dawn to see that she was still there. My dream come true.

"Enter," came the booming voice of Captain Starnes, when I knocked on his door at 0845. Walking in, I nodded to the Captain, who was behind his dark mahogany desk and then I nodded to Lieutenant Clarke, who was off to my right.

"Have a seat, Sage," the Captain directed, but I remained standing, and he continued, "we have some new, sensitive information that we need to discuss. Alexei Vinokourov has recently been reunited with his missing daughter."

"What? What daughter? If it was known he had a daughter, then why in the hell wasn't I told about her before now? That information should have been given to me during my debriefing on Vinokourov."

"You will check your tone detective," Captain said with quiet authority.

"My apologies, Captain, for the tone, but not the sentiment."

"First of all, LAPD did not know of her existence, until yesterday that is, when Special Agent Trey Mathieson came to my office to offer his assistance."

I turned around and sure enough, there was that prick Trey, smirking back at me. I narrowed my eyes at him, turning back to the Captain.

"Sage, let's hear what Special Agent Mathieson has to add to our investigation and then I will address your concerns. I take it you two have already met."

"Captain Starnes, Lt. Clarke, Detective Cartier, the FBI became interested in Vinokourov and his organization when your investigation into his activities was shelved five years ago. We take great exception to the murdering of helpless children, as I'm sure you do, and we do not take lightly the deaths of officers killed in the line of duty. So when Deputy District Attorney Delacourt went missing after the death of her family, we felt it prudent to watch Vinokourov and his operations. We realize key evidence was lost or stolen, leaving no choice, but to suspend the investigation. However, we have been monitoring Vinokourov since then. A year ago, when he allegedly kidnapped and murdered your daughter, Captain, we had planned to approach you then, but waited to see where your investigations might lead you."

"Now wait a damned minute," the Captain barked out, "there is no allegedly about it. He took my daughter and murdered her. We had reopened the human trafficking investigation and were making progress, until he was tipped off, yet again."

"Pardon, Captain. What I meant to say was, we are quite certain that someone within his organization was responsible for her death. What we don't know, with clear certainty however, is whether or not Alexei himself, had anything to do with it. There's been conflicting information presented. But let me continue, we had hoped that each of our investigations would lead to different avenues, but that both would aid in bringing him down. Running into Sage at Club M had not been planned, but was not unexpected, given that we'd ended up on the same path. I assisted him the other night with gaining the attention of the players in tight with Vinokourov. Sage, you've been dealing with that Ivan Dubrovsky, what do you think of Low-rung," he chuckled, "as you call him?"

"He acts like he's a bottom feeder, but I've come to think it's all an act. He has at least one side project that he's running right under Alexei's nose. Do you know about the college guys he's recruited to drug and rape coeds, while filming the whole thing?" Trey shook his head. "He was bragging about someone named MO the other night at Club M. How this MO had brought new rape videos to play in the Luxe room. When I asked him about it, he bragged how this was his secret side project."

Looking at Trey, "and you got that one video for me that was playing the other night. From the sounds of it, there are sure to be numerous copies playing at various clubs around the city."

"I think you're right about Ivan, he's definitely more than he seems and bears watching. But, let's get back to Vinokourov's daughter. We've been told that he did not know of her whereabouts until sometime in the past few weeks. He was attending his niece's ballet performance, when he'd reportedly recognized his daughter. However, she is still unaware of his existence."

"Is she someone that we could use? Could she be our means to get closer to Vinokourov?"

"Well now, that's an avenue we would definitely like to explore, but that depends on you, Sage. Would you like to tell us about the girl you rescued at L'Inked? The one you've been spending time with over the past several weeks?"

I stood there unbelievingly, unsure that he was actually referring to my Ava, surely not. "Are you talking about Ava DeLaney? No...no fucking way. Are you kidding me? There is no way she's Vinokourov's daughter. You must be mistaken." I felt like throwing up; he was the one responsible for killing Tomi's entire family and her presumably. I dropped into the seat the Captain had directed me to earlier. Resting my elbows on my knees, I cradled my head in my hands, escaping their scrutiny, if only briefly.

"Well, Sage, would you like to tell us about Ava DeLaney and your association with her? We know about the rape, her winding up at L'Inked. Her transpo to Cedars Sinai for the rape exam and how you stayed by her side. I've heard about your interaction with Officer Todd, whom we are watching, by the way. Then, I met you at Club M. Where I saw Ava in that video you wanted so badly, bound and..."

I was out of my seat and had the drop on Trey, before he even had a chance to finish his sentence. I needed an outlet for my anger and frustration and that prick was the perfect target. I had him pinned on the floor, in a choke hold, before anyone registered what was going on. "You will not talk about her. Do you hear me, Special Agent Mathieson? You will forget you ever saw her in That...Fucking...Video." Lt. Clarke was pulling on my arm, but I had the strength of the enraged and was not budging.

"Detective Cartier, Stand Down...Now." The Captain's booming voice and Lt. Clarke's continued pulling at my arm, made it through the red haze that had consumed my brain. I sat back on my heels, staring mutely and defiantly at Trey. He was gasping for breath, his face slowly returning to a more normal color. I kept my hands resting on my thighs, hiding the fact that they were shaking, as I attempted to gain some semblance of control. Several minutes and multiple deep breaths later, I rose to my feet and walked over to where Trey still sat on the floor.

Never taking my eyes from his, I stuck my hand out, offering to help him off the floor, which he accepted. Once standing, I continued to stare at him, eye to eye. That would be the only apology I would offer. I walked over to the windows and looked out, my back to the room in defiance and challenge.

"I won't talk about Ava, ever. She's off the playing field, as far as I'm concerned and will not be a part of this investigation. She will not be used as a pawn to bring Vinokourov down." Looking over my shoulder at them, I said, "I will not allow her to be used, in any way. Do I make myself clear? She is mine and I won't allow it."

Lt. Clarke knew exactly what I was saying, as I'm sure Trey did. While the Captain may not fully appreciate what I was saying...he understood there was no way I would allow them to put my Ava into harm's way. She'd been hurt enough, by her so-called father, whether by intention or by association, it didn't matter. He was ultimately at fault and I held him personally responsible for her rape and he would pay for those crimes against her, one way or another.

❧ 20 ❧

AVA

SAGE WOULD HAVE my ass if he knew I had gone to the ballet studio by myself, especially since it was already after eight in the evening. He was extremely protective, but I'm not sure he appreciated the angst I had been experiencing since the rape and the failed first audition. There was this special place, inside my head, where I went when I was dancing and now I couldn't reach it. I had been feeling completely lost and disconnected from my ballet...locked out, standing in the cold, shivering. Madame had commented, more than once, about how my dancing had seemed flat. That it had lost that fresh innocence of a few weeks ago, well she would be right about that. My innocence was definitely gone, stolen from me rather than lost, along with my beautiful ballet.

I dropped my bag onto the ballet floor and stood facing the vast, empty space. My heart was racing with the prospect of performing yet another epic fail. So I had come alone tonight, knowing I didn't possess the emotional fortitude to face judging eyes, while struggling with my ballet. I thought it might be best, just this once, to embrace the darkness, dancing within the shadows. I didn't want to shine too bright a light upon my failings, as they were glaring enough, without the bright lights and reflective mirrors.

Music played softly in the background. I began my warm-up routine and drifted along in the familiar, loosening my ankles and sore muscles. I finished with some bar work, then walked to my iPhone and selected my solo music to play.

Standing in the middle of the shadowed studio, I closed my eyes and I searched for the connection to my ballet. I could feel it, though it remained frustratingly out of reach, still lost to me. The music started and I began dancing my solo easily enough. The routine had been memorized to perfection, but felt flat and rote, with no emotion flowing through my moves. I could feel my soul struggling, suffocating under the weight of this heaviness I found myself shrouded in.

I kept dancing the routine over and over, but to no avail. No matter how much I wanted to recapture my joie de vivre, my joyfulness in life and in ballet, the more elusive it had become. Sweat was pouring off me, as were the endless tears from my heart. I was beyond frustrated, feeling completely lost and hopeless in the dark. Exhausted, I collapsed to the floor, unintentionally landing in front of one of the mirrors and coming face to face with my reflection. I had no desire to gaze upon myself, but once I looked at the girl in the mirror, I couldn't look away from her tear soaked eyes, barely recognizable as my own. The grief and despair clouding her grey eyes had captured me.

Where was Ava? If she was in there, I couldn't find her. She was someone else now, someone I didn't want to be. I wanted to get back to the real me, before the rape and before everything, including my virginity, had been stolen from me. I had suffered loss before and managed to make it through, but dear Lord how much more? I closed my eyes to the stranger in the mirror, her suffering more than I could bear. Breath hitching in my throat, I tipped my head back wanting to scream to the heavens. I wanted to curl into a ball and cry myself to sleep, like a toddler without my favorite toy. Where'd they hide the rewind button? The do-over button? The fucking easy button? I laughed almost hysterically to myself.

Hot tears were dripping onto my arms, but cooled quickly. I hugged my knees tightly and contemplated what to do about the mess my life had become. I knew I had to reconcile the fact that I had lost my ballet. Oh, I could do the moves with precision and beautifully so, but I had lost my way. The emotions fueling my ballet had been severed and were free floating elsewhere, no longer anchored to my artistic heart and soul, and I was left to feel forsaken.

Cradling my head in my hands, I unleashed the grief that would no longer remain contained and stuffed into that little box. I grabbed my hair and pulled hard, welcoming the pain upon my tender scalp. Jumping up, I stormed over to my iPhone and changed the music to something dark and gritty, feeling far removed from light and airy. All I could feel was the darkness. All I could see was the reflection of a stranger, looking back at me through desolate eyes.

Exhausted in both body and mind, I stood in the middle of that floor again, waiting for new music to start. I had to try something...anything, even if it was different, or die from trying. I had waited for so long to pursue my dreams and I wasn't about to give up without a fight. Haunting music began filling the space, a subtle layering that wouldn't be fully appreciated until later. It slowly resonated through my soul, causing the smallest of sparks, and I prayed that would be enough.

I was determined to find my way back and began swaying to the music, with no real form and no particular moves, just dancing my way through the darkness that coated me still. The layers of music were building note upon note, the sound richer and fuller, just as my dancing became sharper and more precise, evolving in synchronicity with the music. Thought had been suspended and I was pure feeling and sensation, shedding all that had been soft. The suffocating shroud was lifting, revealing that the old Ava was gone. I kept stretching for that place inside, but it was different now, darker, bolder...scary. I didn't know who was dancing anymore, but this Ava had found her way in and was dancing with my lost emotions.

As I came out of a fouette turn, navigating my way through these new emotions, I had that creepy-crawling feeling that somebody was watching me. Scanning the room, I looked around frantically, as the sensation became stronger. My heart jumped into my throat choking me, when I realized there was someone leaning against the wall, over by the door. My shaking hand came to my throat and a gushing sigh left my lips, when I realized it was only Sage. He was watching me intently. There was no emotion showing on his face or in his blue eyes, so I couldn't tell what he was thinking, but I could guess. More than likely he was pissed that I had come by myself, but I couldn't help it, I had to and I would just have to explain why. We walked towards each other, unable to deny the irresistible pull between us. I was sweaty from chasing my demons about the room and I surely looked a hot mess, but I refused to check my appearance, knowing there was nothing I could do about it.

When I reached Sage, he swept me into his arms, sweat and all. His left hand gripped the back of my head and his mouth was devouring mine with a soul searing kiss, weakening my knees. Having no time to react, I willingly followed his lead. He was gripping my hair tight now, though I don't think he realized how tight he was pulling on my scalp. But, when I finally let my head drift in the direction he had been pulling, his mouth left mine and skated down my neck. Apparently, he did know what he wanted and I was the ignorant one. With better access to my vulnerable throat, he nipped his way down to my collarbone, biting gently and causing me to moan out loud. Sage's hands drifted down to my butt, lifting me so that I wrapped my legs around his waist and he went after my mouth again. Good Lord, could the man kiss.

Sage had me against a wall somewhere, before I even registered that we had moved. Pressed in tight, he rubbed his hardened cock, against my heated core, with a delicious friction sure to send me over quickly. Pulling his lips away, he rested his forehead against mine and he took a few labored breaths.

"God, I was so mad at you for coming here alone and was all set to give you a piece of my mind, until I watched you dancing with such determination. Your face was glowing with passion. So intoxicating to watch, I had wanted to run across the room and devour you where you stood." He slammed his hungry mouth back into mine, demonstrating just how much he wanted me still.

"Give it to me, Beauty. I know you're almost there," he said between labored breaths, gusting against my cheek. Just his husky, passion-filled voice was enough to send me over. "Let go, Ava, I'll catch you."

With that command, Sage increased the pressure, picked up the pace, and I exploded like a brilliant supernova. The intensity and duration of my incredible orgasm was controlled and directed by Sage. How he could get my body to respond, with just the command in his voice, was a bit of a mystery, but there it was. His words, his very presence intoxicated me, overwhelmed me, and I couldn't get enough of him.

I had been channeling all my angst and frustration into my dancing, which had morphed into my instantaneous arousal, so that the release of tension had left me feeling deflated, like a wilted balloon and I crashed hard. My emotions were raw and bleeding. I began sobbing uncontrollably, still held in Sage's capable arms. He turned my legs, so that I was cradled in his arms and carried me over to one of the benches and sat down. My face was buried in his neck, anointing him with my tears.

"I can't do it, Sage. I can't dance anymore. It's not the same. I can't find my way back to that Ava, the beautiful Ava. She's lost...so lost."

"Be gentle with yourself, Beauty, don't try to force it. Everything in life changes, nothing stays the same. Maybe your dancing was destined to go in a different direction. I'm no expert, but you looked and danced beautifully just now. Try embracing this new way, let your body guide you and your heart will follow. Just give it time."

"I know you're right, but I want to be the old me. I think she's gone. They stole her from me, ripping her from my body. That Ava is dead and I don't know how to be this new Ava, or if I even want to be."

"I love this Ava, here in my arms, old or new. You'll find your way, Beauty, be patient. I'll be with you all the way and together we can discover all there is to know about this new Ava."

❦ 21 ❦

NATALIA

I WAS AT A loss for what to do with my time. I didn't have ballet practice and I hadn't heard from Marcus in some time, not that I wanted to...the rat bastard. So I found myself ghosting about Alexei's home in the Palisades. I had my own place, but liked to come here for the free food and paid shopping trips. Well, to be honest, it wasn't like I paid for anything anyway, Alexei did. I was rather spoiled and not afraid to admit it.

All was quiet though, Alexei was at some meeting, so I was all alone and bored beyond tolerance. Grabbing my purse and my keys from the bedroom I kept here, I made my way down the hall, thinking I could use a little retail therapy to settle my angst. Towards the end of the hall, I heard a loud voice coming from one of the other bedrooms. I slowed to see what was going on, especially since the housekeeper Anya and I were supposed to be the only ones home.

As I neared the room, I recognized Ivan's voice, though raised in anger. I would never forget his demeanor at the house in Pasadena, or the way he treated Ava and the dark aura that had clung to him and practically shouted...'don't fuck with me.'

Picking up the pace, I planned to hurry on by, no need to draw attention to myself, but that was until I heard Marcus's name and then Ava's mentioned. Keep walking Natalia, keep walking, but no, curiosity got the best of me. Good thing I wasn't a cat. I stopped just outside the cracked door to shamelessly listen in, knees shaking and breath held.

"Yes, that's what I said...you'll do as you were told...he's getting suspicious...yes...well, he was too careless...I took care of Marcus...do you want to die in the same manner, I'm only too happy to oblige. Yes...at Club M."

I couldn't contain the gasp that fell from my opened mouth. I tried to walk away, but I stood frozen in place, paralyzed with fear. The door opened with macabre slowness and Ivan stepped out, leaning against the doorjamb...indolently crossing his right leg over his left, with the phone still pressed to his ear, listening. He just stared straight at me...eyes devoid of emotion.

"Yes. I will take care of her myself, don't concern yourself there. A moment, Yosef, I need to attend to something here."

"Natalia, I suggest you leave and forget I was here," he said, after placing his caller on hold. "Our friendship means very little to me, but for the sake of those years I watched you mature, I will let you leave, but this one time only. Go."

I could hardly get my body to obey his quiet, emotionless command or my mind's frantic screams for me to run. I stood there, for what seemed like hours, held captive in his deadly gaze, before I was able to move. I felt the weight of his stare drilling into my back, as I stumbled down the hallway, my legs barely able to keep me upright and moving forward, shaking as they were in fear. The front entrance had never seemed so far away, but it represented safety and freedom, even if an illusion, but at this point I would take anything.

As I was opening the door, I heard Ivan resume his conversation, but this time, I shut the door before I heard anymore.

"Yosef, we'll have another issue to discuss tonight..."

❧ 22 ❧

AVA

A DISTURBING SENSE OF disconnection and disorientation was clouding my head, reminding me of when I awoke in that filthy alley after the rape, which didn't make any sense. My heart rate went from slow and steady, to racing and manic, in a matter of seconds. Why was I feeling this way again? I knew I had been tired, but not to this extent. My eyes felt leaden. Shaking my head for clarity had only resulted in waves of nausea and a violent urge to vomit. Turning onto my side, I curled into a fetal position, pulling my knees to my chest. Taking slow, deep breaths, I gave myself a mental pep talk...there will be no puking, because despite the large amounts of saliva pooling in my mouth, I refused to give in and let the contents fly. Good Lord, I hated to vomit. Laying completely still seemed to help, but whatever I was lying on was about as comfortable and as warm as a slab of ice. Where in the hell was I?

"Ah, so she's awake," said a low, accented voice.

I jumped at the unexpected words. Instantaneous fear coating my skin in a cold sweat. I searched around frantically, but everywhere I looked, there were shadows and focusing my eyes proved difficult. That eerie, disembodied voice was lost to the darkness, hiding from me. But, now that my eyes were wide with fear, I could see I was lying on the cold cement floor, yup totally comfortable. God Ava, focus! Taking a deep breath, I squinted my eyes, hoping that would help me to see, and I looked for where Mr. Accent might be hiding.

"I'm pleased to see the drugs are wearing off. I was tired of waiting for you to wake up. Since you took so long, our time together will have to be cut short. I expect your father will be along soon, but not too worry sweet, Ava, I will put the wait to good use."

"What? What are you talking about? You've taken the wrong girl. I don't have a father, Mr. Accent. I mean, obviously I had one, at some point, but not now." I was incredulous and despite the situation, couldn't keep that from showing in my voice.

"Ava, you'd do well to mind that smart mouth. I won't hesitate to punish you. I've done it before, but I think you may have forgotten how well we have been acquainted...intimately acquainted."

Frantically searching the shadows, I noticed the outline of a man moving towards the dimly lit corner, where the only source of light glowed. I could just make out his dark, slicked back hair and a mustache, but that was all, the rest of him was an indistinguishable blur. From what I could tell, he didn't seem to be familiar, but....Oh...My...God...he had to have been there, during my rape. Hyperventilating, I couldn't go through that again, there was no way, especially with no drugs on board to blunt my memory. I had to get out of there. I wouldn't lay there helpless and docile like before, see how he likes me now, awake and fighting.

"You won't be going anywhere, my delicious Ava."

Damn it, cursed with emotional transparency.

"Yes, Ava, your thoughts are written clearly on your face, even in the shadows, I can see what you're thinking. I could drug you again, like last time, but I won't. No, I want you fully aware of what is happening and I will have you begging for more, oh yes. See if I don't."

The sadistic glee in his voice caused my heart to accelerate into my throat. I prayed the man coming to rescue his daughter, would consider helping me instead. He must be frantic though, thinking someone had his daughter. Squinting at my captor, I struggled to recall him and what had happened. All I managed was to increase my headache. The last thing I could remember, was finishing my second audition for the LA Ballet. I had been fortunate enough, along with several other dancers, to be afforded a second chance to dance. I wasn't sure about the others, but I had royally choked at the first audition. This time, I had performed a darker solo, one that this new Ava seemed to excel at and my pas de deux was with a different partner. I wondered how much time I had lost this go around? Why, of all times, did I have to fight with Sage? He won't even know that I'm missing. Stupid, I was so stupid.

"Ava! Do pay attention," Mr. Accent barked, scaring me out of my head, where I had been reflecting on how stupid I was. Shit! There I go again, pay attention Ava. Geez, pay attention. Damned drugs. I needed to sit up, not only was I uncomfortable, but I didn't like being so vulnerable, laid out on the floor like I was. Keeping a wary eye on Mr. Accent, I pushed myself up sideways, until I was resting squarely on my butt, though swaying back and forth with dizziness. There was no way I could stand up, at least not yet. Scooting backwards to the brick wall behind me, I rested my back against the rough brick and pulled my knees to my chest. I felt more secure wrapping my arms around them, even though I knew it for the delusion that it was.

"Comfortable are we now?"

I didn't answer, doubting he cared whether or not I was comfortable. I continued to stare in his direction, while subtly pushing my back into the wall, hoping the pain would keep me focused on the here and now. I had to stop getting lost inside my head. But, fighting waves of nausea and intermittent disorientation wasn't helping.

"Finally, I have your full attention," he said with an air of hurt and disgruntlement. I was hard pressed to keep my mouth shut at that. It was his sadistic ass that drugged me. What I really wanted to do was scream, 'Fucking really?' I was the captive audience here, what did he want from me? It's not like I had any control over being attentive. You...Drugged...Me! I prayed none of *that* showed on my transparent face.

"Where were we? Now, Ava, if you would be so good as to cooperate, all will be fine. If not? Let's just say, that would be preferable."

Fear surged through my bloodstream and thanks to the burst of fight-or-flight, I was instantly sober. Mr. Accent was pacing back and forth in front of me and I scoped out the room. Everything was gloomy, which made it difficult to see. But, it looked like there was a door behind Mr. Accent and to my right. There were no windows, or at least not that I could see, or that provided any light. To my left, there was a bench or something, it was hard to tell, but there just wasn't much to this warehouse-like room. I returned my gaze to Mr. Accent. I had no idea what he was planning for me, but I wouldn't remain docile to his plans.

"Do not underestimate me, Ava. I may have cultivated an air of subservience and a general lack of intelligence, but I am neither, quite the opposite in fact. That my delicious Ava, is all you will get out of me. For you see, I am not one of those stupid villains that wax poetic about what they are doing and why. So you can stop looking for an escape Ava, you won't be leaving this room," he said with a low, maniacal laugh, causing my stomach to drop in dread.

With a gleeful look, in his remorseless eyes, he pulled something from his pocket. I couldn't tell what it was at first, but I gasped in fear and watched in horror, as he pulled out a gun, raised his hand and fired at me, with no hesitation whatsoever. The pain was unlike anything I could have ever imagined, as it tore through my body like wildfire.

I fell over onto my side, realizing I would die, right here and now. I was too young. I had unfinished business. No, no...the light was fading, closing in on a single spot. I whispered Sage's name, one last time, and as everything went dark, it spilled across my lips in a silent prayer, never to be heard.

❧ 23 ❧

sage

"MASON?"

"Who's this?"

"Sage. Have you seen, Ava? I can't find her."

"No. What's the matter, Sage, did you lose something? Something that should be right under your nose...hmmm?"

"Shut the fuck up. This is serious, there are things going on, things you know nothing about and Ava could be in danger. So again, have you seen Ava today?"

"No, I haven't....hold on."

Mason was yelling to Daniel in the background.

"Daniel said he hasn't talked to Ava since yesterday. He went with her to the studio. She'd wanted to practice for today's auditions. I take it you haven't heard from her since the audition today?"

"No, we had a disagreement. I was hoping that she was there, with you guys."

"She's not here. May I ask what the argument was about? Must have been bad, if she hasn't reached out to you."

"Normally, I wouldn't bother responding to that, but this is urgent and time is of the essence. I told her, in confidence, that I was a detective working undercover for the LAPD. She wasn't supposed to tell anyone, but she told you and Daniel. Now the investigation's jeopardized. I know she trusts you guys, but I don't, not with her life or the lives of anyone involved in this investigation. She swore you guys wouldn't say anything and maybe you haven't and won't, but where is she, Mason? Why can't I find her? This isn't like Ava, not at all."

"Hold on."

Holding was the very last thing I wanted to do and I paced the office at the precinct, waiting. I had come to the office to talk with Lt. Clarke about a few things regarding the investigation. He would be here in a few minutes.

"Sage, I spoke with Daniel. He said, that at the studio yesterday he was chatting with Marcus, who kept saying how worried he was about Ava. Said how she hadn't been the same, since the night they'd all gone out to Circus Disco. Ava hasn't told anyone about the rape, so Daniel didn't say anything. But, when Marcus kept going on and on about her safety, Daniel told him there was nothing to worry about. He told Marcus, that between the two of us and her cop boyfriend she was well protected. He feels terrible and bailed, running out of the house to start looking for her."

"Fuck! I should have never told her. Damn it! If you hear anything, I want to know immediately," I said then hung up on Mason before he could respond. I was about to storm out of the office, when Lt. Clarke walked in. And wouldn't you know it, trailing directly behind him was Special Agent Trey. Oh joy, the topping on my shitcake.

"Sage, is your computer up and running?" Lt. Clarke asked without preamble.

"It is. What did you need?"

He hands me a DVD to put into the computer, nothing further was said, but the tension was palpable. They came around the desk, waiting for whatever was on that DVD to load and run. I looked at them both, but neither was giving anything away. Guess I'd know soon enough. I turned to Trey when he started talking.

"We obtained this DVD from a source deep within Vinokourov's organization. You better sit down, Sage."

At first I thought to ignore the prick, but something in his tone made me think better of it and I took a seat, just as the disc began to play. I sat in stunned silence as I watched what appeared to be a "snuff" video. My stomach clenched in revulsion at the brutality with which it was executed. Shock was my next emotion, when I realized the star of the video, was none other than Marcus Oliver. I looked at Lt. Clarke and Trey in question. Lt. Clarke answered me.

"Information has come to our attention that Marcus was responsible for organizing and directing Ava's rape. We think Alexei may have had him killed in retaliation. Sending a clear message to the others involved in her rape and to those wanting to usurp the reigns of his little empire."

My initial feeling was one of, exultation and vengeance, eye for an eye. He'd raped my Ava, so he had gotten what he deserved. But, that was swiftly followed by revulsion and remorse for his death, though not for the brutal rape he had suffered at the hands of his killer. Nope, no remorse for that!

"Ava is missing. I was just about to leave to go look for her. I wanted to touch bases with you, Lt., regarding Ivan and those rape videos he recruits the college guys for. In light of the Marcus snuff video, I think that night at Club M, Ivan was referring to Marcus, when he said MO was bringing in some new videos. They had to be working together. I wonder if Ivan was there the night Ava had been taken? Or there during the rape? Participating?"

Standing rapidly, my chair flew backwards, crashing into the wall and bouncing off.

"I'm going to kill that little..."

"Not another word," Lt. Clarke warned. "Not one, Detective," he said with a meaningful stare.

I was seething with anger. That low-rung fucking wannabe, Ivan. He was so much more than he appeared, he had to be. Despite Clarke's intervention just now, there was no way I would let Ivan get away with what he did to my Ava, not without some type of retaliation, some kind of retribution. Be it legal or not, he owed restitution for what he did, and I planned to collect the debt and in full measure.

"What's this about Ava DeLaney? She's missing?" Trey asked, breaking through my mental musings.

"That's yet to be determined. I haven't heard from her and have this crawling sensation on the back of my neck. I've learned to trust that and my instincts are telling me something's wrong and that she's in trouble. Her friends, Mason and Daniel, are out looking for her, hitting up all her usual haunts. We're hoping that after the audition today, she decided to run some errands. Or maybe it didn't go well and she wanted to have some time alone, to decompress..."

I walked over to the windows overlooking downtown and paced back and forth. I was hoping against all hope that Ava was just busy and had forgotten to check in, but I didn't believe it and I couldn't make myself swallow the lie. I could feel the Lt. and Trey behind me, but I was ignoring them for the moment, collecting my thoughts and formulating a plan. As I turned to the two, they were looking at me expectantly, knowing I would come up with a plan and we would execute it together.

"We need to move on this new information now. We can assume Ava is in danger and Ivan is responsible. I'm leaving to confront Alexei. You're either with me or you can fuck off," I said, as I walked out the door. Trey and Lt. Clarke fell in behind me and we exited the door, en route to confront Alexei and to find my Ava.

⊶{ 24 }⊷

AVA

NAUSEA AND DISORIENTATION were like old friends now, but at least this time, I knew what was going on. First off, I wasn't dead. That asshat shot me! The pain had been so overwhelming that I had thought I was dying. It must have been something to knock me out, being that I was groggy and nauseous again. As I became more aware of my surroundings, I realized I was lying on a hard surface. One that was only marginally softer than the cold floor I had been lying on earlier. How much earlier, was the question.

Taking stock, I noticed my shoulders seemed stiff, but when I attempted to adjust them, I couldn't. Tipping my head back, I could see my wrists had been wrapped tight with rope and fastened to a hook in the wall above my head. The harder I pulled, the tighter the rope became. I stopped yanking to free them, since that was getting me nowhere. I lifted my head to look about the room and if my jaw could have dropped to the floor, it would have. I was practically naked, wearing only my bra and panties. The fear that had been gripping my gut into tight knots, swelled to the point I thought I'd choke on it. Oh God. I was in the same room as before, only now I was lying on that narrow bench seat I thought I had seen.

Deep breath, Ava, deep breath. Trying to control the shakes that had gripped my body, was proving futile. In closing and opening my eyes, I had hoped the world would reset itself, back to normal, but no such luck. I looked for a way to at least sit up. My feet were on the floor on either side of the bench seat, but when I tried to move them, I realized my ankles had been secured to the bench, keeping my legs spread apart. Now I was panting in fear, I couldn't do this again, I really couldn't. When I couldn't see a way to escape, tears of fear and frustration escaped to wet my temples and soak my hair. Saliva began pooling in my mouth with the need to vomit. Turning my head, I lifted my shoulder to the side, the rope pulling tight on my wrists and I began retching, but thankfully my stomach was empty. I spit out an abundance of saliva onto to the floor that had been pooling in my mouth...fuck 'em...I could be choking for all Mr. Accent cared.

The door opened and Mr. Accent sauntered into the room, as if my thoughts conjured the madman himself. I spat once more onto the floor, clearing my mouth of the residual saliva, all the while staring directly into his dark, demonic eyes. Despite the precarious situation that I found myself in, I'd had enough of being the victim and I would go down fighting.

"Ava, Ava...tsk, tsk! What are we going to do with you? Hmmm...Well, I know what I'm going to do *to* you," he said, while staring at my body, undressing me completely with his evil eyes. Not that it took a lot of imagination, since I barely had any clothes on. My stomach turned with fear and nausea. I watched him, as he stared at me. How in the hell was I going to get out of this? When he began to unbuckle his belt, I thought I might be able to find something to vomit up after all.

⊲{ 25 }⊳

ALEXEI

YOU JUST CAN'T find good help these days. Ivan was missing, his little understudy Marcus was dead, by Ivan's hands I suspected, and now there were loud voices in the outer office. Giving in to the inevitable, I stood to investigate, but as I did, my office door slammed open and three men stormed in. My personal assistant was trailing behind like a lost puppy, ringing his hands. I sighed to myself and shook my head, case in point, my personal assistant was totally spineless.

"You can't just walk in unannounced," my PA was stammering, at the backs of the three men who had barged in.

"It appears they can do just that. You may leave, Sergei, I will take it from here." With barely a glance in his direction, I added, "Take the rest of the afternoon off." I watched as he left, pulling the door closed behind him.

"Well, gentlemen, to what do I owe the honor of your disruptive company? Shall we start with introductions...hmm?"

"We know exactly who you are, Alexei Vinokourov."

"Well, Mr. Cartier, I seriously doubt that you do, but that's a discussion for another day. What can I do for you today?" Assessing the three men, what an odd pairing. Two members that have frequented my sex clubs and a Lieutenant with the LAPD. They all seemed to be vibrating with energy. Except Cartier, who was channeling some dark anger straight at me, if I wasn't mistaken. Naturally he spoke first.

"Vinokourov, I'll skip all pretense and posturing, because there isn't time for that bullshit. We are looking for Ivan Dubrovsky. Where is he?"

Well wasn't that the question of the day, but I waited him out. I wasn't about to give away that I had no clue as to where Ivan was.

"Before you try feeding us a line of bullshit, we need to find your second in command. We have reason to believe he has abducted a young woman, one that he had previously abducted. See, we are fairly certain that he participated in the abduction and rape of this young woman, but somehow she managed to get away. However, not before significant damage was done. I think you might know who we are talking about, Ava DeLaney. Ring a bell for you, Vinokourov? How does it make you feel to know that you are responsible, even if indirectly so, for the abduction and rape of your very own daughter?"

Cartier couldn't have picked a better weapon to gut me with and he very well knew it. The nauseating discord I felt was internal though, I wouldn't show them any weakness.

"You will tell me what you know, what you suspect, and you will tell me now!" I gritted out through clenched teeth.

"Oh I don't think so. Where would Ivan have holed up? Do you know of any places where he could have taken Ava? Somewhere that wouldn't draw attention? Furthermore, why would he take her? What's his end game? Is he blackmailing you? What the fuck is going on?" Cartier lashed out in rapid-fire.

"Why, thank you for taking a breath. Now let us begin, because if you are correct then our goals are in alignment. If Ivan truly was involved with her kidnapping and rape, and has Ava again, he will rue the day he ever went against me. I will stop at nothing to have him buried and I guarantee you he is well aware of that. So again I ask you, what is going on and what lead you to these conclusions? Furthermore, explain the connection between the three of you and be quick about it. We don't have all day."

Before I knew what was happening, I had two hundred pounds of angry male coming at me with his fists flying. Cartier had righteous indignation and worry fueling his anger, and I had the love of a daughter that I longed to rewind time to protect. It felt good to release some anguish, the remorse that my life had been the inadvertent cause of her pain and trauma. But, with that realization, I stopped cold, taking every punch Cartier delivered, with no deflection offered. Every blow that landed, was a fraction of what I deserved for putting her life in jeopardy. I felt and heard my nose crack. Felt the warm spurt of blood onto my chin and shirt. I looked at Cartier in confusion when he had stopped pummeling my face and stood there staring at me with a raised eyebrow.

"Are you just going to stand there? Fight back man, where's the sport in me beating the shit out of you?"

"I deserve every blow that lands, but if you have quite finished, maybe we could get back to the business of finding Ava." I took the pocket square out of my suit pocket and held it to my nose, which was still bleeding and I pinched the bridge. It was either broken or dislocated.

"Sit in the chair, Vinokourov." Cartier directed.

With those terse instructions, I sat in the chair. Cartier approached intently, wearing a smirk and a glint in his blue eyes. Reaching out quick as a snake, he reset my nose. Of course, I had to contend with a fresh spurt of blood.

"Fuck me! You could have at least warned me." I was thankful, but perhaps a little disgruntled and in pain, but I deserved it to be sure. From the corner of my eye I saw Trey smirking. We had known each other a long time, friends of sorts, but I was about to stand up and beat that smirk right off his face. He must have seen the look of retribution in my eyes, for he turned his face away to hide the evidence, fucking prick. Returning my attention back to Cartier, I realized he had seen the entire silent exchange, between Trey and I. Time for some damage control.

Sighing audibly, "Tell me what you know...please."

Cartier glared at me, before getting back to the business at hand. "Ava is missing. She didn't return from her audition with the LA Ballet. We have looked everywhere and have been unable to locate her. I thought she might just be blowing off some steam because we'd had a little disagreement." He cleared his throat at this.

"Oh, do tell." I cleared my throat to mock his obvious discomfort though mine actually did need clearing with all the blood flowing down the back of it. I then continued, saying, "What was this disagreement about?"

"That's irrelevant, Vinokourov. Where is Low-rung?" When I looked at him questioningly, he supplied Ivan's name.

❦ 26 ❦

sage

I WASN'T SURE IF Alexei really knew where Ava might be, but we were running out of options. I had no choice but to trust him at this point. Once he realized Ivan might in actuality have Ava again, his entire demeanor had transformed. He attempted to take over the whole find Ava operation, but that wasn't going to happen. I allowed him to lead us to this warehouse because I was frantic to reach her side, but that was as far as I would go.

Time was our enemy. God only knew what we'd find once we got there. I planned on killing that sadistic mother fucker with my bare hands, jail or no jail. She was mine to protect and to avenge. I had shifted into a state of hyper-vigilance, my heart steady, breathing calm and even. I called this my killer mode. The Lt. and Trey assessed me on the trip across town, but I had given nothing away. The only one actually speaking my language, oddly enough was Alexei, the cold bastard. He was acting as if he too loved Ava and would die to protect her.

We ran into a small warehouse, close to where Club M was located. It was too quiet though, and our footsteps echoed loud through the empty hallways. The element of surprise was definitely lost. Fuck! We were blind, not knowing the building, or where Ava might be located. It was slow going. We were being cautious, yet thorough in our search, not wanting to have to circle back because we missed something. We started our search by canvassing the first floor, the Lt., Trey, and I were operating smoothly with silent communications and Alexei had been right there with us, keeping time.

We went up some stairs, down a corridor, and around a blind corner when all hell broke loose, as we stumbled across a couple of guards. I pointed the business end of my Glock at Frick and Frack.

"Hands out where we can see them. Now! Where are Dubrovsky and Ava DeLaney?" I was eyeing them and the surrounding area, a darkened hallway. My three sidekicks were assessing the area too and I could feel them right beside me.

"Here or downtown boys, where's Ivan?"

Frick tried to make a run for it, but Trey was on him in a second flat, pinning him against the wall. For a scrappy guy, he was strong. Unfortunately, this had caused a lot of noise, but once everything settled back down, we heard some distant screaming, sounding distinctly like Ava screaming my name. I turned, bellowing her name in response and I took off in the direction we heard her screaming. I continued to call out to her as I ran down the corridor. Alexei was hot on my heels. As I rounded the corner yelling out her name, there was Ivan, the rat-fuckingbastard, with his gun raised and shots fired before I had a chance to raise my Glock. My enraged bellow abruptly stopped as the air was knocked out of me with the impact. I saw Ivan take off into the darkness.

I turned slowly towards Alexei, attempting to raise my arm. I wanted to tell him to go to Ava, but all that escaped my lips as I collapsed onto the floor was a frothy, bloodied whispered Ava. The darkness and the ravenous fire in my chest consumed what was left of my words.

❧ 27 ❧

AVO

"SAGE! OH GOD...No...no...no...no"
Oh God, please let him be okay. Mr. Accent and I had
heard loud voices coming closer to where we were. The bastard
pulled his pants up, grabbed a gun I hadn't seen, and taken off,
out the door, like the fucking rat he was. I could hear loud voices and I recognized Sage's among the cacophony of sounds.
Then I heard a sound I would never forget in all my life. The
sound of a bellowing Sage stopped abruptly by the retort of
multiple gun shots.

Screaming at the top of my lungs, I pulled on my wrists
which were still bound to the wall with the damned rope. They
were getting bloody from my pulling so hard.

"Sage! Please someone, anyone, please come set me free.
Please. Oh God, I'm begging, please release me."

I was getting ready to scream out again, when of all the people Mr. Vinokourov barreled into the room. He was wild eyed
and looked as if he had just taken several hits to the face. I tried
to work up some embarrassment, over being naked, but there

wasn't much I could do about it and it's not like I chose to be sporting skin only.

My heart was breaking, which was all I could focus on. I couldn't hear Sage anymore, couldn't feel him. I felt severed and my soul gone. I looked up at Alexei Vinokourov and I couldn't help but think, something about him seemed familiar, but I couldn't concentrate on anything, but the fact that I needed Sage right now. Alexei took a pocket knife out of his pants and he cut the ropes binding me to the damn bench, first my ankles, then my wrists. He gently helped me to sit. Then proceeded to unbutton the first few buttons of his dress shirt, pulling it over his head and placing it over mine.

I cleared my throat, which felt raw from screaming for help, and for the need to scream out in denial. I asked Alexei where Sage was.

"Ava, I need you to come with me, okay?" The gentleness in his voice was almost my undoing.

It really wasn't a question apparently because as he was saying this, he had bent down and picked me up, cradling me in his arms. He held me tight against his chest, like he was carrying a cherished child. I felt frail and helpless in this moment and I allowed him the liberty.

"Please," I whispered brokenly against his chest, "please tell me where Sage is."

"Ava...I don't know where he is right now, but I know he was shot by Ivan. Let's get you out of here and to the hospital to be checked out."

I didn't bother arguing or putting up a fuss. I didn't have the energy or the will. Sage was gone, I could feel it. What was the point? I felt like I was dying on the inside, a slow insidious death that was creeping through my soul and stealing my will to go on. I knew most people would think there was no way I could love someone, heart and soul so quickly. But, the strongest bonds are forged in the hottest flames, and we had virtually combusted. There was no denying we were drawn to each, from that first moment at L'Inked when I fell into his arms. We had both been walking through our own personal hells. Combine that with all we had been through together, and it felt as if an integral part of me, his portion of what made me, made us, was gone. I would never survive half alive.

❧ 28 ❧

Sage and ER Staff

"WHAT DO WE have?" Dr. Berghoza asked the paramedic.

"Officer shot in the field, multiple chest shots at close range. He arrested in the field, but responded to a brief round of chest compressions and epinephrine. He has been breathing spontaneously since then, but with increasing distress, has a non-rebreather mask with oxygen at fifteen liters. Guy over there, said he was FBI and he insisted on coming in with him."

Breathing wasn't much of an option at the moment, what with the heavy feeling constricting my chest and the fire ripping through it.

"We noted increasing cyanosis, tachycardia, and hypotension. Breath sounds profoundly diminished on the left side," said the paramedic.

"Get O neg blood ready to roll on the rapid infuser, start two more large bore IV's, and get ready to intubate his airway. Have a chest tube ready for a probable hemothorax. Notify surgery we'll be rolling in with multiple penetrating wounds, suspected lung damage, and have perfusion available for cardiopulmonary bypass if necessary and cell saver for certain."

Who the hell are they talking about? Ava, where's Ava...I need to get to Ava. Where's my Ava? Why won't they answer me?

"Doctor Witting, Doctor Berghoza...he's in V-Fib."

"Pull the crash cart over. Pads on, ready two hundred joules...all clear, all clear, all clear...shocking."

"Begin CPR, epinephrine one milligram IV. Bag/mask assisted ventilations for now. Let's put that chest tube in, might buy us a small window of time and start that uncrossed, O neg blood stat, and keep them coming."

"Still in V-Fib, shock again two hundred joules...all clear, all clear, all clear...shocking."

"Epinephrine one milligram IV, chest compressions looking good, EKG waveform showing good perfusion."

"We've got a rhythm back."

"Call surgery, we are transporting now. Spike those next units of O neg with blood tubing to hand push on the way, let's go people, time is of the essence."

"Fuck, we lost him again!" exclaimed, Dr. Witting.

"Resume chest compressions. James get ready to straddle his hips on the gurney. Keep the compressions going, we are transporting to the OR now. Let's go!"

It feels like I'm moving...away though, away from my Ava. Wait...

"What are his chances, Dr. Witting?" Trey asked.

Dr. Witting shook his head.

❧ 29 ❧

AVA

BEFORE I KNEW it, we were at Cedar's again. If I never saw this hospital again, it would be too soon. Once settled in the exam room, the same rape response team came to see me.

"How are you, Ava?" Dr. Wong asked when she saw me.

"Dr. Wong," I rasped at her in a strained voice, "we really do have to stop meeting like this. I'm beginning to think you may be stalking me." With that ridiculous statement, I shrugged my shoulders, giving a little, self-deprecating laugh. "I've seen better days, Doc, but I'll live. Please, tell me about Sage. Did they bring him here too? He was shot I think. Please tell me, is he here?" My voice trailed off at the end, I wasn't sure I truly wanted the answers I sought. I was holding on by the smallest of measures, I truly feared for my sanity in this moment.

"Yes, my dear, you may have to file a restraining order against me. I am clarently stalking you through the hallowed halls of Cedar's."

At my obvious surprise at her use of my word, she winked at me.

"You actually mumbled clarently to yourself last time. I thought it quite the clever word. As for Mr. Cartier," she paused and my heart paused with her, "I don't have any answers, as to his whereabouts, but before we get started I will ask someone to find out, okay?"

"Okay, Dr. Wong," I replied on a long exhale.

As I waited for Dr. Wong to return, I contemplated the reality of another rape exam. Last time, I had Sage to hold me together. He'd been a virtual stranger at that point, but between his strong, comforting presence and the drugs that had, thank the good Lord, blunted my perception of the whole ordeal, I had managed to make it through. This time however, I didn't have Sage, my heart turned over at the thought, nor the drugs to alter my mind. I wasn't above begging Dr. Wong for drugs this time. Hell, I would more than welcome the comforts of oblivion. I really didn't want to do this again, but perhaps it would be different this time...considering. I stared dispassionately at my wrists, turning them this way and that, assessing the damage. They were raw from where the ropes had been tied, but I had made them worse when desperately trying to escape to reach Sage. Why didn't they hurt? They should, they were raw and bleeding...they looked painful, but they weren't. They were just numb. Perhaps the pain in my soul had left no room for physical pain. I shook my head as Dr. Wong came back into the exam room.

"I have a question before we proceed any further. Were you raped again, Ava?"

The words were stuck in my throat. What saliva I could accumulate I swallowed hoping to wet my dry, scratchy throat.

"No, Dr. Wong, I wasn't, though almost. Sage and Mr. Vinokourov came just in time. I was drugged, but I don't think anything happened because he kept saying he wanted me wide awake and fully aware this time." I ended my answer with a bit of a sneer, aimed at Mr. Accent for being denied.

"Ava? May I be Lisbeth for a moment and not Dr. Wong?"

I nodded my head in consent, causing my long, tangled hair to fall forward, and I swiped at it impatiently. Ugh, what I wouldn't give for a pair of scissors about now. I looked up at her expectantly and the compassion in her eyes was my undoing. The wall of numb that I had tried to hide behind dissolved in the face of such compassion and remorse. I knew. I just knew what she was going to tell me. I tried to stand, but before I made it an inch off the exam table, Lisbeth was there pulling me into her arms.

"Ava," the sadness in her voice said what her words had yet to convey.

"I know he's gone. I feel it..." I was sobbing now, my whole body shaking uncontrollably with the force of my grief. I felt ready to splinter, my mind and spirit fracturing once and for all. Lisbeth gently brushed the hair from my face, where it was sticking to the wetness of my tears. He had been alone, oh God I couldn't stand knowing he had been all alone when he had died, surrounded by only strangers.

"I'm sorry, Ava, they just told me he was taken to another area hospital, where he died in the emergency room. I was told his commanding officer was with him. He wasn't alone, Ava."

I cried against Lisbeth for quite some time, unable to control the force of my grief. But eventually, I ran out of tears. Can you dehydrate yourself crying? I was thirsty, oddly enough. I could feel Lisbeth pulling away and I let go of the good doctor. She waited a moment, allowing me to gather what little strength I had left, and I looked into her eyes.

"Ava, I won't be doing another rape exam, unless you feel that we should."

I shook my head in the negative. There was no way I would consent to it in any case as that was well beyond my mental fortitude at this point.

"In that case, I would like to give you some intravenous fluids for the dehydration and draw some lab work, just to check everything over and give you another antibiotic. In the meantime, there is a Mr. Vinokourov who would like to come in and speak with you for a few moments, after we have all the other stuff concluded. Would that be okay with you, Ava?"

"Yes, I'd like to speak with him, once we've finished and I have a few clothes on," I said, with a bit of a raised eyebrow, hoping she would get the message.

"Of course, I'll have some scrubs brought to you." I could hear the empathy in her voice.

Labs were drawn, an intravenous catheter was placed, and lactated ringers were started, the antibiotic was going and I was dressed in scrubs. I pulled my hair up into a messy top-knot, that I secured with a re-purposed tourniquet, the elastic-thingy they had used to draw my blood with. One of the nurses had brought me a warmed blanket, and I thanked her profusely for her thoughtfulness.

I was finally settled, when I heard a knock on the door, and Mr. Vinokourov poked his head in. I bid him enter and I swear in that one moment, my world wavered, seeing a younger version of this man, but without time's stamp upon his features. He was barely through the door, when I hit him with a barrage of questions.

"Why were you with Sage? Why were you there? How did you all find me? Why are you so familiar to me? Where is Mr. Accent? Why did he shoot Sage? Why?" I had more questions, but I ran out of steam trailing off exhausted. I sat there helpless, at the mercy of my environment wanting to run, but with no means to leave, and not wanting to go home. I stared at Mr. Vinokourov focusing on him instead of the misery I currently found myself in. He was gazing at me softly, through grey eyes that reminded me of my own, though his were more silver than grey I thought. He looked rather nervous, which didn't seem to be a natural attribute for him.

"Ava, I will answer all of your questions, but first I have a few questions I need to ask you, and then I need to tell you a story. Can you bear with me for a few minutes?"

Had I known, this one conversation would completely alter the perception of my entire life, I might not have consented. But, as they say, hindsight is crystal clear.

❦ 30 ❧

AVA

THE LOS ANGELES Ballet was hosting a special performance tonight, featuring Riley Spencer, a concert pianist. I had been chosen as the soloist to dance to her accompaniment. This would be my first performance, as a principal dancer, and I was quietly bursting with pride. I had anticipated being nervous tonight, but I wasn't, not after the events of my life these past few months. I appreciated this opportunity, for the gift that it was. Tonight was for celebrating, as my dreams were finally coming true.

When Riley and I had first met, we'd hit it off straight away and becoming fast friends, much like Willow and I had. I was blessed in that regard, as I had Willow and now I had Riley. She was a delicate little thing, only a few years older than me with blonde hair that glowed like silver moonlight under the stage lights. Practicing with her had been a true joy and while she had far more experience than I had, she was extremely grounded.

For as long as I could remember, I had been an eye person, noticing the glowing orbs before any other feature. Riley's were exceptional and for multiple reasons. First, they were a unique whiskey color, setting her apart and lending her an ethereal aura. However, it was the untold stories held within the whiskey'd depths that drew you to her. I had thought my life was bad, until I looked deep into eyes, so haunted and sad, that I had almost dropped to my knees in pain and grief. Her story was there, just waiting to be told, but I couldn't imagine what atrocities she had seen or endured to have permeated her eyes with such pain. I had wanted to gather her tiny frame into my arms and absorb all her pain. After meeting Riley, I had finally closed the chapter on my pity party for one.

Willow had come to the theater with me one day, two weeks ago. To keep an eye on me I'm sure, but we ignored that. She had brought her violin and was playing, while I warmed up. Riley had come to practice as well, but we hadn't realized she was there; we had both been lost to the music. So, when Willow had finished the piece she'd been playing, Riley's soft applause had ushered out the last haunting note of Willow's weeping violin. We'd watched in awe as Riley had floated across the stage towards us; she really was a magical creature. I shook my head at my whimsical thoughts.

"You must be Willow?" Riley said, going directly to Willow and embracing her free hand, into both of her delicate ones. They were about the same height, fun-sized, as I liked to call Willow. Whereas, Riley was delicate, and Willow was curvaceous.

"Ava has told me all about you. What a pleasure to finally meet you, Willow." Another distinctive thing about Riley, was her voice. It had a low husky quality to it, as if at one point she had injured her throat. "The program directors are coming down in a few minutes. Willow, you will accompany me on your violin."

With that little ditty, she had walked over to the piano to warm-up, leaving Willow and I staring at one another with twin expressions of surprise and our mouths hanging wide open. We'd finally shut our mouths, smiled hugely at one another, and had gone back to warming up. Willow was at the piano now standing next to Riley, who was explaining something to her. Nodding her head, Willow raised her violin, up and at the ready, and they began. Despite having never played together, you wouldn't have known it by how smooth and seamless they were.

This could be just the break and recognition Willow had needed for her career. I started dancing the choreography, getting lost in the beautiful harmony they were creating, and I had missed when the directors had come in. My ballet was different now, but I had come to terms with the fact the old Ava was dead and buried, never to be resurrected. I was becoming acquainted with this new version of me, and she wasn't too bad, just a little unique. Yes, unique, that's it, so much better than weird.

We had been practicing with Willow for the past last two weeks, and I had been practicing with Riley for the better part of a month now. Riley didn't have to practice with us, but I think she found solace in our quiet company, getting just as lost as we did in the comfort of our crafts. Riley was always quiet though, speaking very little, and conveying almost everything with her body language. She could go an entire practice session without uttering a single word.

We would be finishing and I would look at Riley, saying, "You do realize, you never said a single word to me, the entire practice, and I didn't even realize it till just now. How do you do that?" Her only response would be a little knowing smile.

The grand entrance I was about to make was bittersweet. It was my first performance as a principal ballerina and as a soloist. I had Willow and Riley on stage with me, and my other family members, Mason and Daniel, front and center. Only Sage was missing. My heart pinched with a pain so extreme, I reached out to hold the wall just to keep myself upright, and I locked my knees as I tried to breathe through the pain. Most of the time, I thought I was coping quite well, only to be swept off my feet with the pain and remorse of remembering the day of my rescue, well over two months ago. But it was Sage's abrupt cry and the eerie silence that followed that were still haunting my memories. Sighing deeply, I closed my eyes and I sent a prayer heavenward. Once composed, I slowly opened my eyes and a lone tear escaped my control, rolling softly down my cheek. I quickly wiped at the runaway, least it leave a sullen track across my beautiful makeup. Oh how I wished Sage could have seen my debut. I couldn't think on that now, focus Ava, he would have wanted you to revel in this moment, and that is exactly what I planned to do.

I walked out onto that magical stage, at the Grand Auditorium with my head held high, owning those ancient boards below my pointed feet. Wondrous emotions were bubbling inside me, and I floated to center stage. I could feel him, as if he were right there standing beside me, running his hand gently along my tear stained cheek...my Sage. He and my moms were there in spirit, I could feel them, and I would give them the best damn ballet performance they had ever seen. I looked over at Willow and Riley, each looking at me with such sweet smiles on their faces. I was emotional and from where they stood, they could easily see the shimmering of unshed tears. I gave them both a little nod of reassurance, and took my place at center stage, and I assumed the starting position for the piece we were about to perform.

Willow actually started the performance with an achingly sad solo. It wasn't long, so I held my position until Riley joined in on the piano. I pushed everything else away and I got lost in the melody and lyrical nature of the music. This was a very emotional piece and the choreography reflected it perfectly. It felt tailored-made to my current emotional state and my new dancing style. I was pulled into the music with every note, connected in a way that had me pouring my heart into every movement. My soul felt raw, the edges bleeding all over the beautiful stage. I tried to rein my emotions in, but it was of no use. Once unleashed from their cage, they'd not go back willingly. I had a feeling once we were performing live, I wouldn't be able to disconnect, and I'd been right. Luckily, I knew this piece so well, that my body was fluid with muscle memory. At times, I had my eyes closed and every emotion was pouring out unfiltered. Tears made silent tracks down my cheeks, having their say, whether I willed them or not.

As the performance came to its beautiful finale, I found myself slowly re-entering the world of The Grand Auditorium. With my eyes adjusting to the bright lights, I focused on the stage around me. I was at center stage and just before me covering the stage was a beautiful carpet of roses. I looked up in amazement, and was greeted with a standing ovation, and a wildly clapping audience. I curtsied and about fell over, not very graceful I thought, but my legs were shaky from the emotional drain, and the unexpected audience response. One of the ushers brought over a bouquet of exquisite, long stemmed roses in a blushed pink. I closed my eyes and took in their heady fragrance, curtsied again to the audience, then sashayed off the stage.

Once offstage, I headed towards where I left my jacket. My head was still so caught up in the performance, and intoxicated by the heady fragrance of the roses, that I wasn't paying attention to where I was going. Reluctantly, I pulled my face from the flowers and then stopped abruptly, dropping the roses unnoticed onto the floor. I cried out and took off at a dead run, launching myself at the vision before me. He had been leaning indolently against the doorframe of my dressing room, waiting patiently for me to look up from the flowers. I jumped into his arms and wrapped my legs around his waist. He caught and held me without issue, though I could have sworn I heard a small grunt of pain, but I wasn't sure. The very next second, I was sobbing uncontrollably and I couldn't hear anything above that. I was destroying my beautiful stage makeup, but couldn't make myself care.

"Hey now. It's okay, Ava. Look at me, Beauty." With that soft command, he pulled me back and raised my chin to inspect my destroyed face. As he looked me over, I drank him in with joy soaked eyes, and fat tears of happiness were overflowing. Luckily my costume was a flowing, light chiffon dress, versus a stiff tutu or we would have had some issues. That thought had set off a round of sobbing giggles.

"Was that any way to treat those beautiful flowers that I gave you?" Sage admonished in a teasing tone. I pinched him in response. My hysterical sobbing turning to silent tears. I swallowed, took a deep breath, and attempted to gain control, so that I could ask an actual question, and not just cry like a two year old.

"How," I took another shuddering breath and tried again, "how are you here? Where have you been these past couple of months? Oh, Sage." I couldn't continue any further. The grief, remorse, and longing I tried to stifle these past few months, overrode whatever control I thought I had. Sage continued holding me, rubbing soothing circles across my lower back, patiently waiting for me to gain control of my emotions. He might be waiting a year or two. The next thing I knew, we were in my dressing room, and we were sitting on the love seat, and I was still nestled against my Sage's chest. Reverently, he placed gentle, open mouthed kisses on every heated surface he could reach, anointing me with his sinful lips.

"I'm sorry, Beauty," he stated simply, though that one little sentence was packed with emotion. He set me gently beside him, and then kneeled on the floor before me, head bowed in supplication. He stayed that way for such a long time that the only sound was our gentle breathing. After a while I grew restless, concerned with his silence and lack of movement.

"Sage, why won't you speak to me or look at me? Please...please, Sage." I scooted forward, so that my knees were on either side of his hips, embracing him. Sitting up straight, I reached out my hands, and lifted his eyes to mine. Pain and devastation were written plainly through the depths of his blue eyes. He held mine captive, letting me see all that he was, offering everything to me, his naked emotions, he was stripped bare before me. My dark knight begging forbearance, forgiveness for some imagined transgression, but I didn't care what he thought he needed; I would never make this proud man beg.

"I love you, Sage, no matter what I love you. Just touch me. Let me feel you. Show me that you are truly here and alive, explanations can come later. I need you now." With that, I sat forward, crashing my mouth to his, so hard I was sure to have a fat lip, but I didn't care. I hugged him with my legs, pulling him in tight, cradling him against where I was desperate to have him. He immediately hardened in response to my aggression. I pulled his hair, desperate to have him imprinted upon me, marking me. I pulled away from his beautiful mouth and directed him to my exposed neck.

"Mark me, Sage. I want to feel the edge of your teeth, I want the pain, I need it. God, I want to feel alive again."

Sage wasted no time complying with my plea, devouring my exposed neck with his hungry mouth. I pushed into him, into his teeth, wanting it all, and he didn't hesitate or hold back. My hands were exploring him, holding him tight, least he try to escape. I reached for the top button to his dress slacks, undoing it, and pulled the zipper down, mindful of the fact, he often went commando. My questing hand found his tumescence, already oozing for me.

"Please, Sage, now. I need you in me. Right...now, I can't wait another second more."

Sage continued devouring my neck, working his way down to my aching breast, his hand was between my legs, moving the panel of my leotard to the side. He aligned his cock with my saturated entrance, and without any hesitation at all, slammed home. I cried out at the abruptness, but reveled in the overwhelming sensations of him plunging into the depths of me repeatedly, until he stopped abruptly. Seating himself all the way to the depths of me, he pushed himself in, past the point of comfort.

"Feel me, Ava. I am now and I will always be a part of you. I will be completely imprinted upon you, and your soul, that there will be no distinguishing one from the other. I am you, and you are me, and we are forever one."

With that bald statement, he continued thrusting home, past the point of comfort, but I was loving every bit of it. Before long, I was climaxing for the first time in months, and for the first of many that night. Sage pulled the top of my outfit down and greedily latched onto my erect nipple, worrying it with the edge of his teeth, and then sucking it into his hot wet mouth, alternating back and forth driving me crazy. Admittedly, crazy was a short trip. He pushed me hard and fast over that first peak, then slow and gentle over the second. By the time he was working me up and over the third, I was trembling, saturated, and fairly incoherent, hoarsely babbling whispered inanities. Sage thrust home a final time, before moaning out his grunting release. Once coherent he maneuvered us, until we were laying on the sofa. He was nestled deep within me still, cradled between my open legs, perfectly at home. He kissed me sweetly on the lips, before completely losing it. He rested his head on my shoulder, his body shaking with his apparent distress. I couldn't stand it. I hugged him tight to me, telling him over and over it was okay, that we'd be okay.

"Please Sage, don't be upset. We will work it out, whatever is distressing you so."

He lifted his head, a huge smile plastered across his face, and started belly laughing, his whole body shaking mine with the force of his laughter.

"What in the hell were you babbling there at the end, Ava? I swear you were praying to every known god and perhaps a few lesser known ones too." He started cracking up again. I was trying not to laugh with him and kept a straight face, while proceeding to admonish him for his rude behavior.

"It's not my fault, mister. I think I may have been praying for deliverance from your licentious attentions." I ended that little statement with a sniff of disdain, lasting about two-point-one seconds, before I started laughing uncontrollably, a nice release of all the tension and grief I had been experiencing. We laughed together for a minute or so, smiling so wide, my face hurt from using muscles that had been neglected these past couple of months. When our laughter concluded, we continued staring at one another, cataloguing all the minute changes that had occurred over the past few months. Faint lines of pain were bracketing his eyes, and mouth, and with my fingertips I gently traced the clear evidence of his suffering.

"Sage, tell me why I see such tremendous suffering in you. What happened after I heard the shots ring out, your grunt of pain, and the painful silence that had followed? Tell me, where have you been?" I swallowed the tears of grief that I had endured from thinking him dead, but I didn't want to burden him further with the pain I had been feeling.

❧ 31 ❧

sage

How could I tell her that I had died several times, before the doctors had been able to stabilize me? That the damage from Ivan's unfortunately placed bullets had been extensive, and had taken hours to repair. I stared down at her loving face, alight with humor and love, and reflected on my time during rehab. It was only the memory of her face, her smile, and her laughter that had pulled me through those dark days of pain. The thought of holding her and loving her hard and fast, then slow and leisurely, had motivated me to push through the pain's limitations. I'd left rehab, well before the doctors had wanted me to, waiting only long enough to tolerate being without oxygen and pain meds. I'd be the first to admit that I liked to be in control of everything, and I had not liked the altered state of mind or loss of control that the pain meds had allowed.

My wounds, only barely healed were screaming at me just now. They were making sure that I knew they were still there, as if I could forget. I had no business leaving, but I couldn't stand to be without Ava for more second. Once that little prick Trey had told me that Ava would be doing this special performance, there was no way I would have missed her first performance as a principal.

But no, I wouldn't be telling her all that had occurred. I would protect her from how severe it had been, as it served no purpose to distress her when nothing could be changed. I kissed her gently, longing to love her over and over again, but for now this one gentle, thorough kiss would have to suffice.

"After Ivan had shot me, I heard you scream, but then there was just...nothing. I don't remember much of anything after that. I awoke in the recovery room after surgery, but they'd sedated me shortly after because I was going crazy in my attempts to come to you."

Thoughts of what Ava had been subjected to at the hands of Ivan haunted me still. Potential scenarios had looped through my head driving me insane, until I had been in a rage to kill that low-rung rat bastard. As a consequence, they had kept me sedated for days just to keep me from tearing out my sutures, the sedation allowing my body the time it needed to recuperate.

"Once my head was on straight and I wasn't trying to imitate a raging bull, I'd had weeks of debriefing with the department and the FBI. Their collective decision was that Sage had to remain officially dead." At her gasp I hurried to continue.

"Or I should say, we had unofficially leaked a report stating that I had died as a result of injuries sustained in an undercover operation, and that is why you were led to believe I had died. We needed your reactions to be real, not feigned, because we knew someone in association with Ivan and Alexei, would be watching you. We still haven't found Ivan, he's gone to ground, and could be anywhere at this point."

I felt her shift a little beneath me, and I looked down at her face to assess what was going on in that head of hers. She seemed uncomfortable all of a sudden. It was probably when I mentioned Alexei and Ivan both. I could allay her fears as to Alexei, I'm sure she thought there was still tension between us. As for Ivan, I would protect her from him with my life and I didn't plan to be far from her side, not until Ivan and his close associates were caught.

"Ava, look at me. Beauty, I know Alexei is your father and it's okay. We've been working together though my contribution has been in a limited capacity. I can't tell you everything that is going on, but it'll be fine, just trust me a little longer. As for Ivan, please don't worry. I promise to protect you with my life. He will be caught Beauty, please don't doubt that. Every rat must surface eventually."

"Alexei...he...we...we have been getting to know each other. I have been trying to unlearn things or rather un-think things, I have thought to be true my entire life. Inaccurate things about Alexei, my father and about him, and my mother Grace. Oh, Sage, they truly loved each other. He was devastated when she died. He didn't know where I was because they'd stolen me away to protect me. I can't imagine what that must have been like for him. He lost the love of his life, and the daughter they had created, his only child, within hours of each other. My heart breaks for the family we could have been."

I gathered her even closer, if that was possible, kissing away her tears, absorbing their beauty into myself. She had been through so much, these past months and the courage, humor, and poise that she'd maintained through it all, amazed and astounded me. I would never be worthy of her, but I'd do my damnedest to be deserving of her love.

"I'm here, Ava, to stay if you'll have me. I never want to be parted from you again. I realize we haven't known each other for long, Beauty, but I love you and that's all I need to know. For some crazy reason you love me too, so what else is there? Some people have less than that."

I took a deep breath to continue, but before I could utter a single syllable, someone was pounding on the door to Ava's dressing room, and we could hear the very recognizable voice of Alexei. I dropped my forehead to hers, sighing loudly. Kissing her quickly on the lips, I hopped off the sofa to right our clothes, and cover our various parts. Hopefully, he wasn't toting a gun, as I had only just recovered from my last gunshot injury. We were consenting adults, I hoped he remembered that.

I walked over to the door, opening it with the best fuck-off scowl I could muster. Alexei walked past me without a second glance. I guess fathers trumped lovers every day of the week. As I turned from closing the door, I saw Alexei embrace Ava, in the European way, holding her shoulders and kissing her softly on both cheeks.

"Darling, you were incredible tonight, so like your mother Grace. I was drawn back in time, reminiscing. I could see Grace in my mind's eye, floating across the stage in New York. You have surpassed her in skill and technique, and she would have been the first to tell you so."

I saw a tear escape her eye, and I was at her side in seconds, wrapping my arms around her waist from behind. I felt how she nestled in tighter, stepping back into my embrace, comforted by my presence. I kissed the side of her neck, unable to stop the impulse, despite how Alexei was scowling at me. It's best that he understand now what was going to be occurring between Ava and I. He may be her father, but I would be her husband, if she'd have me. I had my grandmother's ring in my pocket, and when presented with the perfect opportunity, I would be dropping to one knee. I would ask her to take a chance on me, and my demons, consenting to be my lover, my wife, and the best part of me.

"I should be angry with you, Alexei, for not telling me that Sage was indeed alive." She raised her hand, stopping the words that were ready to spill from his lips. "I understand why you didn't though, and I will forgive you both for keeping me in my grief filled darkness."

Gut punched was how I felt just then, and by the greenish look of Alexei, he felt much the same. A more beautifully phrased reprimand, I had never heard. I would find a way to make it up to her, a promise I made to myself and to her.

"Ava, I am truly sorry for that. We didn't want to leave you in the dark, but we had no choice." The regret shading Alexei's voice was clearly evident. Ava pulled from my arms, to embrace her father, consoling him when in reality, we should be consoling her, but that was my Ava always thinking of others first.

"Alexei, I think we should tell Ava about our, not so little surprise now." Thinking that Ava might really kill us over tonight's event.

"Ava, I know you were adamant about not having a celebration, but we planned a small party, at my place to celebrate your solo. I'm leaving now to be sure security is tight and all is in order. Sage will bring you over after you're ready. I took the liberty to acquire a dress for you...I think you'll like it." Alexei looked away for a moment, but not before I had caught the look of anguish and love swirling in his eyes. He leaned forward to kiss Ava softly on the forehead, before practically running out of the dressing room, damned coward.

Turning Ava to face me, I dove back into her mouth, before she could say a single word to the contrary about the party. I'd just have to convince her with my mouth and body...again.

❦ 32 ❧

AVQ

AS WE DROVE from the Grande Auditorium to Alexei's home in Pacific Palisades, I watched the scenery pass by in a slow blur, not really tracking any of it. I was replaying the moment I had opened the package Alexei had left for me. I couldn't stop touching the diaphanous material of the dress that had been nestled inside the beribboned box. I had been so irritated with Alexei and still overwhelmed that Sage was alive.

"Where do suppose he gets the nerve to choose a dress for me, that was rather presumptuous don't you think? I know he's my father and all, but of all the high-handed neanderthal moves." I was a bit miffed, to say the least as I untied the ribbon surrounding the box. Sage was smart enough to keep his mouth shut, only nodding his head in agreement...knowing we had our own issues yet to discuss, he chose wisely.

I lifted the lid off the garment box and nestled atop delicate ivory tissue was a note addressed to me with, *'Please Read First'.* Opening the note it read:

Ava,

I hoped you might like to have something of your mother's.

I saved all of Grace's belongings.

I couldn't bring myself to part with anything.

I thought you might like to wear this beautiful dress of hers for your special night.

I had it refurbished. She would be so proud of you, milaya.

I love you, Ava. I never stopped.

Alexei

"Oh God, Sage. I'm afraid to look, to touch." My hands were trembling, as various emotions moved through me in alternating waves.

"I have nothing of Grace's, nothing except a few videos that Maman had saved from her dancing at NYC Ballet. I'm so afraid. I've yearned my entire life to know more about her, but was resigned to knowing very little, or no more than what Maman had known. I truly thought I had come to terms with the unknown, and had found peace, but the chaos of my emotions just proved that, for the lie it was."

The end of that statement had come out in a choked whisper, as tears had clogged my throat. Ever my savior, Sage had pulled me into his arms, comforting me, and my grieving heart. After the storm of emotions had calmed, I had braved unfolding the tissue to look upon the dress that had once belonged to my mother. I gasped, as I lifted the dress out, the delicate tissue had clung to it, as if loathing to be parted from such perfection, but finally, reluctantly had floated to the floor at my feet, revealing her dress, my beautiful dress. I couldn't have chosen a more perfect dress had I chosen it for myself.

*   *   *

I felt Sage's Mustang roll to a stop and I realized we had arrived at Alexei's home. I turned to Sage, offering him a small smile, acknowledging that I had been lost in my head for the entire trip over. He came around to my side of the car, opening the door, and he offered his hand to help me out. I must admit, I felt like a movie star, and I gave Sage a million-watt smile. Off to the right, at a surprisingly respectful distance were some local journalists covering Alexei's high profile party. A flash of their camera signified our photographic immortalization, our moment of unbridled happiness captured by the camera's discerning eye. Sage couldn't resist giving the photographers another picture moment by gently kissing my cheek next to my ear, and lightly touching my bare shoulder with his hand.

"Beauty, you steal my breath. I want to take you away, and far from here, just the two of us with no unwanted interruptions. I love you, Ava," on a sigh, those beautiful words were whispered into my ear.

As I floated to the entrance of Alexei's home, my silver peep-toe sling backs barely made a sound. The gentle breeze from the Pacific flirted with the hem of my dove-grey chiffon dress, making it dance about my ankles and tickle my toes. As Sage ushered me to the front door, I could feel the warmth of his right hand through the delicate material clinging to my lower back. The double doors were opened by attendants before we ever breached the trellised entrance.

When we stepped inside the foyer, we were ushered by another attendant down a long hallway lined with framed, black and white photographs. I wanted to stop and study the beautifully captured subjects, but would have to come back later to appreciate them. This was my first time coming to Alexei's home, though not the first invitation. I hadn't been ready to take that next step, but tonight seemed a perfect time. I had Sage on my arm and the buffer of a large party to temper any awkwardness. We were still feeling each other out, in the getting to know one another stage. I was trying to unlearn things, I had believed to be true, but that was much harder than one would think, and he was trying not to pressure me. I hadn't decided, whether or not, to be upset with Alexei. I couldn't believe he had kept me in the dark about Sage, though I suppose I do understand. We were still learning how to become family.

When Sage and I arrived at a set of double doors, the attendant knocked, and we were told to enter. What the hell! For some reason that irritated me, like we were peasants seeking an audience with our feudal lord. When we walked through the doors, I was ready to give Alexei a piece of my mind, which must have been evident by the smile he gave me. But then, I looked past Alexei to the grandeur of the room,which was bursting with people whom were all clapping for me and it quite took my breath away. I blushed hotly, both for the unexpected reception, and my incorrect thoughts. I winked at Alexei and gave him a small, self-deprecating smile, because really, what else could I do?

Alexei made his way over to Sage and I, pulling me into his arms for a tight hug, far from his typical European greeting. I hugged him back in full measure, learning and accepting the imprint of this man, my father. I turned my face into his chest, hiding the evidence of my tears. I took a few calming breaths, inhaling his essence, and I was immediately calmed. I had found that dwelling on what my life might have been, what I had missed out on, caused nothing but an aching heart. So, I had made a pact with myself, deciding not to think about those things I couldn't change. I was having only marginal success, truth be told. I think Alexei felt the same way and we were navigating these strange waters together.

I stepped back, just as Alexei was pulling away, neither of us wanting the hug to seem awkward. I felt Sage's hand at my waist, and I stepped into the warmth and protection of his side with a grateful sigh. Looking about I realized we were in a ballroom of sorts. I was overwhelmed by the amount of people there, in celebration of my first solo performance, though thankfully they had stopped clapping and they were now smiling and chatting amongst themselves.

As I looked about the room, I smiled when I saw that my close friends had been invited as well. Mason and Daniel, the brothers of my heart, stood side by side, engaged in conversation with a guy I had seen once before, Trey something. I gave them a little wave when they looked my way, and they tipped their heads synchronously in acknowledgement. I laughed, men never change.

Willow and Riley were chatting it up in the back. Actually, Willow was chatting, and Riley was nodding her head with an endearing and rare smile gracing her beautiful face. The three of us had become really close...they were the sisters I had secretly wished for as a child. I saw Willow glance over towards Mason and Daniel, to wave hello, but then watched as her hand dropped, aborted mid-wave. When her face flushed red, then quickly paled, I started walking towards her, but she shook her head at me, imploring me with her eyes to stay where I was. I looked back to Mason and Daniel still talking with that Trey guy and shook my head not understanding her obvious distress. Trey looked towards Willow, assessing her from head to toe, then he zeroed in on Riley with a look of adoration, and I shook my head at him, obvious much?

My attention had been drawn back to Sage and Alexei, as the serving staff were in the process of passing out flutes of Cristal Champagne, something I had never tasted before. I took a sip and the effervescent bubbles exploded in my mouth with an orgasm of flavor. Good Lord, no wonder people paid so much money for the pleasure of sipping these tickling little bubbles. I giggled to myself, though looking back at Sage he had obviously heard me. I smiled up at him, then blushed yet again when I realized no one else had been sipping their champagne. A moment later, the gentle tapping of a crystal glass, the universal sign for attention, had its requisite effect as the room grew hushed with silent expectation.

"Good evening, to you all. I bid you welcome to my home. I'm Alexei Vinokourov, your host for the evening."

Laughter echoed about the room, as if anyone wouldn't know who he was. He smiled at everyone for humoring him, then winked at me, as I had done to him. In my peripheral vision, I could see people's heads going back and forth, like watching a tennis match. I'm sure they were trying to reconcile this playful side of Alexei, one they had probably never seen before, with his usual reserved demeanor. He beckoned me to his side, with an outstretched hand, and taking a deep breath, I stepped away from Sage's sheltering frame, to join my father.

I was trembling on the inside, but held my head high, and smiled in genuine affection, as I took my place at Alexei's side. As I walked towards him, I noticed Natalia standing off to his left side. Her eyes made brief contact with mine, before she looked away. She had been extremely quiet since Marcus had disappeared and she had taken time off from the LA Ballet, where she was a part of the company. Alexei's voice pulled me from my thoughts.

"I wanted to take a moment to welcome and thank you all for coming. We are here tonight, to celebrate the premiere solo performance of Miss Ava DeLaney for the LA Ballet. I had the pleasure of first meeting Ava when her and Natalia were practicing their solo performances for the LA Ballet open tryouts. The moment she took the stage I knew..." he cleared his throat, clearly gathering his composure. I held his hand a bit tighter.

"I knew she was destined for greatness. She had floated across that stage, owning every board, yet with a reverence not

found in one so young. I was utterly captivated, as was her audience tonight. When I watched Ava that first time, something
about the way she held herself, her carriage, her impeccable
lines reminded me of someone, a woman I had loved and lost
many years ago. However, once we were introduced that famili-
arity was undeniable."

As Alexei took a breath to continue, I hazarded a look at
Sage. He looked as if he was about to shut Alexei's mouth with a
well placed fist. Sage didn't want Alexei to announce that he was
my father. I shook my head at him slightly and smiled. We knew
this would be revealed eventually, might as well be on our own
terms. Alexei was looking around a bit, searching for someone.

"Natalia? Where's Natalia? Come up here, oh niece of mine."

Natalia made her way over to his left side, a small smile gracing her lips.

"Now, where was I?" We all laughed a little at that.

"Please would you raise your glasses high. Here's to a night of
many firsts. To all my friends and family, may I officially introduce to you, Ava DeLaney. My daughter...lost to me these many
long years."

I heard a small gasp that had to have been Natalia, but the
'here, here's' and clapping were drowning everything out. We all
took a sip of our champagne, though I chugged mine, needing a
little liquid fortification, but such a waste as it hardly caressed
my palate to play with my taste buds. I looked over at Natalia to
see what was going on with her. I knew we would never be best
friends, but I had thought we had at least progressed to the
stage of aloof friendliness. Her being my cousin, must truly be a
blow to her sensibilities. When I saw her face though, she had
lost all trace of color, all trace of haughtiness, and was looking at
me as if seeing me for the first time. Her eyes were overflowing
with sadness. These were not happy tears that slid silently down
her pale cheeks.

"I'm sorry." With that quiet, yet heartfelt apology, she turned around to leave. I stood there momentarily at a loss as to what had just happened. Shaking my head, I turned back to Alexei who was chatting with an older couple. I stood there conversing with the elderly couple, wondering what was wrong with Natalia, at the same time wondering if my grandparents, Grace's parents, would have been much like this wonderful couple. They were very effusive in their praise of my performance, and apparently were great supporters of the performing arts in and around LA.

The only warning I had, before being tackled to the floor was the widening of the elderly couple's eyes. I landed hard enough to steal my breath, and heard the unmistakable crack of a gun, as my tackler landed atop me, losing their breath as well. Lifting my head, I could see the room was in chaos, moving rapidly, yet as if pulled backwards through mud. People were running and appeared to be yelling or screaming, but my hearing was only just coming back, so everything was still muffled. I couldn't see Sage or Alexei anywhere, but then my scope was limited, due the heaviness of the person on me and my view from the ball-room floor.

I threw my arms over my head, as more gunshots rang out, as if that would stop the deadly missiles. I was wishing the person above me would move, they couldn't really protect me from fly-ing bullets, not really and they felt rather heavy. Things were still chaotic, but I chanced a little hip movement hoping the person would get the point, as it was warm and sweaty between us. I barely managed to slide out, getting no help from the person above.

I looked around and saw that, most of the guests were in var-ying stages of cautiously righting themselves. Everyone had a wide-eyed, scared look which I'm sure I must have been display-ing as well. I turned to look behind me, where my tackler was located and cried out scrambling to my knees to hover over my would be savior. I went to cover my face with my hands, but when I raised them to hide the vision before me, they were dripping, covered in her blood, Natalia's blood.

I reached forward with a shaking hand to check her pulse, but could see she was clearly gone. I gently closed her sightless blue eyes, leaving a red streak of blood across her delicate lids, and hung my head in silent prayer. Chaos still reined in the ballroom, but I felt like I was in my own private little bubble, removed from the whole of it. That was, until Sage enfolded me into his warm embrace and picked me up to cradle me against his chest. I buried my face in his neck, letting loose of my fear, and remorse, my grief over having lost yet another family member, though I hadn't known until recently that we were even related.

We left the room and traveled down a hallway, ending up in a room that was more than likely Alexei's home office. It now looked to be an impromptu command center. Several men were on their phones, barking orders, and I heard sirens in the distance coming in quick. Sage placed me on a small settee that was nestled close to the fireplace, but away from the windows. Luckily, there was a woolen throw draped across the back and the seat because I was covered in blood.

Sage brought over a full tumbler of some kind of amber liquor, whiskey or scotch I had no idea and it didn't really matter. I was shaking so bad, I couldn't hold the glass to drink it anyway. Sage knelt in front of me, shielding me from the room, though I doubted they were paying any attention to us.

"Take a small sip, Beauty, it'll help the shaking," he said, while holding the crystal tumbler to my trembling lips and tipping the glass. My incoordination was clearly evident, when most of it dribbled down my chin. Shaking my head in disgust at my weakness, I raised my eyes to his and I watched as he took a large swallow of the amber liquid. Thinking he was just going to drink it himself, I was shocked to stillness when he leaned forward to seal his lips over mine, then ever so gently trickled the warmed liquid into my mouth. The intimacy of the kiss, coupled with the amber liquid, as it slid smoothly down my throat, quickly warmed my insides. The potency of both, subdued my shaking only to be replaced by a fine internal trembling, of a nature altogether different. Sage ended the impromptu infusion, by sealing his mouth over my bottom lip to catch the last few drops that had spilt there.

I wanted to cradle his beautiful face in my bloody hands, but tucked them under me to prevent the urge, not wanting to ruin our little respite from the chaos. So I attempted to convey all that I was feeling with my eyes, not trusting my voice to carry the words from my heart. Sage never ceased to amaze me, because in the very next instance, with his laser blue eyes focused on my grey ones, he pulled his charcoal dress shirt off, leaving him in his white t-shirt.

"Sage..." I whispered afraid the others would hear me. "What in heavens name are you doing? We aren't alone."

Curse his ass. He just smiled at me, while picking up my hands and the tumbler of scotch. He cradled both in his dress shirt, poured the scotch over them and then proceeded to cleanse them of Natalia's blood. His thoughtfulness brought tears of gratitude to my eyes, and they spilled over onto my cheeks. Love and remorse, happiness and grief, were trying their damnedest to tear me apart. I closed my eyes, floating along with the turbulent current, hoping the competing emotions would eventually calm before the waves could pull me under again.

❧ 33 ❧

AVA

"AVA, AVA! WHERE'S Ava?"

We heard Alexei bellowing my name. He was somewhere down the hallway, but it was hard to tell where with the way his voice was echoing. My gaze shot to Sage's. He shook his head, indicating that perhaps Alexei didn't realize that I was safe and in his office. The pain I heard in his next outcry was that of a mortally wounded heart, taking its final breath, and had me bolting from my stupor and running to my father.

Entering the ballroom, I stopped in my tracks. Alexei was cradling Natalia gently against his chest, rocking her back and forth saying her name, over and over, in quiet benediction. I looked away, hoping to erase the tragic image they created, but it was of no use, as it would be forever engraved upon my mind to recall and replay. Taking a deep breath, I gathered what strength I could muster, because if ever I needed to be strong, it was now in this moment. I would lend my father whatever strength I could, anything to pull him from his sorrow.

I walked over and knelt down, wrapping my arms around him

from behind. Together we gently rocked Natalia, my silent tears soaking into his suit jacket. LAPD, and oddly enough my paramedic Brian, rushed into the room clearly intent on attending to Natalia, but before they could get near us Sage had intervened. What could they possibly do about a gaping hole in her back and chest? They were good, but they couldn't resurrect her. Thankfully, they left us alone, allowing us to mourn for our family.

Alexei draped his jacket over Natalia, the only protection and privacy he could offer her at this point. I had no idea how much time had passed when Alexei and I had finally stood, with our hands clinging to one another. We looked about the room with no clue as what to do...feeling lost, but not wanting to acknowledge it. Sage walked over pulling me into his arms, grounding me to the here and now. I kept ahold of Alexei's hand, not wanting to relinquish the contact with my father, sensing he needed it as much as I did.

It looked as if the detectives and officers with the LAPD were processing the scene as best they could, considering the circumstances. Mason and Daniel were over in the far corner and were safe, my heart sighed in relief. Willow and Riley were there too, clinging to one another, but in the corner proper, with Mason and Daniel protecting them with their bodies.

Trey walked over with another man, twin expressions of sobriety across their faces.

"Sage, Alexei," Trey acknowledged. "Ms. DeLaney, Special Agent Trey Mathieson, FBI and Lieutenant Clarke, LAPD." They each shook, my less than clean hand, without hesitation.

"Ava, can you recall anything that happened before the shooting?"

Before Sage could object to my questioning, I answered.

"Alexei had made his speech, welcoming everyone. Then, the announcement about how I was his daughter. I heard a gasp and I turned to see who had made it, Natalia had. When I looked over at her, she had a look of devastation and remorse on her face. She was crying and had whispered she was sorry." I looked at them, one by one seeking answers. I wanted the truth as to why she was sorry, but more importantly as to why she was dead.

"I have no idea as to why she would have said she was sorry," Trey continued, "but we have reason to believe, she may have known something about Dubrovsky's plans or perhaps his future whereabouts. She had been dating Marcus, and he had been in close association with Ivan before Marcus was killed. As you know Marcus and Ivan were responsible for drugging and raping you."

"What?" I practically yelled. "What do you mean Marcus was killed? Marcus is dead, not just missing?" He may have been responsible for my rape, but that didn't mean I wished he was dead, maybe in jail rotting, someone's bitch, but not dead. My head was in chaos, I guess I should be used to it by now, but I wasn't. I hated this feeling of everything being out of my control, like a puppet dancing to someone else's tune.

"Please tell me what any of this has to do with me. I don't know anything. I don't remember anything, nor do I understand what is happening. Other than I'm rather tired of people trying to kill or rape me. Was that bullet intended for me? Is that what this is all about? Was Ivan trying to kill me and not Natalia? Good Lord, had she not tackled me that bullet would have torn through me. I'm right aren't I? Tell me, I have a right to know," I practically screamed.

I turned to Sage, looking him full in the face. I would not relent, I wanted some damn answers and right...fucking...now! Just before I truly lost it, Trey intervened. He said my name in a gentle tone, like he was attempting to calm a wild, frightened creature using only his voice. I turned to vent my spleen and stopped mid-inhale. It just wasn't in me to be aggressive and demanding, screaming at people, no matter how demented I felt.

"Trey," I sighed, "would you please tell me what is going on, I'm too tired to beg for answers."

Sage moved to my right side and Alexei to my left. I felt protected and supported. I wasn't a wimp, but damn a girl could only handle so much before she broke. I straightened my deportment, Madame would be proud, because if nothing else, I would carry myself beautifully.

"Ivan sent one of his minions to kill Natalia. We've apprehended the shooter and he's in the custody of the LAPD. However, we have no idea where Ivan is. We are worried that in his delusional mind that he blames Ava for everything that is going wrong with his world, including the downfall of his little kingdom. Ava, we want to put you into protective custody until this is resolved."

"The hell you will. Why wasn't this discussed with me before now?" Sage queried with a tone of retribution.

"Sage, this option only became necessary after tonight's events," Trey stated simply.

"No, absolutely not. The last person taken into protective custody, as a witness in this investigation was Deputy DA Tomi Delacourt. Who went missing from that supposed, protective custody, and to this day is presumed dead." Sage turned to the Lieutenant, "of all people, Clarke, you should know I would never allow such a thing."

The look he gave Sage definitely supported that fact. He knew Sage would be vehemently opposed to Trey's suggestion. Sage turned back to Trey.

"I'm taking Ava tonight and we'll disappear for a while. The Lieutenant knows how to reach me if it becomes necessary," Sage said with a finality that offered no room for discussion.

"Alexei, may I have a moment." Not really a question, more a statement of fact. Sage had barely uttered the words, and they were walking away together, presumably to discuss my future. I looked at Trey, eyebrow raised, and he offered me the most un-expected response...a lopsided grin and one backed with the full weight of his charm. Unable to temper my reaction, I smiled back at him. I shook my head at Trey's obvious manipulation of Sage. He had totally played him, getting Sage to do exactly what he had wanted, at least that's what the grin and the devilry gleaming in his eyes said to me.

On my way over to the corner, where Mason and my crew were huddled, I glanced over to Sage and Alexei. They were still deep in negotiations, by the looks of it. I stepped into Mason's comforting arms, once I reached him. Then Daniel held me and the girls too. These friends were my family and I'd be lost with-out them. I didn't realize Trey had followed me over, until I heard his voice behind me.

"Ava, won't you introduce me to your friends?"

I felt Willow stiffen against me and then give a little sigh of resignation. I turned towards Trey, at the same time I reached for Willow's hand, holding it tightly in mine.

"Special Agent Trey Mathieson, may I introduce to you my family. Mason Alexander, Daniel Creighton, Willow Sinclair and our newest member, Riley Spencer."

"Nice to meet you all. Have your statements been taken and recorded yet?"he asked to which everyone said yes.

"Miss Spencer, Miss Sinclair, you ladies played together beautifully. You only met this past month? What an honor it must have been Miss Sinclair, to accompany Miss Spencer at such an auspicious occasion. Perhaps this will open some doors for you."

"Special Agent Mathieson," Willow started, though it sound-ed more like a derogatory curse, than his name, "yes it's true, we only met this past month, but we have a similar work ethic, and our styles complement one another. While I may not have had the experience that Riley has had, I more than held my own."

Willow had ended her statement by raising her chin defiantly, daring him to say something to the contrary. My heart hurt for her, because despite her bravado, and apparent openness, she held her hands so tight behind her back, that they were turning white. I was just about to intervene, when Riley stepped forward taking the focus off of Willow.

"Special Agent," Riley raised her hand to forestall his interrupting, which he clearly wanted to.

"Was there something specific you were wanting to ask me or any of us?" Her quiet words resonated acutely, despite the low raspy nature of her voice.

I was watching Trey through the entire exchange and his expression was puzzling. If I were to name it, I would say he looked enraptured, as he was hanging on Riley's every word, though she'd only said a handful of them. There was something almost desperate and hopeful about his expression. He didn't strike me as someone who let his emotions show often, but this deep emotion appeared beyond his control. I looked over to Willow and she looked as if someone had just gutted her with a dull serrated knife, her pain was palpable. She looked away, bowing her head as if in defeat. What in the world was going on here?

"Willow is an accomplished violinist and I have no doubt she will have multiple offers to play first chair, if she should want to," Riley said, the hoarseness of her voice worsening the longer she spoke.

"I didn't mean to imply that Willow was not as equally talented. I do hope that she can catch a break, she's a beautiful and extremely talented young woman," he said, looking over at Willow meaningfully.

Willow looked up briefly, but looked away just as quick, but not before I saw her cheeks flush with color.

"You sound as if you have a cold, you should rest, Miss Spencer. The drama of the night can't be helping any. Tell me, will you be heading back home soon? Where was it you lived again?"

Willow dropped my hand again and I could feel her kick into protective mode. She may be fun-sized and all, but she was extremely protective and loyal. This should be interesting, but Sage walked over to the group just then, interrupting the mounting tension.

❦ 34 ❧

AVA

THE CHAOS OF LA was fading in the distance as we travelled north. I was holding Sage's hand, while the lights from the dash bathed us in a gentle glow and bluesy jazz played softly in the background. I turned towards him, my eyes caressing his strong jaw, as he concentrated on the road ahead of us and he constantly checked behind us. I couldn't decide what to feel right now because once again my head was in turmoil. I should be used to it by now. My world was careening out of my control, though the one thing I knew with a certainty was that Sage would protect me, with his life if need be.

Silent tears slid down my cheeks with so many things to mourn. Natalia, leaving the father I was just getting to know, and my family of friends. To say nothing of the career I had dreamed of my entire life, now in ruins at my feet. My immediate future was ahead of me, at an unknown destination, hiding from Ivan, and his demented obsession. What lay beyond that, I had no idea and decided not to dwell on it. I would take each day as it presented itself, considering I really had no other options, though I was trying to convince myself this was all my choice.

When I asked where we were going, the only thing Sage would divulge was that we were going to a safe place, and one that no one knew about. I would trust him to keep me safe. Sage gave my hand a squeeze, his thumb gently caressing the top of my hand with light strokes.

"Relax, Beauty. We'll be safe, absolutely no one has followed us, and I didn't tell anyone where we were headed, not even the Lieutenant knows where we are going. So there's no need to worry. This is only temporary Ava, the Lieutenant and Trey will have Ivan in custody before too long, and if not, we can re-evaluate what to do then. While we're waiting," he glanced at me, his blue eyes glowing, "we'll have uninterrupted time alone together."

With that statement, he lifted my now clean hand and brought my wrist to his mouth. He nipped at my pulse point unexpectedly, then tempered the sting with opened mouth kisses, sucking at the rapid beat, fluttering under the press of his lips and nip of his teeth. I couldn't control my heart or my body's reaction, it was visceral and instantaneous. My body attuned to his and enflamed with need.

"Sage..." I moaned out breathlessly, my heart beating in my throat, stealing my ability to speak.

He sucked my ring and middle fingers into his warm, wet mouth, and I nearly came undone. His wicked tongue was wreaking havoc on my already frayed control, grief and fright, morphing into passion and need.

"If you don't stop teasing me, I will not be responsible for what happens next." I sighed, knowing this was going nowhere at the moment, but appreciating his pulling me from my funk.

"How much longer, Sage, I'm ready to pull my hair out. Can we stop soon and stretch our legs or something?"

"Soon, Beauty, we'll stop soon."

He kissed my hand, then placed it back on his leg, though safely wrapped in his. We'd been on the road for hours now and knew I was just overly tired. Looking out the window, I saw the lights of passing towns, but I wasn't focusing on any one thing, but allowing my heart to settle. A few minutes later, Sage pulled over and into a parking spot along the beach.

"Come, walk with me."

He came around to my door and helped me to get out. We left our shoes by the Stang and walked, hand in hand onto the cool velvety sand towards the water. The surf was quiet, just a gentle slide to and fro, wetting the sand just beyond my toes. Sage pulled me into his arms and we looked out over the water, so peaceful with the moon shimmering across the surface, like liquefied moonbeams. As we stood there absorbing one another, bathed in moonlight and the gentle breeze, a sense of tranquility washed over me whisking away my grief. Sage turned me towards him, holding both my hands in his and leaned forward to place a reverent kiss upon my lips. I sighed into his mouth at the sweetness of his gesture.

"Ava, I know your emotions are chaotic and everything seems out of control, but you'll get back to the life you had, to the dreams you made. I promise this is only temporary. I want more than anything for you to have your heart's desires; your happiness is what matters to me. Before I met you, Beauty, I had no idea I could love this way, this desperately, this completely...this hard. You broke through my defenses to invade my darkness, Ava, you've nestled in so deep, I don't think my soul could breathe without you."

The moonlight was just bright enough for me to see the love and sincerity swimming in his eyes. I felt something sliding onto my finger and looked down at my hand to see Sage had slipped a ring on and was positioning it just so. The setting sparkled and winked up at me and when I looked up at Sage, it was to watch him dropping to both knees before me and wrapping his arms around my hips, hugging me tight. When I would have joined him, kneeling in the sand, he stayed me with his words.

"No, Beauty, let me kneel here before you. Let me show you, through my actions and my words, what you mean to me."

The breeze was ruffling his longish dark hair, causing it to fall across his forehead in disarray. God he was so beautiful to me.

"I have loved you from almost the moment you fell into my arms. I can't do without you, my Beauty, my heart. Will you have me? Will you step into the darkness with me? I know we haven't known each other for long, but I know you're it for me. I promise you...all of me, tarnished soul and everything, but wholly and completely yours."

I stepped back, pulling myself from his arms. He let me go, though reluctantly, his arms clinging then dropping to his sides. I looked at him for a moment, then looked away, but not before I saw his look of pain. He dropped his butt to his heels and he gazed away. I walked away from his dejected form, but circled back around Sage and dropped to my knees behind him. I wrapped my arms tight around his shoulders and he reached up to grip my wrist, tight to his chest. I put my mouth to his ear, nipping his earlobe hard between my teeth.

"I don't need you humbled before me, Sage. I'll take you and all your raw edges, tarnished and bleeding, if need be. You are everything to me. Time is of little consequence to the heart, to the soul. I am already yours Sage, surely you see that, surely you feel that."

Before I knew what was happening, we were facing each other and Sage was devouring my mouth, like a man dying from thirst, and I was the only source of water and he was determined to drown. I could be so lost in him and never want or need to be found.

"I'm yours Sage, forever and always, don't pass go, don't collect two hundred bucks, stuck in jail with me for life."

Sage burst out laughing against my mouth.

"Are you really talking Monopoly to me right now? See now that's why I love you so much. Forever, Ava, you are my forever."

"Yes, Sage...Our forever."

About the Author
Paris Andren

As a self-described optimist, Paris finds something to smile and laugh about every day. She claims to have a potty mouth to rival a truckers and all her friends would readily agree. Walk over and hold her expressive hands and Paris is quite suddenly mute. Passionate about words, Paris has a head full of stories that will be making their way to a virtual page near you.

Paris started her college career in literature, but when her infant son was hospitalized she decided to change her field of study and graduated into the medical field, as a Nurse Anesthetist. With her husband by her side, she's come full circle to pursue her writing. She writes in loving memory of her daughter, Andrea.

LET'S CONNECT

www.pariswrites.com
twitter.com/ParisAndren
www.facebook.com/authorparisandren

If you enjoyed *Pointe of Darkness* and want more of Sage and Ava and the LA Dark world, sign-up for the Paris Press Release newsletter at pariswrites.com that way you won't miss out on the next book in Paris Andren's, *LA Dark Series*.

Whose story are you dying to hear about next, along with more Sage and Ava that is? Drop me an email, and although I've started the next book, I would love to hear from you, my readers, as to who should be next.

Resources for
Help and Intervention

"Human trafficking is a form of modern-day slavery. This crime occurs when a trafficker uses force, fraud or coercion to control another person for the purpose of engaging in commercial sex acts or soliciting labor or services against his/her will."

Get Help.
Report a tip.
Request services.

traffickingresourcecenter.org

"Help Is Just A Phone Call Away, No One 'Deserves it'..."

"There are a number of resources in most communities, but if you have nowhere to turn, two national hotlines can quickly connect you with local help and assistance:"

National Domestic Violence Hotline at 1-800-799-SAFE (7233)
National Sexual Assault Hotline at 1-800-656-4673.

Online support for rape, abuse, and incest national network RAINN

rainn.org
rainn.org/get-help